SYDNEY COVE, BOOK 1

To Love Anew

BONNIE LEON

Revell

a division of Baker Publishing Group
Grand Rapids, Michigan

Published by Revell
a division of Baker Publishing Group
P.O. Box 6287, Grand Rapids, MI 49516-6287
www.revellbooks.com

Fourth printing, April 2009

Printed in the United States of America

Library of Congress Cataloging-in-Publication Data
Leon, Bonnie.
  To love anew / Bonnie Leon.
      p.   cm. — (Sydney Cove ; bk. 1)
    ISBN 10: 0-8007-3176-X (pbk.)
    ISBN 978-0-8007-3176-2 (pbk.)
      1. British—Australia—Fiction. 2. Young women—Fiction. 3. Australia—
  Fiction. I. Title.
  PS3562.E533T6 2007
  813'.54—dc22   2007010820

Scripture is paraphrased from the New King James Version. Copyright © 1982 by Thomas Nelson, Inc. Used by permission. All rights reserved.

Acknowledgments

Special thanks to Jayne Collins, an Australian who lives in Queensland and has been my research partner. She's a teacher, a historian, and a woman who is passionate about her country. Because of her sacrifice of time and her dedication to this project, I am able to present this story with confidence. Thank you, Jayne, for your assistance and your encouragement.

1

London, 1804

Hannah Talbot stared at the freshly covered grave. The ache in the hollow of her throat intensified and tears seeped from her eyes. "Mum," she whispered, and then her words choked off. She tried to swallow away the hurt.

Wiping her tears, she closed her eyes. How was this possible? It seemed only days ago that she and her mother had been laying out a pattern for a woman's gown. It was lovely, made of pink-and-white-striped taffeta. Her mother had chatted about how fetching the young woman would look at her debut.

Reality swept through Hannah, agony swelling with its truth. *She's gone!* Her legs felt as if they might buckle. "How, Lord? How can it be?"

Her eyes roamed over the churchyard. There were many headstones—so many loved ones gone. Each time she came to visit she noticed other gravesites. Today she'd stopped at a cluster of headstones, all belonging to one family. They'd been taken within weeks of each other.

Some graves had only crosses. Hannah thought it sad that a person's final resting place didn't display their name. Fortunately, she'd managed to procure enough funds for a simple casket and headstone.

A chill wind swept across the frozen ground and shivered through the limbs of bare trees. "Why, Lord? Why my mum?"

The day her mother had come down with fever, the late winter sun had slanted through the windows of their tiny home. They'd worked in the sewing shop at the front of the cottage. During a respite, they'd sipped tea and talked of the coming spring and how much fun it would be to picnic in the countryside beyond the London streets.

A sharp draft of air caught at wisps of brown hair and tossed them into Hannah's eyes. Brushing them aside, she pulled up the collar of her coat and closed it more tightly around her neck. "I miss you, Mum," she said, as if her mother might hear. "I don't know how to live without you." She took in a tattered breath.

Kneeling, Hannah pulled her hand out of her pocket and rested it on the frozen mound. She could feel the coldness of the ground through her glove. Outside the gate, a carriage rambled past, its inhabitants tucked safely inside. Hannah watched as it rolled down the street and moved on around the corner. Once more, her world turned quiet. She was alone.

Hannah stood. The churchyard suddenly felt menacing. She tried to concentrate on warm memories—hours at her mother's side learning the intricate stitches needed to create fine garments, listening to stories of her mother's youth and of her father and grandparents. Her mother often spoke of God—his statutes and his love.

She stuck her gloved hands back inside her pockets. "I shan't come back," she said. "You're not here. There's nothing of you here." She took a deep breath and smiled softly. "You're in our Father's presence, just as you always said you would be one day. I want to be happy for you. And I am, really . . . happy for you and for Papa. It's me I'm crying for. Forgive my tears. I know you wouldn't want them." She sniffled into a handkerchief.

It was time to open the shop. Hannah knew she must go. Yet, she lingered and stared at the frozen pile of earth. What if this was all just a terrible dream? If only it were. Or perhaps her mother could return. Jesus's friend Lazarus had. She closed her eyes. *Lord, would it be too awfully selfish of me to wish her back? I miss her so.*

Hannah remembered her mother's last days. She'd lain abed for weeks, shivering with fever and then clammy with sweat. Bit by bit she'd faded, and then one morning she was gone. It would be selfish to drag her back from the Father's arms and the glory of heaven. Hannah hugged herself about the waist. "No. I won't ask," she said. "I love you too much for that."

Her hands shaking with cold, Hannah pushed a key into the lock and turned it. The door fell open just a bit and a bell chimed softly. Hannah smiled. She loved the little bell hanging from the doorknob. It had been her idea. She was no more than seven when she'd seen one just like it at the millinery shop. Hannah remembered how fast her feet had carried her home. "Oh, Mum," she'd cried. "Mr. Whittier has the finest bell at his store. It hangs from the door. And when the door opens it makes a lovely sound. Could we get one? Please?"

Her mother had explained that it was an unnecessary expense, and Hannah had tried to put it from her mind. A few days later, the first customer of the day arrived and Hannah heard a soft tinkle when the door opened. Jumping up and down and clapping her hands, she hugged her mother and then opened and closed the door at least a dozen times, just to hear the gentle ringing. She thought it sounded even better than the one at the millinery shop.

Pushing the door shut and closing out the cold, Hannah felt the familiar whisper of Jasper, her old tabby cat, as he rubbed against her skirt. She picked him up and held him close, pressing her face against his long fur. He felt warm and his purr vibrated contentedly. "Good morning. Did you find any mice to eat? I hope so, I'm afraid the larder is nearly bare. Perhaps there's a bit of milk yet."

She lifted a pitcher of milk from a shelf on the back porch, then broke a thin layer of ice on top with a wooden spoon and poured some into a tin. "There you go," she said, setting the bowl on the floor. Jasper eagerly lapped it up.

"Now, for some warmth," Hannah told him, and moved toward the coal stove. Opening it, she peered inside. There were a few hot coals left. After dropping in a handful of straw, she scooped coal out of the hod and placed it on the fledgling fire. Closing the door, she set the hand shovel back in the coal scuttle and then stood beside the stove, hoping to warm her body. If only she could afford to build a large, hot fire. That would feel so much better, but there was little coal left and her money was gone. Fear flickered to life, but she forced it from her mind. It would do no good to think on the things she could not change. The Lord would provide, somehow.

Moving to the tiny kitchen behind the shop, she took the last of a loaf of stale bread and carved a thin slice. Next, she spooned cheese from a ball and spread it on the wedge. She folded the crust around it and took a bite. The mix of strong and mild flavors tasted rich, and the emptiness in her stomach felt better. She sat in a wooden rocker and Jasper jumped into her lap. Stroking his soft fur, she fed him a bit of the cheese and bread, and he settled, chewing contentedly.

The bell jangled and Ruby Johnston stepped in. Her open, friendly face fractured into hundreds of tiny lines when she smiled. "Good mornin', dear. How ye faring?"

Ruby's presence warmed the inside of the shop and Hannah's heart. She adored the robust, square-built woman. As far back as Hannah could remember, Ruby had been part of her life. And since her mother's death, the kind woman had spent many hours at Hannah's side. "Oh, you know, I'm managing. Went to Mum's grave this morning."

Ruby raised an eyebrow. "So early? Ye spend a lot of time there. Ye think it wise?"

"Probably not. I just want to be close to her."

Ruby sat on a straight-backed chair. "She's not there, ye know."

"Yes. I do know." Hannah scratched the underside of Jasper's neck, burying her fingers in his thick coat. "I've been considering not returning."

"Just as well, I'd say. Too cold these days. And it's not seemly for a young lady to be wanderin' 'bout a graveyard. I don't think yer mum would want that."

"You're probably right. Every time I go I feel lonelier. I miss her so." Hannah swallowed the last bite of bread. It ached all the way down. Shaking her head, she said, "How can she be gone? She deserved to live."

"That she did, dear. But one can't know the ways of the Lord. We just have to trust him."

"Truly. And I'm trying. But life seems pointless without her, and I don't know how I'll keep the shop open. I've already had patrons withdraw orders."

Hannah could see apprehension in Ruby's brown eyes, and creases lined the older woman's forehead. "It's a shame. Yer a fine seamstress." Ruby smiled. "But it's not the end of the world. There'll be new orders, I'm sure."

"I hope you're right. I'm not the seamstress my mother was."

"No. That yer not, but ye do have a fine hand all the same."

The bell jangled as the door opened. Keeping her chin high and her shoulders back, Ada Templeton stepped inside. She had a way of looking down at people, even those who stood taller than she, which weren't many for she carried quite a lot of height for a woman. Leaning on a cane, she moved into the room, peering suspiciously at Ruby. Her eyes went to Hannah. "Child, it's chilly in here. You need to add more coal to your fire."

"Yes. I quite agree," said Hannah, thinking that she would love to add more if only she could. She pushed out of her chair, dropping Jasper onto the floor. He raised his back and tail and strolled toward the kitchen.

"I've not been able to finish your gown, Mrs. Templeton. With my mother's death and all the arrangements, I . . ."

"Your mother has been gone two weeks or more. Isn't that right?"

"Yes."

"I'd say you've had more than ample time to get your life in order, including your work." She tugged at a glove. "No matter. I expected this." She bobbed her head and a bow on her showy lace hat tottered. "Your mother was very capable. I can't expect you to be as skilled or as clever with designs as she. I've found a fine seamstress who said she'll be able to fulfill my needs and will also complete any unfinished work."

Hannah was flabbergasted. "I know I'm not as accomplished as my mother, but I'm quite capable. I can have the dress done for you promptly."

"I can't wait." Ada turned toward the door. "Please deliver the dress to—"

"She'll not deliver anything for the likes of ye," Ruby stormed, moving toward the woman.

Ada gasped and backed away.

"If ye want yer gown, *ye'll* be takin' it with ye and ye'll take it now." Ruby moved past Ada and hustled to the back of the shop where gowns in varying stages hung. "Which one is it?" she snapped, grabbing one gown after another. She swung around and looked at Ada. "Which one?" she demanded, bristling like an angry mother hen.

"Why, the purple—"

Before Ada Templeton could finish her sentence, Ruby grabbed the gown off its hanger, flung it over her arm, and strode toward the woman. "Here ye go, then. Take yer dress and be off with ye. We've no need of business like yers."

"Well! I never!" Ada Templeton clutched the dress to her chest. She turned to Hannah. "You'll not stay in business long with this kind of behavior! I don't feel the least bit sorry for you, young lady. You've brought this on yourself." With that, she stormed out of the shop.

Hannah stared at Ruby. She didn't know whether to laugh or cry. She loved Ruby, but her dear friend had a fondness for giving in to her emotions. "Ruby, I needed that sale. I could have handled her."

"Ye wouldn't have, luv. She already had her mind made up."

Ruby dropped into a chair. "I am sorry, though, for raising such a fuss. Maybe I did muck it up. I truly am sorry. It's just that I can't abide those hoity-toity ladies. She had no right to treat ye badly."

"I know you meant well, Ruby." Hannah moved to the stove and lifted a kettle. "Would you like a cup of tea?"

"I would at that. I'm all out at my house."

Hannah poured two cups of the weak tea. After serving Ruby, she returned to her rocker. "I wish I had a sweet to offer."

"Not to worry. These days, none of us have money enough for pleasures."

Hannah stared into the pale golden drink. She wanted to cry, to let her tears spill freely and never stop. But then, she'd spent so many tears already, she wondered if she had any left. She looked at Ruby. "I don't know what I'm going to do. The rent is owing, and Ada Templeton isn't the first to withdraw an order."

Ruby nodded her head in sympathy. "It's not fair, none of it."

"Mum often said, 'Life isn't supposed to be fair, but it can be good.' I try to be thankful for the small things." She took a sip of tea. "I need her so badly. She's the one who kept me steady—always reminding me of God's love and compassion. She believed he watched over and cared for all his children all the time."

Hannah set her cup in its saucer. "I'm confused, Ruby. If he is such a merciful, caring God, why would he take my mother? She never asked for much, except to be able to work and to keep food on the table and a roof over our heads. I never heard her speak an unkind word."

"Caroline was the closest thing to a saint I've ever known." Ruby smiled. "She was a good friend to me and my family." Her eyes glistened.

"Of course, you miss her too. Here I've been complaining about my loss and I've forgotten how much you've lost."

"Oh no. Not to worry 'bout me. Friends aren't the same as family. I know that. I remember my own mum's passing. I've not stopped missing her."

Quiet settled over the room as each woman's thoughts stayed with their loved ones. Hannah set her cup and saucer on a small table and walked to the tiny window at the front of the shop. She gazed outside at falling crystalline flakes. "Snow has started. I hope it doesn't get too bad."

"I'll be glad to see spring."

Hannah turned and looked at her friend. "What am I to do? There isn't enough money for rent, and not only have I lost work, I've not had any new orders."

"I wish I could take you in, luv. You know I would if I could. But with my daughter and her little ones and that brute of a husband . . ." She looked away and shook her head.

"Please don't feel badly. I don't expect to be taken in. I want to care for myself." Hannah brushed a wisp of hair off her face. "I doubt I'll ever marry. I need to find a way to be independent."

"You're a lovely girl," Ruby said. "You'll find a man."

"I'm already past twenty-one. And I've had no proper suitors. I dare say, I'm not so fine-looking."

"You're quite comely. You've lovely hair and your brown eyes dance with light, child. The right one has just not come along yet. And it's possible you're just a bit too particular. I remember that one young man—the carpenter—he was quite taken with you."

"That may be, but he was more taken with himself. I just couldn't abide that."

"Well, what about the smithy? He's a fine gent."

"Oh yes. But he has one flaw—too great a love for the spirits."

"Someone will come along, and he'll be just the one." Ruby smiled and stood. "I heard of a gentleman named Charlton Walker. He's a magistrate, I believe—a fine gentleman."

"A magistrate? What are you thinking? He'd never be interested in someone like me."

"No. No, deary. You didn't let me finish. He's in need of an upstairs maid. Might tide ye over for a bit. He has a wife and children who'll need some mending done from time to time too, I might think."

"Yes. I suppose." The idea of being a housemaid raised no enthusiasm in Hannah. She didn't want to work for someone else. She was a seamstress. She loved the way a piece of cloth came to life when it was matched with the right pattern and then clothed a fine figure. Even simple fabric could become something special. "I'll think on it."

"That's fine, dear. Well, I'd best get myself home. My children and my husband are certain to be hungry." She rested her hands on Hannah's shoulders and kissed her cheek. "Let me know what I can do, eh?"

"I will." Hannah offered Ruby a smile. "Thank you for your kindness." She watched Ruby go and then closed the door and returned to the stove to add more coal. The outdoor chill had invaded the room.

Perhaps I should contact Mr. Walker. If things go on as they have, I'll soon be put out of my home.

The thought of ending up on the streets of London sent a chill through Hannah. The city was congested with disreputable sorts who would have no conscience about taking advantage of a solitary woman. She doubted she'd make it through even one night.

16

2

Hands clasped behind his back, John Bradshaw walked between rows of workbenches. Occasionally he'd catch the eye of a craftsman. He'd nod and move on.

One young apprentice smiled broadly and said, "Good day, sir."

"Good day to you." John stopped and looked at the planer the man was constructing. "Fine work, lad."

"Thank ye." The young man bobbed his head and turned back to his task.

John continued on. The boy had apprenticed at the factory only a few months, but already he demonstrated a high level of aptitude for machinery work. He would do well, and most likely serve out his days happily constructing and assembling tools.

Years of tedium stretched out before John as he imagined his life overseeing the business his father had built. He knew he ought to be thankful for his prosperity, but adventure was more what he wanted. With a sigh he tightened the bow holding back his dark, shoulder-length hair and then smoothed his waistcoat.

Noticing a new apprentice who appeared to be having difficulty, John approached him. "Can I be of service, young man?"

The worker brushed thick red hair off his face and turned to look at John. He held up a partially assembled hammer. "I am havin' a bit of trouble, sir. Not sure how this joint ought to fit."

John's mind carried him back to his early years in the shop. It had been just him and his father. He'd struggled to learn the business of toolmaking; it wasn't something he truly enjoyed, but he had liked working with his father. Those had been good days.

He took the hammer and examined it. "You've got it just about right. Might I suggest . . ." He pushed the head forward a bit. "Ah, there. It just needed to be tilted a bit more up front." He handed the tool back to the lad. "You'll get it. No need to worry." He clapped the boy on the shoulder.

"Right, sir."

John moved on, briefly examining each employee's work.

The air was heavy with dust and the smell of cooking metals. His eyes rested for a moment on the founder as he poured a mix of melted lead and copper into a mold. Another man worked furiously at the bellows, keeping the blaze blistering hot.

In spite of the fire, the shop felt chilled. John glanced at an ice-encrusted window. *If only winter would pass. I've enough of the cold.* He tried to envision spring's revival and could almost smell the aroma of damp, green grasses. He craved the outdoors and places beyond London. The machinery business no longer suited him, nor did the city.

John stared out the window, but it was so dirty he could barely see across the street. All the windows were in the same condition. *No wonder it's gloomy in here,* he thought. *I'll see that they're cleaned.*

The idea of managing one more trivial task railed at him. He wished his father had created a business of importance, something more challenging to the mind. Building tools seemed of little significance. Surely the Lord had something more noteworthy for him to do.

The familiar pull to explore the world and establish a legacy nagged at him. *Enough.* He'd been down this road before. It always ended up back here. He glanced about the shop. *It's better than nothing. The business is thriving. I'm able to provide well for myself and for Margaret.* His mind momentarily settled on his wife. From time to time, she could be a bit demanding, but most generally she was kindhearted and loving. *I've reason to be thankful.*

How many times had his father tried to convince him of the value of what they did? "This is a good, solid business, son. Where would people be without tools? And we provide jobs for fellow citizens." He'd smile and pat John on the back. "One day it will be yours."

His father had known that John's untamed spirit wanted more. But he'd understood the importance of stability and had striven to teach his son the value found in steadiness. Some of what he taught did catch on, and though John stopped complaining, the desire for daring endeavors never ceased to tantalize him. When he was only twenty, both of his parents were taken by the sweating sickness and the business became his.

A sudden urge to get away swept over John; he needed to be outside. No matter how cold it was outdoors, it would be better than one more minute inside this shop.

"Sir." The man who'd been working on the hammer approached. "Is this more to your liking?" He held up the tool.

John examined it. Ran his thumb over the handle, and then rested it on the joint where the metal head met the wood. "Much better." He smiled and returned the tool.

Wearing a pleased expression, the apprentice hurried back to his place at the bench. Watching him, John let out a slow breath. He felt weary. Perhaps a walk along the Thames would help.

I'd best let Henry know I'll be gone, he thought and headed for the office. Opening the door, John stepped into a small room crowded with desks, cabinets, and bookcases. His twenty-two-year-old cousin, Henry Hodgsson, looked up from a registry he'd been working on. "You look a bit tight."

"I am feeling worn down. I was thinking a walk might help."

"A pint would do you more good." Henry kept his quill close to the paper. As always, he held his shoulders rigid.

"It's a bit early for that, wouldn't you say?"

"Never too early to imbibe in the benefits of the vine." Henry smiled. "What do you say to tipping up a pint together?"

"I think not."

"Ease up, man," Henry said, his blue eyes glinting.

Henry could be amiable when it suited him, but more often than not he was obnoxious and secretive. John tried not to spend more time with him than was required. On more than one occasion he'd regretted bringing Henry into the family business, but when the young man had come seeking employment, John couldn't turn him away. They'd worked together for two years now, and although Henry had a good mind for figures, he possessed few scruples. John seemed to be forever getting him out of some scrape or other.

"Give me a moment; I'm nearly finished here," Henry said. He turned back to his work. "We've done well this month. There'll be sufficient funds to pay the workers and still add a good deal to the coffers." He dipped the pen into a bottle of ink.

"I've work to do here. I ought to stay," John said, preferring to keep his associations with his cousin to business.

Henry looked at John, mischief on his face. "No more work for you today. Time for a respite." After setting the pen on the desk, he snapped the ink bottle shut. He dusted the ledger with sand, sifted it over the page, and tossed the remaining powder into a trash bin.

"I suppose one short drink won't hurt," John said, walking to the coatrack. He picked up Henry's hat and coat and tossed them to him. "Suppose I've seen enough of this place for one day." He grabbed his tricorne hat and pushed it down on his head, then pulled on a knee-length coat.

"I've a real thirst," Henry said with a wicked grin.

John opened the door and stood aside while Henry strode out, still settling his hat on his head. Pulling the door closed, he followed the younger man down the steps and onto a congested London street. The cold air felt invigorating. He walked quickly, his long legs carrying him farther and faster than Henry's short, stocky ones.

"I'm not about to run to keep up with you," Henry said with irritation.

John looked behind him. "Oh. Sorry." He slowed to a stroll and studied the partially frozen Thames. A ship moved down the unfrozen channel in the middle of the river. "Have you ever considered what you might do if you had a different life, something exciting and meaningful?"

21

"No. I'm content." Henry eyed John closely. "You thinking of stepping away from the business?"

"No. Course not." His eyes lighted on a martin and he wondered why the bird had not flown away before winter had arrived. Using its beak, it groomed its deep blue feathers, trying to clean away soot that had settled on them, just as it had on everything else in the city. It was a hopeless task. The bird would never triumph. Even if it cleaned its feathers today, they'd be coated with the city's grime tomorrow.

Henry cupped his hands and blew into them. "What is it you'd do if you did walk away?"

John pried his eyes away from the pathetic bird. "Don't know exactly. There's a lot I haven't seen. And the years are passing." He glanced at Henry. "I'm not so young anymore."

"You're only twenty-six. You sound like an old man."

John smiled slightly and gazed down the street. "Time passes quickly. I don't want to wait until it's too late."

"Too late for what, man? You live first-rate. You have a charming wife, a grand home . . . a lucrative business. What more do you want?"

John didn't know how to answer him. He didn't really know what he craved—only that it was something other than what he had. He moved swiftly down the street.

Henry hurried to keep up. "Where is it you'd want to go?" He spread his arms wide. "This is the center of the world. What could be better than living in London?"

John glanced around, taking in the ocean of businesses and cottages crammed together in an untidy hodgepodge. A filthy street separated the muddle. Pedestrians, carts, and animals plowed through or stepped over a virulent stream washing down one side of the lane. A mongrel of a dog lifted its leg on the front door of a cottage while a woman tossed some sort of waste from a second-story window. A persistent brown fog encased the putrid-smelling city.

"I could think of better places." John chuckled.

Henry shook his head. "You have what all men long for. You've the money and the good name that brings you whatever you wish. You're refused nothing. And you're still unhappy?"

"You're right, of course. But I'm not unhappy. It's just that sometimes I'd like to have the opportunity to begin again." John thought about the hunger he'd never been able to still. He smiled. "I rather think an excursion to the Americas would be grand."

"The Americas?" Henry shook his head. "And what would you do there?"

John thought for a moment. "I might have a hand at one of those plantations I've heard about and live the life of a country gentleman."

"Don't mind telling you I'm pleased to stay right here." A strange expression touched Henry's eyes. "And what of Margaret? She'll have none of it, you know."

"You're right there. She'd not find pleasure in such an adventure."

Henry tipped up his hat slightly. "She's rather attached to this city and not doddery enough to retire to the country. You'd be hard-pressed to pry her loose from here." He grinned. "And I dare say London would miss her."

Lifting a brow, John said, "You mean the shopkeepers would miss her and my money."

All of a sudden the sound of bells ringing accompanied the incessant noise that already permeated London. More bells joined the first, and they grew louder and louder. "Those confounded youngsters," Henry lamented. "Could they not find some other form of entertainment?"

"Have you so quickly forgotten our own youth?" John asked. "It seems to me that once upon a time you were one of the best of bell ringers." He grinned.

"I was young."

"And so are they."

Henry stepped around a frozen puddle. A small, white dog ran under his feet and nearly tripped him. Instantly enraged, he kicked at the animal, managing to catch it just below the ribs. The dog yelped. "Out of my way, mongrel!"

A boy ran after the canine while a group of his friends stood on the walkway and glared at Henry. "Ye didn't need t' hurt me dog, mister. He meant no harm." The boy lifted the filthy animal and clutched him against his chest.

John looked at Henry, expecting an apology. Instead, the man kept walking.

"Sorry, lad," John said. "No harm done, eh?"

The boy bobbed his head, tucked the dog under one arm, and dashed back to his friends. The small band ran up the street, and John hurried to catch up to his cousin.

"Ah, here we are," Henry said, stopping at the door of the pub. He grinned at John, his blue eyes glinting. Pushing open the door, he disappeared inside.

John followed reluctantly. A blast of warm, stale air hit him as he stepped inside. There were only a handful of patrons scattered about. "A bit early for the crowd, I'd say." He tipped his hat toward the barmaid. "Afternoon, Abbey. How you faring?"

The buxom woman smiled. "I'm doin' well. You?"

"Good."

"We need a pint," Henry said. He sidled up to Abbey and circled her waist with his arm. "I've found myself an angel." He pulled her close.

Abbey managed to wriggle free and stepped back. "An angel, indeed. I doubt you'll find what you're looking for here."

Henry laughed. "I suppose that today a pint will have to do." He gave her behind a friendly swat. "Course another time, eh?"

She glared at him. "I'll never have time for the likes of you."

A scowl touched Henry's face for a moment but was quickly replaced by a smirk. "You can't blame a man, now. You're a tempting morsel."

Unhappy with Henry's antics, John crossed to a table and sat. He pulled out another chair. "Sit down, Henry." His tone demanded obedience. He placed his hat on the table in front of him.

Henry slid into the chair. "Just havin' a bit of fun," he said, watching Abbey make her way back to the bar.

"Barmaid or not, she's a decent sort and deserves our respect."

Henry reached into his breast pocket and lifted out a snuff box. Flipping open the lid, he dipped out a fingertip full of snuff and sniffed it into one nostril. He held out the box to John.

"No thank you. It's a disgusting habit."

Henry shrugged and put the box back into his pocket. He watched Abbey at the bar.

John was beginning to wish that he'd taken a walk along the Thames. His eyes rested on a group of men at another table. One of them looked familiar. He'd seen him here several times before. If memory served him, the man had been mouthy and a hothead. "You know that fellow?"

"Who?" Henry glanced at the cluster of men.

"The one there," John nodded at the group. "The younger one, wearing the blue shirt."

"Oh yeah. Name's Langdon. Langdon Hayes." He repeated the name with disdain. "He's a whelp, rich and spoiled. Comes in now and again." His attention returned to Abbey.

Although full-bodied, she moved with the grace of a dancer as she approached the table. She set the ale in front of the men. John gave her four pence. "Quiet today."

"It's early, yet." She smiled. "Ye need anything else?"

Henry's roguish smile appeared. "I was—"

"We're in no need of anything," John cut in. He brushed back a loose strand of dark hair, lifted his drink, and sipped. "Good ale. Always serve the best here."

"We do at that." Throwing John a look of mischief and Henry one of disdain, Abbey tossed thick, long hair off her shoulder and moved away.

"I dare say, she tempts a man," Henry said, continuing to stare at her.

"She's not the sort for you."

"I'm not talking marriage, man. Just one night . . ."

John's irritation grew. Henry was too often taken with the ladies, and when in that frame of mind, he made no attempt to hide his lasciviousness. He even seemed partial to Margaret.

John studied the man. He had to admit that, although not a statuesque person, Henry was rather good-looking. He had a straight nose and strong chin and made sure his hair was neat and worn fashionably. And he was intelligent, as well as an asset to the business.

"Perhaps I'll have another go at Abbey, eh?"

Leaning on the table, John looked squarely at his cousin. "You're incorrigible. I doubt you'll ever marry."

A crooked grin lifted Henry's lips. "You are most certainly right." He took a long swill of ale.

John leaned back in his chair. "Marriage might be good for you. Margaret's been a fine wife to me. You'd be lucky to have someone like her."

Henry didn't look at John, but kept drinking until his cup was empty. He smiled as if he had some kind of secret. Holding up his empty mug, he said, "Abbey, luv, get me another." She quickly replaced the empty goblet.

Leaning back in his chair, Henry sipped his drink. "So if you went off on an adventure, what would become of the business?"

"It would be your responsibility." Even as John said it, the idea unsettled him. What would his father have thought about placing Henry at the helm? John took a long drink. The discontent of his mundane life pushed him on. "Perhaps it is time I started spending some of my hard-earned money—"

"That's the spirit." Henry downed another mouthful of brew. "I offer my services. But you can't be serious about the Americas?"

John shrugged. "Maybe. I want to return to France and Italy. I haven't been for some time." He grasped his cup between both hands and stared down into the dark ale. "I will most likely stay here. I'm afraid my course is set. Adventures are for dreamers."

He glanced at the group of men across the room. Langdon stared at him, his expression cold.

Henry caught his look. "I'd like to drag him down from his high horse."

"Ignore him."

"No fighting today, Langdon," Abbey called. "If you can't keep your temper under control, we'll put you out."

Wearing a smirk, Henry cocked his hat backward, then moved his thumb down the brim and thumbed his nose at Langdon. "That's what I think of you," he said just loud enough for John to hear.

His eyes lit with anger and a penetrating gaze glued to Henry, Langdon stood and strode toward him.

I don't need trouble. John downed the last of his ale. "Time we returned to work."

"I'm not done with my drink yet," Henry said, keeping his eyes on the young man charging toward him.

Langdon stopped about two feet from John and Henry's table. "So, you think I will let such insolence pass?"

Henry pushed to his feet. "If you're looking for a fight, I'll give you one."

Langdon's smile broadened. "I'll be glad to comply."

Henry moved toward the man.

"There's no reason for a fight," John said. "We were just about to leave."

The two men squared off, ignoring John's appeal. They circled one another. Langdon moved in, swinging at Henry with his right hand. Henry blocked the blow and managed to land one of his own. Langdon's head snapped back, but he acted as if he'd not been hit and came back at Henry with ferocity.

Langdon stood a good four inches taller than Henry and outweighed him by a substantial amount, but the reckless young man charged him anyway.

John jumped into the melee and tried to pry Langdon off of his cousin. "Enough. Enough of this," he said, doing his best to protect Henry and still break up the fight.

In the end, Henry landed on the floor. He was barely conscious, and blood spilled from gashes on his face and mouth.

"All right, that's enough. You've beat him." John stepped between the two men and reached for Henry. "Let's go then, lad."

"Leave him be," Langdon snarled.

John turned and faced him. "You're done," he said with authority. "You've beaten him." He turned back to his cousin. "We'll be on our way."

"You want to finish his fight?"

John didn't respond, but instead helped Henry to his feet.

"I said, leave him," Langdon bellowed.

Looking dazed, Henry leaned heavily on John. Langdon grabbed for him.

John stepped out of his way, dragging Henry with him. "Back away, I say."

Langdon lunged at John. He grabbed Henry and shoved him aside, then threw his closed fist at John's face. John ducked and the blow missed. Looking crazed, Langdon came at him again. This time he struck him across the side of the skull.

Pain and bright lights erupted in John's head. The room whirled. He fought to keep his feet under him. Before he could focus, Langdon threw himself against the unwilling participant and shoved him to the floor. John landed on his back, hitting so hard the air rushed from his lungs.

Struggling for breath, John looked to Henry for assistance, but he leaned against a wall looking stupefied. *He's of no help.* John pushed to his feet.

Langdon pulled a knife out of a sheath hanging from his belt. Holding it high, he moved toward John.

"That's enough!" yelled Abbey. "No weapons!" She moved toward the men as if she might try to put an end to the fight, but she stopped short. There was nothing that could be done if none of the men in the pub were inclined to step in.

Langdon lunged toward John, who barely managed to move out of the blade's reach. Again the man slashed at him, this time slicing through John's shirtsleeve and into his upper arm.

Feeling the sting of the blade, John glanced at the wound. Blood stained the fabric of his shirt. He moved toward Langdon, knowing this fight was for his life. With everything he had, John struck the younger man hard across the chin, and then followed with another punch the thug managed to avoid.

Langdon came back at him, driving the knife toward John's throat. Grabbing the enraged man's arm, John fought to push him back. The sharp edge of the blade felt cold against his skin. And then sensing a weakening in his adversary, he took the advantage, thrusting the man's arm back and down.

All John could think about was keeping the blade away from himself. He forced it toward Langdon, and then with all the energy he could summon, he plunged the knife at his attacker and drove the blade into the man's abdomen.

Langdon let out a howl. Clasping his stomach, he dropped to the floor and lay groaning. Blood soaked through his shirt and spilled onto the wooden planking. Sweat ran down his face in rivulets. He glared at John and, in panting breaths, said, "You've killed me."

"It was you who forced the fight." John looked about. "Is there a surgeon here?"

No one answered.

"Come on. Let's go." Henry staggered toward John. He grabbed John's hat and pushed it down on his head. Snatching up his own, he dragged his cousin toward the door.

"We can't just leave him." John pulled away and took a step toward Langdon.

Henry fastened a hand on John's arm. "He'll be all right."

"We must do something."

"Nothing can be done now."

Henry hauled John out the door and shoved him into the street.

"Stop worrying," Henry said. "That fellow will likely be back tomorrow downing his grog. You'd do better to think about yourself." He patted John on the back. "You did a fine job."

"Yeah, and a lot of help you were."

"He caught me off guard is all. I'll thrash him next time."

"There'll be no next time. This is your fault."

"He deserved it."

Trying to release tension, John lifted his shoulders and then dropped them again. Searing pain from his wound shot through his arm, causing him to wince.

"You better see to that," Henry said, nodding at the bloody stain on John's coat sleeve.

"It's nothing."

Henry glanced down the street. "Time I got home. I'll see you tomorrow."

Taking quick, short steps, Henry walked away.

John glanced down at his bloodied clothes. How had something as simple as having a drink turned into such misfortune? He headed toward home.

After cleaning and bandaging his arm, John had barely sat down to his dinner when a knock sounded at the door.

"Now, who can that be?" Margaret asked, dabbing at her mouth with a linen napkin.

The housemaid bustled toward the front of the house. The sound of voices came from the vestibule, but John couldn't make out what was being said. A few moments later, the maid returned, eyes wide. "There're two constables 'ere t' see ye, sir. I put them in the study."

Alarm pulsed through John. He looked at Margaret. Her brown eyes were wide with uncertainty, but he didn't give her a chance to ask what the trouble could be. "It'll be all right," he said, pushing away from the table. Keeping his shoulders back and trying to remain calm, he walked to the study and opened the door.

3

The bell hanging from the door of Hannah's shop chimed. *Father, let it be a customer*, she prayed. Business had continued to be poor.

"One moment please," she called from the back room and then pushed a bolt of cloth onto a top shelf. After smoothing her skirt and tidying her hair, she hastened to the front of the cottage. "Good mor—" she started, but the words died. Cecilia Smith, the householder, stood just inside the door. Hannah's stomach turned. Cecilia was certainly here to turn her out.

Managing a smile, she said cheerily, "Good morning. It's a fine day for February, wouldn't you say?"

Cecilia shifted her infant son from her right hip to the left. "Yes. Fine indeed." Her expression was somber. "Ye know why I've come. I need the rent. I can't wait longer."

"Yes." Hannah searched her mind for inspiration; there must be something that would rescue her from the streets. She moved to the kitchen and retrieved a crockery bowl from a shelf. Scooping out a handful of coins, she said, "I have some of it." She moved toward Cecelia. "As I explained, since my mother's passing I've had a temporary decline in business.

33

I'm sure things will improve." She pressed the money into the householder's hand. "I assure you I'll pay the rest before the month is out."

Cecilia looked down at the money in her hand and then let out a slow breath. "Ye know I can't wait. Mr. Whitson wants the entire payment. If I come to him with this, I'll be out on me ear." She turned regretful eyes on Hannah. "I got me kids to think of." Her eyes fell to the floor. "There are tenants that want to move in. And they have the money."

Hannah fought down rising panic. "Perhaps Mr. Whitson's wife needs a fitting. I can take care of that for her. And right away too."

"Mr. Whitson's a widower."

"Does he have a sister, then?"

Cecilia simply stared at her.

Hannah's mind frantically searched for an idea—something. Nothing came. "Can't you ask him to wait just a few more days? I'm sure I can manage by then." Hannah knew she was simply putting off the inevitable. For without some sort of miracle she'd be just as destitute in a week or two weeks as she was at this moment.

Cecilia set her jaw and shook her head. "Can't do it. I already give ye more time than I ought. I can't wait another day." She looked down at her little boy and smoothed his hair, then turned her gaze back to Hannah. "I hate t' do this, but I got no choice."

"What am I to do? I haven't any place to go."

Cecilia looked at the coins in her hand, then held them out to Hannah. "He'll not know if ye paid me or not. And ye'll need somethin' t' tide ye over." She pressed the money into Hannah's hand. "It's all I can do."

Hannah didn't want the money. It only meant that all hope of staying was gone. She stared at the coins, then reluctantly closed her fingers and pushed her fist into her apron pocket.

"Ye have to go. Today."

"I'll be out before noon," Hannah said, barely able to breathe. "I've only a few things to pack. You can take the rest of what I have to cover my back rent."

Looking nearly as devastated as Hannah felt, Cecilia moved to the door. "I'll be back this afternoon," she said and left.

Hannah dropped into a chair, and resting her elbows on her thighs, she covered her face with her hands. "Lord, what am I to do?" She freed her tears.

Hannah allowed herself only a short cry. She must be reasonable. Taking a long, shuddering breath, she wiped away the wetness and stared at the window. "Where shall I go? Where?"

Scanning the tiny house, she contemplated what she ought to take. There was little left that hadn't already been sold or offered in place of rent. Her eyes fell on a satchel sitting near the door leading to the kitchen. All that would go with her must fit into that bag.

***

Hannah wrapped half a loaf of bread and the last of her cheese in a cloth and added them to the satchel, which was already overflowing with clothing, sewing supplies, and mementos. On the bureau by the bed, a gold chain with a cross rested in a stoneware bowl. It had belonged to her mother. Hannah lifted it, studying the delicate necklace. Heartache swelled within her as she draped it about her neck and secured the clasp. She rested her hand on the cross, pressing it against her skin. The coolness of the metal felt soothing and brought her the comfort of feeling closer to her mother, if even for just a moment.

Jasper mewed and rubbed against Hannah's skirt. He always understood her moods. She picked him up and smoothed his fur. What was he to do now? She couldn't take him with her. *He's a good mouser. Perhaps Ruby will want him.*

Grief swept through Hannah, and she buried her face in Jasper's thick fur. "Oh Mum, what am I to do?"

It was time to go. Hannah walked to the front door and stared at it, but she couldn't make her hand reach for the knob. Instead she turned and looked at the room. This was the only home she'd ever known. It was small and plain, but it was safe. She could still feel her mother's presence. Sometimes when it was quiet enough to hear the sweep of the clock's pendulum, she'd remember the evenings and how her mother would rock and knit in her peaceful, quiet way. And on occasion she thought she could hear the soft click of the knitting needles.

Hannah closed her eyes and tried to capture some of what she'd known here. The memories were elusive, the stark truth keeping them from her.

Gathering her courage, Hannah said, "Those days are gone. And there's nothing can be done about it." She picked up Jasper and tucked him under one arm, then hefted her satchel and draped it over her shoulder. She opened the door and the bell jingled. Startled, she stared at it. She'd nearly forgotten to pack it. Retrieving the little bell, she dropped it into the satchel. With a heavy sigh, she stepped outside and closed the door.

She hugged Jasper. "It's time to see what God has for us," she said, trying to sound optimistic. Her throat tightened and fear reached for her. *I must have faith,* she told herself. *Mum never wavered.* Hannah could hear her mother's wise words. How often had she said, "The Lord never forsakes his children, Hannah"? Her voice sounded like a song. She'd smile and add, "He's with us always, forever watching over his beloved."

Hannah forced herself to walk away. The warmer temperatures that had graced the morning turned chill. Huddling inside her cloak, she tried to walk with a determined stride as she headed for Ruby's.

When Hannah was little, she'd spent many days at Ruby's house. The kindly woman always seemed to be baking. Hannah's favorite treat had been her special bread. In a rhythm, she'd roll the dough and press it down with the heel of her stout hands and then form it into perfectly shaped loaves. Hannah would wait while it rose and then was baked. She could still smell the sweetness of it as it came steaming out of the oven. Ruby would cut a piece for her to eat while the loaves cooled.

Ruby's home had always seemed close, but today the distance felt like a journey. As she neared the house, Hannah slowed her steps. What would she say? She'd kept many of her troubles to herself, not wanting to worry her friend. Now she wished she could retreat from what she would see in Ruby's eyes when she told her what had happened. She didn't want her pity nor the guilt her friend would feel at her inability to help.

There simply was no room at Ruby's. Her cottage was smaller than Hannah's, and her daughter and grandchildren lived with her. They were already squeezed tight. And Percy, Ruby's husband, was an unfriendly type. Having a houseguest would not sit well with him. If Ruby defied her husband, she'd bear the brunt of his displeasure. Hannah needed to help her friend understand that she could care for herself. She only hoped that Percy would allow Jasper to stay.

When she reached Ruby's, she didn't knock right away. Instead, she stood on the stoop and tried to work out what she ought to say. An acceptable explanation eluded her. Summoning courage, she raised her hand.

Just then she heard tapping at the window and looked up to see Ruby's friendly face gazing out. She waved her in, but before Hannah could grab the knob, it turned and the door swung open.

"What ye doing here standing out in the cold? Come in. Come in." Ruby opened the door wider.

Hannah stepped inside. "Good day to you."

"Afternoon." Ruby eyed Jasper and the satchel hanging from Hannah's shoulder.

Hannah still couldn't think of anything to say.

"So, they kicked ye out, eh?"

"Yes. I had to come and say good-bye. I'm not sure where I'll be just yet. I considered the Bakers, but they have six children, and the widow Barnett is on the verge of being evicted herself." Hannah gazed at the floor, mortified.

Ruby's brow knit, but she managed to smile. "Well, could ye do with a bit of tea? Got some just this mornin'." She placed an arm around Hannah and ushered her to a chair. "Ye sit and I'll make it." She moved toward her kitchen and then glanced back at the cat. "Ye can put him down too. He'll be fine." She got cups from a cupboard. "Good thing my daughter took the children with her this mornin'. Give us some time to ourselves."

Giving Jasper a pat, Hannah set him on the floor. "I was wondering if I might leave Jasper here with you. He's a good mouser so he won't need much in the way of food." Hannah sat on the settee.

38

"He'll be fine for now." While Ruby poured the tea, she hummed a folksy tune. "Glad I had some brewing," she said, handing Hannah a cup. She sat in a straight-backed chair. For a few moments, the two women sipped their tea in silence.

"So, do ye have a plan?" Ruby finally asked.

Feeling miserable, Hannah looked at her friend. "I haven't a notion. I've been praying and praying, but nothing seems clear to me. What do you think I ought to do?"

Ruby thought a moment. "I'd be more than happy to let ye stay 'ere, but ye know how Percy is. He'd never stand for it. He'd make us all miserable."

"I don't expect you to take me in. That's not why I came." Hannah set her cup on the table. "I need a place for Jasper, and I couldn't go without saying good-bye."

The two women's eyes met, and silence settled between them once more.

Ruby interrupted the quiet. "What about the . . . no. That won't work. The Johnsons just moved in. That means there are four families in one tiny house. I'm sure they won't allow anyone else." Ruby sipped her tea, making a slurping sound. "What about that Mr. Walker, the magistrate? Perhaps he still needs help."

"Do you think he might?" Hannah felt hope stir.

"Maybe. All ye need do is ask." She grinned. "Oh, that would be lovely. I hear he has a grand house. And there are children. Wouldn't that be nice, to live with a family?"

Inside Hannah quaked at the idea of working for someone as prominent as a magistrate, but she said, "That would be excellent."

Ruby smiled. "That's it, luv. Ye'll go and see them tomorrow. It's a bit late today. I have a friend, Lucille. Her daughter works for his neighbor. I'll find out if they're still needing a maid."

Hannah stood on a walkway leading to the front door of an imposing three-story brick home. The Walker estate took up nearly half a block. The house stood close to the street and was squeezed between two other lavish homes. In spite of the crowding there was a small yard with a tiny flower garden. This time of year it held only well-trimmed greenery, but Hannah could imagine what it would look like in the spring.

There were four chimneys reaching from the roof, which reassured Hannah that the home was well heated. Numerous windows looked down on the street, but most had closed draperies, shutting out the light. *Curious,* thought Hannah. *The children must have need of light for their studies.*

Hands shaking, she tidied her hair and smoothed her skirt. Taking a deep breath, she tugged on the bell pull. Keeping her spine straight and shoulders back, she stared at the door and waited. The knob turned and the door opened, revealing a small, sturdy-looking woman with silvery hair. Her demeanor was as starched as her apron.

"Yes. What can I do for you?"

Hannah swallowed hard. "My name is Hannah Talbot and I'm here to inquire about the position of upstairs maid." She couldn't keep her voice from trembling. "Is the position still available?"

"It is." The woman studied Hannah. "You're just a wisp of a thing. Doubt you could do the work."

"I'm much stronger than I look."

"Come inside, then. You're letting in the cold."

"Thank you," Hannah said. Thinking the woman didn't seem the least bit friendly, she stepped inside.

40

"Wait here," she said and marched toward the back of the house.

Hannah looked about. She'd been in many fine homes, but never one quite this opulent. An exquisite chandelier hung in the center of the vestibule, showing off the marble floor. The walls were covered with a robin-egg blue brocade paper with floral sprays. And the window draperies were fashioned from heavy, gold fabric—quite elegant. A nymph-like statue sat at the bottom of a sweeping staircase, beckoning one to hurry up the stairs. The house was still and hushed.

Sharp clicking steps echoed from the back of the home. Hannah clasped her hands in front of her.

A slight woman with a pinched expression walked toward her. She was followed by a skinny man with thinning red hair. They both seemed tightly strung.

"I'm Mrs. Walker," the woman said. "You've come to see about the position of scullery maid?"

"I thought you had need of an upstairs maid?"

"Oh yes indeed, but the person we have in mind must do both. Could you manage?" she asked, her voice laced with doubt.

"Certainly." Hannah kept her elbows tucked in close and kept her hands clasped tightly.

The man studied her, his brown eyes showing intense interest. Hannah guessed him to be Mr. Walker. He sucked on a piece of hard candy that had a strong and distinct odor of mint.

Mrs. Walker moved around Hannah, sizing her up. Hannah felt unnerved and wished she'd never set foot in the house. She didn't like Mrs. Walker.

"You're skinny and frail," the woman said. Before Hannah could defend herself, she continued, "What kind of work have you done before?"

41

"My mother was a seamstress. I've worked with her since I was a girl. I've a fine hand with a needle and thread."

"Your mother's name?"

"Caroline Talbot."

"Never heard of her," she said, her tone dismissive. "And yours?"

"Hannah Talbot." She pressed her lips together to keep from arguing her mother's talents. She didn't dare. She needed this job. "I can get references if you like."

Mr. Walker leaned against a doorway frame. He seemed to be enjoying the exchange.

"That won't be necessary." Mrs. Walker tapped her index finger against her chin and continued to study Hannah from behind dark eyes. "You speak well, girl. Why is that?"

"My mother made sure I was educated. I attended school at the church in my borough."

Mrs. Walker nodded slightly. "It pays six pence a month, plus your room and board. You may have Sundays off."

"That would be fine," Hannah said, careful not to let her relief show.

"When can you start?"

"I have a few things to collect and then I shall return and be ready to work."

"Fine. I'll expect you tomorrow, then." With that, Mrs. Walker turned and strode back down the hallway the way she'd come. Mr. Walker nodded at Hannah, a smile hidden behind his eyes, and then he followed his wife.

Hannah felt breathless. She didn't know whether to cheer or to cry. She stepped outside, breathing deeply of the cold air. If only she could go to her mum.

4

With his back pressed against a stone wall, John sat on stale hay that had been scattered about the prison floor. After nine days of being locked up, he was weary. For in this place one never truly slept. Despite his fatigue, he felt restless. The first few days he'd paced, but finally gave up the useless walking. It took him nowhere and did little to relieve his agitation.

He looked about the large chamber. At least fifty men in varying degrees of ill health were housed in this single enclosure. It appeared most had been here a relatively long time. Nearly everyone was thin, their skin pallid. And what little clothing they had hung loosely, frayed and threadbare.

One of the inmates walked back and forth in front of the wall opposite John. He'd done that most of every day since John's arrival. Another sat and stared at a tiny window, as if he'd find salvation there. John had been here a relatively short time and already longed for such simple pleasures as fresh air and sunshine. The rest of the inmates either slept or sat staring at nothing in particular.

He laid his arms over bent knees and rested his cheek on them, longing for sleep and hoping to awaken from this nightmare. A man lying on the floor on the far side of the cell coughed so long and hard John worried he might hack up his lungs. The man had been sick for days. Life in prison was not conducive to good health.

The stink of human sweat and waste assailed his senses. There was no escaping it, and nothing to be done about it. In fact, John could barely tolerate his own stench. He wondered what was to become of him. His attorney had been to visit only once and no one else had come at all. Where was Henry? He was supposed to be his partner. And it was Henry he'd been defending when he got into this mess.

An ache tightened at the base of his throat. And Margaret—why hadn't she come?

He tried not to think about his upcoming hearing. Each time he did, anxiety set in. Since the fight and his arrest, he'd ceased believing that all things would work out and worried about what else might befall him.

Amidst the moans and groans coming from other inmates, there was a rustling sound within the hay. Lifting his head, he peered through bleary eyes. A large rat scuttled across the floor in front of him. *How bold he is*, John thought, feeling an unexpected sense of respect for the rodent. *Most likely used to the company of men.*

John's thoughts returned to Margaret. He could see her thick auburn hair and lively brown eyes. Why hadn't she come to see him? He hated the thought of her being exposed to this foul place, yet he longed to gaze upon her wholesome good looks, smell the soapy fragrance of her hair and skin, and hear an encouraging word. Sighing, John leaned his head back against the wall and closed his eyes. Where was she?

Steps reverberated against a stone floor, echoing from a distant corridor. John didn't bother to look.

The steps stopped and the jailer hollered, "Bradshaw! Ye got a visitor."

Jolted out of his stupor, John opened his eyes. Could it be Margaret? He looked toward the guard's station. No. It was Leland Martin, his attorney. As always, he wore an old-fashioned white wig and a three-piece suit with a brocade vest. Leland caught his eye and smiled.

John pushed to his feet. He liked Leland. The man gave little thought to style or to what others might think of him, but he was solid and trustworthy. John admired that. Moving stiffly, he made his way to the cell bars.

"How you faring?" Leland asked, his eyes cheerless.

"I'm still breathing. I guess that's something." John studied the man. Something in his watery blue eyes told him to prepare for bad news. "So, what have you learned?"

"It's not good. The man from the pub . . . he died. And his father means to have his revenge."

John felt as if someone had punched him in the stomach. He took a step back. "His dying . . . what does it mean for me?"

Leland didn't answer right away. He licked cracked lips and reached through the bars to lay his hand on John's shoulder. "Have I ever told you how proud your father was of you?"

"At least a hundred times. I appreciate the kindness, but . . . I need to know what I'm to face."

Leland leveled sad eyes on John. "Most likely . . . the gallows."

The floor seemed to drop from beneath John's feet. He grabbed the bars to steady himself. "How can that be? I was simply defending myself in an altercation I'd attempted to prevent. My cousin will tell you. Langdon came after me. It was I who tried to put an end to the fight."

"You don't need to convince me. I believe you. It's the judge

45

we must persuade." He squeezed John's shoulder. "All is not lost. You are highly regarded in the community and have no previous record of wrongdoing, so the magistrate may be lenient. I'll do all I can to attain a lesser sentence for you."

"What might that be? Is there any possibility of my release?"

Leland shook his head slowly back and forth. "Sorry, lad. You've no chance of going free, aside of a miracle. If you escape the gallows, you'll most likely spend the remainder of your life on one of the hulks or be deported to New South Wales."

John could barely breathe. He laid his hand against his chest. Trying to get hold of what was happening, he pressed his head against the bars.

"I'm sorry. You don't deserve this."

"You're right there." John straightened and gripped the bars more tightly. "It was stupid of me to go with Henry. He has a gift for finding trouble and I knew it." He swiped his hair back. "I'd hoped he'd help sort this out. He's not thoroughly depraved."

"He may well be more depraved than you imagine."

"What do you mean?" John studied Leland, who had been the family's attorney for a good many years. He could see there was something more that needed saying. "What's happened?" John asked, not wanting to hear the answer.

Leland stared at the floor, scraping up grime with the edge of his boot. Finally he looked at John, his eyes watering more than usual. "It appears your cousin Henry has departed . . . along with your money and . . . and . . . your wife."

"No. You're mistaken. Henry may be irresponsible and even a bit disreputable, but he'd never steal from me, and why would Margaret go with him?" As the question left his lips, he remembered Henry's womanizing and how often he'd referred to Margaret in a personal way. All of a sudden, John knew why she'd gone, why *they'd* gone.

His voice flat, Leland said, "I went to the bank to withdraw funds from your account and was told there were no funds. That Mr. Hodgsson had closed the account." Leland scratched his head at the base of his wig. "I stopped at his home and was told he'd moved."

"He wouldn't do that to me. You can't be right."

"I then pressed on to your house, hoping to speak with Margaret, but she was gone also, along with her things. I made inquiries and was told that she and Mr. Hodgsson left together. One gentleman, a mister . . . Smith, I believe he said his name was, saw them the morning after you'd been arrested." Leland stopped and studied the dirtied hay strewn across the floor. "Mr. Smith said he watched while a coachman loaded two trunks. He thought she was going on holiday."

His doubts piling up like storm clouds, John struggled to grasp the wrong done to him. "Margaret wouldn't leave me. Not now."

"Your housemaid concurs with Mr. Smith. It would seem your wife has gone off with that mongrel of a cousin of yours. If I were a younger man and if I should meet up with Mr. Henry Hodgsson, I'd take great pleasure in choking the life out of him."

John reached through the bars and pressed his hands on Leland's chest. "There must be another explanation."

Leland grasped John's hands. "I wish it were so." He shook his head. "I offer my regrets."

Angry heat burned inside John and he withdrew from Leland. How could they do this to him? He dropped his arms to his sides. "All right, then. What is to be done?"

"Henry must be found. And scoundrel though he is, he must

be given an opportunity to explain his actions. Litigation may be complicated because he is an equal partner." He lifted his upper lip sardonically. "Of course he has no rights to your wife. But that you must settle yourself." He stepped back and glanced at the jailer and then at John. "Before you can deal with him, we must first see that you are released."

"You said that was impossible."

"Quite. But one can hope."

John fought for calm, but he felt as if he'd been set afire. "What are the charges against me?" he managed to ask.

"Murder. But we may be able to get that reduced."

"To what?"

"Manslaughter."

"What's the difference?"

"Murder means you intended to kill Langdon Hayes, and manslaughter says you did it without forethought." He dusted off his waistcoat. "It could mean the difference between life and death. I'll do my best to have the charges mitigated."

John's mind went back to the day he and Henry had gone to the pub. The thought of his cousin made him want to rage. He shoved the image of Henry aside. There were more important things to think about now.

"There's a barmaid," he said. "Her name's Abbey. She's a good sort, and she saw everything. She would help."

"A barmaid? And a woman as well? I'm sorry to say, she'll be of little use to us." Leland took out his pocket watch and glanced at it. "I have another engagement. I must go." He started to leave and then stopped. "Your hearing is two weeks from today. Do your best to look presentable."

John looked down at his filthy clothing. "And how am I to do that?"

"I'll bring you something." He offered a smile. "Don't lose heart." Leland walked away and was quickly swallowed by the darkness of the prison corridor.

"Looks like yer goin' t' 'ang," another prisoner taunted. John ignored him even when the man acted as if his neck were being stretched and started making choking sounds. Finally with a loud chuckle, the man walked to the far wall and sat down.

John paid him no mind. His thoughts were on Margaret and Henry and their treachery. How could they have betrayed him so unspeakably?

The creak of wagon wheels carried in from outside, and a crowd that had gathered turned boisterous, shouting accusations and cursing. *The death cart*, John thought.

No one in the cell spoke. They listened. John didn't want to hear. He'd seen the sickening sight before—cheers of satisfaction from salivating mobs as prisoners were walked up the scaffolding. They made proclamations of innocence or long confessions of guilt and repentance and then were hanged.

He moved to the far wall and slid to the floor. Pressing his hands over his ears, he tried to shut out the viciousness.

<hr />

Carrying a candle in one hand and a cup of tea in the other, Hannah moved along the dark corridor behind the kitchen. When she reached the basement door, she set down her tea and opened the door. Hinges, rusted from London dampness, creaked. A cold blast of air swept up from below. She didn't much like sleeping beneath the house, but it did afford her some privacy. She was the only one with a room in the manor basement.

Stepping carefully, she descended the stairs and followed a

short, narrow passageway that led to her room. She'd left the bedroom door slightly ajar so all she need do was push on it. She closed it using her hip and then crossed to her bedstand and set down the candle and tea.

Hoping for moonlight, she glanced up at a tiny window that sat at street level. There was no illumination. Exhausted and thankful for the end of the day, she fluffed her feather pillow and set it against the wall. Pulling down her quilt, she sat on the bed and lay back against the pillow and then tugged the blanket up over her legs. The room felt like ice. She bent her legs and drew them close to her. Picking up her cup, she sipped the already cooling tea. It was just hot enough to warm her insides a bit. The ritual reminded her of better times with friends and family. She closed her eyes, yearning for those days.

Hannah shivered and looked about the tiny, shadowy room. The darkness felt oppressive. She was allowed only a candle, no lamp. *It could be worse*, she told herself. *I could be on the street.*

Stretching out aching legs, Hannah wiggled her toes and tried to think on things she could be thankful for. Instead, she held up her left hand, turned it over, and studied the palm. It was chapped and blistered. She'd only been at the Walkers two weeks, but the days had been grueling. She labored from first light to last. And the children never tired of pestering her.

It seemed nothing Hannah did satisfied Mrs. Walker. Her work was always viewed as insufficient. And the cook was even worse. She seemed a miserable person, forever complaining about something or other. She had no pity for others and in fact went out of her way to make others as miserable as she.

Just that afternoon, she'd made a point of addressing Hannah's lowly position and what was out of reach for scullery maids. Hannah had been cleaning dishes when late in the afternoon the cook, Mrs. Keller, walked into the scullery. She sniffed. "Ye smell that? It's fine veal. Whitest meat I've seen." She grinned. "I can nearly taste it—the juiciness of it and oh such a delicate flavor." Eyes alight with viciousness, she poured hot water into the washing tub.

It was too hot, but Hannah fought to keep her hands beneath the surface, refusing to give the woman satisfaction. "I'm sure it will be quite tasty," she said agreeably, continuing to scrub a greasy pan.

"Course ye'll never know how delicious it is. It's not for ye and yer kind." With a smirk, she continued, "I'll let ye know how it turns out." She chuckled and walked back into the kitchen.

Oh, she's hateful, Hannah thought. *Lord, why have you placed me here? What is it you're doing?* She squeezed her eyes shut and tried to staunch hot tears. She felt alone. Holding back a sob, she whispered, "Oh, Mum. I miss you so. I need you."

Hannah forced herself to think about the present. At least she had work and wasn't living on the street. It did no good to dwell on the ugliness of others. She sipped her tea and wished she could feel her mother's presence. But the oppression and hopelessness pressed down, and she felt as if the weight and darkness of the house above rested upon her. Feeling faithless, she thought, *God most certainly is displeased with me. But, Lord, my circumstances seem too much to bear.*

"Father, may your presence overshadow the hatefulness I feel," she prayed, knowing that Jesus had endured so much more than she and from people he'd loved.

With a small sense of tranquility, she set her cup on the table beside the bed and rolled onto her stomach. She hugged her pillow and burrowed beneath the blankets.

She thought back to the lovely days when she and her mother

had worked together creating fashions for the best-dressed women in the city. If only she could have those days back. She would treasure every one.

When she'd come to work for the Walkers, she'd hoped to be able to use her skills as a seamstress to serve the family. Instead, she scrubbed dishes and woodwork and polished the silver.

The children were unbearable little monsters who seemed to delight in dirtying what she'd cleaned. Mrs. Walker was not a permissive mother, but she did have difficulty keeping track of the children.

Mr. Walker was rarely home, but Hannah was grateful for that. She didn't like the man. He watched her and often sought her out for no good reason at all. He'd come upon her and ask an absurd question or inspect her work, and although it had been done respectably, he'd insist she do it again. And there were times when he'd touch her. The contact was always brief and seemed accidental, but Hannah knew it wasn't. She'd seen lust in his eyes. The thought sent a shiver through her.

"Ah well," she told the empty room. "Time for sleep. Tomorrow will be here much too soon." She blew out the candle and pulled the covers up around her shoulders. *Lord, please deliver me from this place and from these people. Is it too selfish of me to ask that you restore my life to what it once was? And if that is not your will, I pray that you will create a new life for me.*

She closed her eyes. As she sought sleep, she thought she heard something at the door. A light cast beneath it and then a shadow passed. She stopped breathing and listened. She heard a noise, as if something were being pressed against the door. Someone was there! Her heart battered wildly.

Who could it be? No one used this part of the house. Should she have need, no one would hear her scream.

5

Afraid to breathe, Hannah clenched her blanket tightly under her chin.

Her heart pounding so hard it felt as if it would beat out of her chest, she stared into the darkness. Again, she saw a glimmer of light along the bottom edge of the door.

She sat up, still clutching her covers. *Who would be down here at this hour?* Wetting dry lips, she asked, "Who is there?" Her voice wavered. "Pray, tell me." There was no reply. "Is someone there?" she asked more forcefully.

She remembered the oldest Walker boy, Peter. He was always up to some sort of mischief. It must be him.

"Peter, that's enough foolishness." She tried to sound authoritative. "Go up to bed or I'll be forced to speak to your mother." She waited for the pounding of footsteps or a mumbled apology. There was neither. "Peter?"

Lying down, she huddled beneath the blanket. The house remained silent. Minutes passed, and Hannah listened, but heard nothing. *My mind must be playing tricks on me.* She closed her eyes and, taking a deep breath, she relaxed tight muscles, but her heart continued to thump. *I'm being childish. I'm sure it's nothing,* she thought and drifted toward sleep.

Something startled Hannah awake. Then she heard it—a grating creak. It sounded as if the door was opening. She sat up. The door rasped.

"Who's there?" No one answered. "Please, who is there?"

The sound of the door closing was the only answer. Then she heard the rustle of clothing. Someone was moving toward her bed.

"Please, who is it?"

There was no answer.

"Who is it?" she demanded.

She could just make out a shadow and rolled away from it. Someone grabbed the back of her nightdress and yanked her backward. A hand was clapped over her mouth, smothering a scream. The person breathed loudly and smelled of sweet lozenges.

Mr. Walker!

Hannah struggled and managed to break free. She scrambled to the side of the bed and leaped to the floor. Facing the bed, she challenged, "Mr. Walker! What are you doing here? Leave my room at once!"

He sounded as if he were panting. Then he stepped into the dim glow of a rising moon. His thinning hair stuck out wildly from his head, and in the moonlight he looked like an apparition.

"My dear, you knew I would come." He half smiled, his teeth luminous. "You've been enticing me since your first day."

He grabbed for her.

Hannah evaded his grasp. "Don't touch me." She clutched the neck of her nightdress closed. "I haven't enticed anyone!"

"You tease me even now."

Hannah edged toward the door. "Truly, I'm doing no such thing. I mean only to do my work and to bring harm to no one."

Clouds must have parted, for the room suddenly brightened as moonlight streamed through the small window.

Mr. Walker wet his lips and lunged at her. With a smirk he ripped away the top of her nightdress.

Hannah snatched at the torn material and clutched it against her as she ran for the door. Before she could reach it, he seized her about the waist and pulled her to him.

"Let me go!" she yelled, fighting for freedom. "I've had no wicked thoughts toward you, sir. You have misunderstood."

"It matters not." He buried his face in her hair and pressed his lips to her neck.

"Sir! No!" Hannah screamed, shocked at the strength of the slightly built man.

"Be silent!" He shook her.

"I'll not be quiet!"

"As you like, then. Your cries will do you no good. No one will hear you." He held her tightly against his body, then lifted her and carried her to the bed.

Quaking, Hannah pleaded, "I entreat you, sir. You can't mean this. I will be ruined."

Ignoring her pleas he pushed her onto the bed and pressed himself upon her. He stared down at her. "Your beauty bewitches me."

He kissed her greedily. Hannah managed to wrench her face away, but his lips only found another target. Pressing them against her neck, he whispered, "Do not fight me. You want this too."

55

"No! I do not!" Hannah pushed against him.

He only shoved her down harder and trapped her arms beneath his hands. He gazed at her, his expression one of pure lust. "You'll do as you're told."

"You can't mean to defile me in this way."

"Pretending innocence will do you no good. I've seen your glances, your provocative ways. You've beguiled me and done so deliberately."

"I've done nothing of the sort." She fought to free her arms. *This can't be happening.* Looking into his licentious eyes, she knew there would be no escaping his hunger.

He kissed her hard on the mouth, and then gripping her hair, he said, "I'll have you whenever I want." He smirked. "You'll do as I say."

God, tell me what to do, Hannah prayed. "It is true, sir," she said, forcing herself to look at him. "You are more powerful than me, in every way. But I always believed you to be an honorable man." She choked back a sob. "To take a woman against her will is not honorable; it is beneath you."

He tightened his hold and jerked her head back against the straw mattress. "If one of us is lacking honor, it is you. For this is not my doing, but yours. And because you have sought me, I shall have you."

***

Hannah didn't know how long the assault went on. It didn't really matter. Her life was over.

When Charlton Walker finished with Hannah, he warned her not to speak of what had happened, saying he'd deny her accusations and stressing that no one would believe her word against his. Before leaving her, he'd also threatened to put her out if she said a word.

Hannah rolled onto her side, tucked her arms in close, and pulled her legs up to her abdomen. For a long while she lay like that, staring into the darkness and feeling dead inside. The attack played over and over in her mind. How could he have done it? How could a man be so vile? *Why? Why?*

Hannah knew she ought to cry, but there were no tears. Closing her eyes, she sought the solace of sleep, but she could smell him. She stank of him. She needed to wash.

Climbing out of bed, she was unable to suppress a groan. She hurt all over. Stiffly, she moved to the wash basin on the bureau. Stripping off her tattered nightdress, she washed with a rough cloth and water. The cold water took her breath away, but its bite felt cleansing. She scrubbed her skin until it stung, but she could still smell him.

He'll come back! It will happen again! And he's right; no one will believe me. The thought made her want to retch. "I can't stay," she said. "I can't."

Hearing a sound from somewhere in the house, she stopped washing and listened. What if he were to come back tonight?

"I must leave. Now."

She pulled on her undergarments as quickly as her shaking hands allowed. Moonlight illuminated bruises already staining her arms and legs. Nausea rose into her throat and she pressed her hand against her abdomen.

"Oh God, how could this happen?" The tears she'd expected earlier now stung. But there was no time for sorrowing. She wiped them away and prepared to leave. Shivering violently, she struggled into her day clothes.

After packing her few belongings in her satchel, she moved

toward the door. She stopped. Where would she go? She had no place, but staying was incomprehensible.

Lifting the satchel to her shoulder, she reached for the doorknob. With her hand resting on it, she prayed, "Lord, I need your help. Cover me with a cloak of protection. And tell me where I'm to go."

Again, she heard something from above. Was someone on the staircase? Hannah's heart battered against her ribs. She opened the door and the hinge whined. She stopped, leaving it ajar, and listened. Hearing nothing, she stepped into the dark hallway. Keeping one hand on the wall to guide her, she moved silently toward the bottom of the stairs. She snuck a quick glance up the stairway. It was dark.

Shaking and sick, she pressed her back against the wall. She had little chance of survival without this post. "I have no choice," she said, hoping the words would bolster her.

She peeked up the staircase again and then feeling her way in the darkness, Hannah slowly ascended the stairs. She was shaking so violently, her legs felt as if they might crumple beneath her.

At the top of the stairway, she stopped and listened. Had he gone to bed? Was he still up and working in his study or reading in the parlor? It had been at least an hour since he'd left her. No sound came from behind the door. Was he waiting for her? Waiting for her to make an escape? Slowly she opened the door, holding her breath. When no sound came, she opened it the rest of the way and quietly moved to the kitchen.

It still smelled of roasted veal and cabbage. Hannah's stomach rolled and she thought she might be sick. She closed her eyes and breathed slowly. Water dripped from the hand pump, making a dull plunking sound as it dropped into a basin in the sink, and wood popped in the hot stove. A loud crack of floor boards startled her and she whirled around. But there was nothing except shadows. The thought of the man filled Hannah with loathing.

She clutched her satchel against her as she moved to the back door. Glancing briefly about the room, she opened the door and stepped outside. In spite of the dangers that faced her, she was glad to be free of the house and its owners.

Frosty air hit her, but Hannah was thankful for the clear night. A nearly full moon lit the streets. She huddled inside her cloak and hurried down the lane. She'd go to Ruby's.

Although the hour was late, the streets were not deserted. She passed several people bundled inside wraps huddling in doorways. Would she soon be like them—dispossessed and wandering? A candle lighter moved from lantern to lantern, illuminating the city one street at a time. She heard the echo of a night watchman, calling out the time—nine o'clock. It seemed much later.

Hannah longed for Ruby's kindly hug, but couldn't bear the thought of telling her what had happened. How could she ever tell anyone?

Feeling as if she were being pursued by some unseen specter, Hannah ran until her lungs burned and her legs ached. She slowed to a walk. Approaching Ruby's house, she stopped and tried to create a reasonable explanation for her showing up at this time of night. Ruby would want to know. *I simply won't tell her,* Hannah decided. *No matter how much she insists that I do.*

When Hannah reached the cottage, she stood on the stoop and stared at the door. Perhaps it would be better if she simply disappeared into the darkness. She looked out at the street with its menacing shadows. No, she couldn't do that. She turned back to the door and knocked softly. A few moments later, she heard a voice from inside.

"Now, who is it that's waking me from my sleep?"

"It's me, Ruby. Please, may I come in?"

The door opened. "What are ye doing out at this time of night?" Ruby focused on Hannah. "Oh dearie, what's happened to ye? Ye look dreadful." She bundled Hannah inside and hustled her to the settee. "Let me get ye a cup of tea."

Shaking and weary, Hannah huddled inside her cloak. She still didn't know what explanation to give. "I'm sorry for disturbing you so late. I . . . I didn't know where else to go."

"What's happened, luv?"

Hannah looked at Ruby. She'd decided to say nothing, but now knew that would be impossible. Ruby wouldn't tolerate her silence. How could she explain what had happened? She could barely even think of it.

Ruby sat beside Hannah. "It's all right, dear. Ye can tell me."

"Well . . . Mr. Walker . . . he . . ." She shook her head.

"He what?" Ruby's voice sounded strident.

"He came to my room . . . and . . ."

"Did he touch you?" Ruby asked, with outrage.

Hannah could only nod.

"And did he have his way with ye?"

Again Hannah nodded, only this time tears burned a hot stream down her cheeks.

"I'll hang him by his thumbs!" Ruby stood and acted as if she'd stride right out the door and then on to the Walkers. Catching hold of herself, she returned to Hannah, her countenance tender. She knelt before the young woman and pulled

60

her against her breast. "Now, now. It'll be all right. Ye'll see. Everything will be all right."

"Ruby," a surly voice called from a back room. "What's going on out there?" A moment later Ruby's husband, Percy, tottered out of the bedroom. He was barely clothed. He rubbed his face and gazed bleary-eyed at Hannah. "Why she 'ere?"

"It's none of your concern," Ruby said. "Go back to bed. I'll see to her."

"She's not stayin' 'ere. We got no room."

Ruby stood and faced her husband, hands on her hips. "I'll not put her out in the middle of the night. No matter what you say or do." She stood directly in front of him, looking fierce.

Percy glared back at her. "She can stay 'til mornin' and then she's got to go." With that, he turned and disappeared through the dark doorway.

Ruby walked back to Hannah and sat beside her. "Don't worry 'bout him. He don't know what he's sayin'." She rubbed Hannah's back. "Ye can stay as long as ye have need."

"Thank you, Ruby, but you don't have room. And I'm not about to cause trouble between you and Percy. But I will stay the night."

"All right for now. Ye need to sleep. I'll fetch a blanket for ye and ye can sleep on the sofa." She walked into the bedroom and reappeared a moment later, a blanket and pillow in hand. "Here ye go, luv. Try to rest. Put all this out of yer mind. It can't be undone so ye might as well just leave it behind ye." She smiled and helped Hannah lie down and then covered her with the blanket.

"Thank you," Hannah said, feeling embraced by Ruby's gentleness.

"Tomorrow will be a new day. Ye'll see." She kissed Hannah's

cheek. "I'll leave the lantern . . . just in case ye might need it."
Before leaving the room, she stood over Hannah for a moment
and gazed at her with sad eyes. "Good night, then," she said
and left Hannah alone.

Hannah turned down the lantern and stared at the window.
Moonlight filtered in, illuminating the room. Something leapt
onto the sofa, startling Hannah. Then she heard a deep, thrum-
ming purr. "Oh, Jasper," she said, pulling him to her chest. She
rubbed her cheek against his soft fur. "Jasper," she whispered.
"How good to see you."

She settled into her pillow, keeping the cat in her arms. She
closed her eyes, comforted by his steady purring. But her mind
took her back to the dark room in the Walker house. Again,
she felt fear and revulsion as if it were all happening again. She
opened her eyes, but the images stayed with her. She would
never be the same.

A cold stone of bitterness grew inside. *I'm defiled and no good
to anyone.* Hannah loathed Mr. Walker. But she also loathed
herself. Maybe she had been at fault. Had she, indeed, beguiled
him?

6

A guard strode toward the locked cell door. "Lindston . . . Bradshaw . . . Steller," he called.

John pushed to his feet. This was it. His prison term would begin on one of the decaying ships known as hulks. He didn't yet know when he'd be sent to New South Wales. It mattered little; his life was no longer his own. The truth of it felt like lead in his gut.

I ought to be thankful to have my life, he told himself. By the grace of God and a good attorney, he'd escaped the gallows. But he couldn't muster any joy. He'd be lucky to survive the six-month passage. All that he held dear was gone. And worst of all, he'd been betrayed by people he trusted. How could he believe in anyone again?

Margaret's saucy smile flashed through his mind. As his anguish swelled, he pushed her image aside. She was lost to him forever. Leland Martin had brought word just two days before. Margaret had died from an undiagnosed ailment.

His throat tightened at the thought. Even with her betrayal it was a loss beyond understanding. *She deserved it*, he thought, his bitterness driving out his grief.

I won't think on it, he told himself as he picked up a bag containing clothing, soap, tooth powder, and a hairbrush that Leland had left with him. They were his only possessions.

The three men lined up at the cell door. No one spoke. One man kept his eyes on the floor, while the other defiantly glared at the guard. John tried to look indifferent.

The jailer yanked open the door and stood watch while another guard put the men in wrist and ankle irons and then looped chains around their waists, tethering them together.

"Get away with ye. And don't make no trouble." The gaoler carried a bludgeon and glared at the defiant-looking bloke. Chains clanking, the three shuffled along the dank corridors of the prison, through a monstrous gate, and outside to a waiting wagon crowded with other prisoners.

John blinked against the bright light of day. He hadn't been outdoors since his hearing. Most likely this would be a brief encounter with the outside world. His mind carried him to the dark hole he knew was waiting. He didn't want to think on it.

With the ousting of one dreadful thought, another replaced it and his mind returned to his trial. Outrage filled him, but it was better than despair.

He'd stood in the oppressive courtroom, his senses insulted by the stinking union of cigar smoke, unwashed bodies, and the stale smell of spirits given off from the many spectators. A bellowing plaintiff and the blustering prosecutor harangued. Before Mr. Martin could utter a word, the judge had already made his decision—guilty. John had been certain he'd hang, but then Leland Martin had skillfully presented his background and his character, and John received a prison sentence instead—one to be carried out in New South Wales. *Life in prison. The gallows would have been better*, he thought dismally.

A guard grabbed him by the arm and thrust him up into the back of the wagon. He barely managed to hang on to his belongings.

"Sit down," the guard ordered.

John sat on one of two wooden benches that ran from the front to the back of the wagon and then glanced about, trying to get his bearings. His manacled ankle was secured to a bolt in the floor. The irons cut into his skin.

While the last of the three men from John's cell was being shackled, the wagon lunged forward and the prisoners started their trek through the city. John tried not to look at staring bystanders. Instead, he concentrated on the buildings and the markets. It would most likely be his last look at London. The fast pace of the city, the cries of vendors, and the merging smells of cigars, coffee, and horse manure that he'd complained of only a few weeks before no longer repulsed him.

How had life gone so awry? He stifled a shudder.

John glanced at the other prisoners. There were ten others locked in just as he was. A skinny young man looked back at him. John could see panic and disbelief in his blue eyes. He wondered if the same expression lay behind his own gaze. Under normal circumstances he would have offered a smile of encouragement, but John had nothing to give. Instead, he looked down at his hands and slid the manacles down to loosen them slightly.

The wagon moved slowly through the streets. John wished the journey over. He didn't like the stares. What if someone he knew saw him? He couldn't bear that. The horses plodded on, and the more of London John saw, the more wounded he felt at being dragged off to another continent. *There is no justice*, he thought, the bitterness inside growing.

They rumbled past businesses and crouching cottages, and John wondered where Henry had gotten to. Was he somewhere along this very route? If he saw him, what would his response be? Rage boiled inside. He deserved a chance to face the man, to tell him what he thought of his deception, his treachery.

All of a sudden, a young apprentice who had worked for John stepped into his line of vision. The lad's eyes widened when they met John's. He quickly looked away and then back again. He held his previous employer's gaze and finally nodded in respect. John managed a slight smile, thankful for the kind gesture.

The wagon turned a corner and rolled over cobblestone streets, heading for the Thames. *So it's the river, then.* The hulks tethered along the Thames might be better than the ones in the bay. Still, his stomach tightened. He'd heard stories about the misery on board the decaying ships.

Transportation for the term of his natural life, the judge's voice reverberated through his mind. *How will I endure?*

His father's voice replaced that of the judge's. *"One day at a time, son."* How many times had he heard that advice? More than he could count. When John had been fearful or had wanted to give up on something that seemed too difficult, his father was there, steady and wise. "You can't scale a mountain all at once," he'd said when John had lamented over learning the machine trade.

One day at a time, John told himself. *I can do today. That's all I need think of. Today will be my first day of survival.*

The cart approached the river and a row of tethered hulks. The derelict ships looked like hideous caricatures of vultures hunched over carcasses, their wings spread possessively. Dread swept through John and his earlier resolve faltered. What awaited him? Bile rose up into his throat and he swallowed, trying to keep his stomach in place.

The wagon jolted to a stop, and the men were unloaded and marched across a gangplank that tied a hulk to the shore. "This'll be your home for a while," one of the guards said, chuckling. "Enjoy your stay."

The prisoners were handed off to marines wearing red-breasted uniforms. They were hustled onto the ship and into a small room, then left to wait. A guard remained at the door.

The prisoners sat on the floor. John rested his back against a bulkhead. A small man who reminded John of a scrawny chicken couldn't keep from crying. As he sobbed, his shackles clanked.

"Stop your sniveling," a prisoner next to him ordered. "You chose your lot like the rest of us. Now it's time to pay the price. Why you crying like a baby?"

"Got me a family," the man said, wiping his nose with the back of his hand. The movement carried the other man's hand with his.

He jerked back on the chains. "Aye! Keep my hand away from your nose."

The man's shoulders drooped. "Don't deserve this. All I done was get me family somethin' to eat. We was starvin'.'"

The prisoner chained to him glared. "You're no different than the rest of us. We all done something we figured we had to do. And none of us is innocent."

The door opened and an officer stepped into the room. Arms folded across his chest, he stared at the men. "Up on your feet." No one moved. "Stand up, I said."

The men stared; some slowly stood.

"Up with you! Now!"

The authority in his voice got the rest of the prisoners to their feet. He nodded to the guard who then removed the men's manacles.

"Now, strip. I want everything off." The guard at the door proffered a wooden club. "I wouldn't want anyone to be bludgeoned on their first day here."

Although still tied to one another, the men managed to undress. Most stood in their underdrawers.

"I said everything."

The underdrawers came off.

The men stood naked and vulnerable. Wearing a smirk, his eyes heated by scorn, the officer looked the men over and then walked out.

"Now what?" a rather rotund prisoner asked.

No one answered.

The men moved to the wall and sat. John pulled his knees up close to his chest, and tried not to think about his imminent future. Instead, he allowed his mind to return to his father. *I'm glad he can't see me now*, he thought, rubbing his sore wrists. He hoped he'd stay free of the irons.

John rested his chin on bent knees and closed his eyes, longing for rest. He was weary, to his very heart.

Without warning, the door was flung open and a tall, heavyset man stepped into the room, followed by a sailor. The first man was so tall, he had to bend to get through the door. "Up! Everyone up!"

The men scrambled to their feet. John's muscles tensed. He kept his eyes straight ahead.

The man walked to the first prisoner in line. "Bend forward." The convict did as he was told. The big man looked through the prisoner's hair. "Straighten up. Open your mouth." He peered inside the man's mouth, checking his teeth, and then examined his body, including the prisoner's private places. After that he moved to the next man and the next, examining each similarly.

When he'd finished, he said, "You're a healthy enough lot. Get dressed." He left abruptly.

The prisoners struggled back into their clothes. The guard opened the door and stood aside. "Out with you. Now."

John and some of the others picked up their belongings. "Leave 'em," the sailor barked. "You'll have no need."

"But they're all I got," one man said.

Instantly the soldier smashed the butt of his gun into the man's face. Dropping to his knees and covering his nose with his hands, the prisoner cried, "Ye broke me nose!"

"Next time you'll do as you're told. Now, get up!"

Still holding his hand over his face, the man stumbled to his feet and staggered after the rest of the group. They assembled on deck and stood waiting, for what they did not know. A sharp, cold wind buffeted them. Marines stood guard, muskets ready.

A man whom John thought might be the captain strode up before them. Hands clasped behind his back, he stood silently for a long while and studied the prisoners. His eyes were hard. "While you're on my vessel, you'll do as told. You'll get your rations twice a day. If you ask for more you'll get less the next day, so you'd be wise to be glad for what you're given. And there'll be no pinching food." He walked to the railing. "You'll have one hour of lamp light a night. We don't waste oil on my ship." He lowered his gaze, peering out from beneath heavy eyebrows. "When I say sleep you'll sleep, and when I say work you'll work. You disobey and you'll feel the lash."

He turned and faced the men straight on. "You won't set

69

sail for a while. 'Til you're transferred, you're mine. There'll be *lady* passengers sailing with you, but don't be getting any ideas. They're not for the likes of you."

John knew this was only a taste of what was to come. He looked toward the city. An ugly brown cloud draped itself over brick and mortared buildings. Chimneys stuck up defiantly from rooftops, as if to say they would continue belching soot into the air, like it or not. And John would take orders, like it or not. For his world had gone askew, and he had no say about its course.

He'd wanted adventure. Had he wished this upon himself? Was it some kind of judgment? If there were a way to return to the life he'd once had, he would gladly go.

But there was no returning now. He'd lost his life—forever.

Before Ruby or her family roused from their sleep, Hannah had quietly slipped out of the house. She'd left a note, explaining her reasons for going. She didn't want to create trouble between Ruby and her husband. Ruby's kind heart wouldn't be able to put her out. She'd shortchange her own family in order to help. Hannah couldn't bear to be the cause of more struggles for the kindly woman. She and her family had trouble enough. Her difficulties were her own and not Ruby's responsibility.

After spending hours walking, she wondered if she'd made the right choice. Her legs and feet ached, her shoulder throbbed from carrying her satchel, and her stomach growled angrily at its emptiness.

She stopped at every business she thought might have work. No one needed help. She didn't know where else to look. *There must be someone who has a place for me. Lord, where should I look?* She heard no answer. But of course she wouldn't, not after what had happened. She was defiled and had most certainly been shut out of God's favor. Unwillingly her mind carried her back to the attack. She could feel him touching her. She could still smell him.

"Aye! Watch out!" shouted a man pushing a cart of vegetables.

Distracted, Hannah had nearly run into him. "So sorry, sir," she called after the man, but he didn't hear as he hurried on.

Children had gathered to watch a Punch and Judy show. Hannah stopped, thankful for the distraction. As the marionettes yelled at each other and chased one another about the small stage, the performance didn't seem at all entertaining. Screaming her frustration, Judy whacked Punch over the head with her broom and the children laughed, but their antics only disturbed Hannah. She moved on, hoping to put the sounds of the play behind her.

The emptiness in her stomach gnawed. The smells of baked goods and the calls of peddlers selling produce only made her hungrier. She stopped at a display of apples. Picking up one, she held it to her nose and smelled its sweet fragrance. Her mouth watered. She could almost taste it. What if she were to drop it into her bag? Would anyone see? She looked about and her eyes locked with the peddler selling the fruit. Her heart skipped. He stared as if knowing her thoughts. She quickly set it back in the pile and, as nonchalantly as she could manage, ambled on.

She kept walking, finally leaving behind the sounds and smells of the marketplace. Weary and feeling faint, she leaned against a building. Two gaunt-looking children, probably a brother and sister, approached a gentlewoman, their hands held out palm up.

71

"Ye 'ave a pence for us, mum?"

The woman opened a small coin purse, fished out two pence, and dropped one into the boy's hand and then the girl's.

"Thank ye, mum." The children tucked their treasures into their pockets and ran off toward the market.

Hannah felt envious. If only it were so easy for her to acquire funds. *Perhaps I could beg*, she thought and tried to imagine herself holding out a hand and entreating someone to give her money or food. The image repelled her. She couldn't. She wouldn't—no matter how hungry she became.

The aroma of baked goods wafted from a shop across the street. Hannah's stomach cramped. Perhaps the owner needed a clerk or a cook. She crossed the road, stopped at the door to tidy her hair and smooth her wrinkled skirt, and then stepped inside.

She admired rows of heavy brown breads and sweet cakes laid out on display. Holding her spine straight, she smiled at a man standing behind a counter. "Good day, sir. You have a fine shop."

"That I do." He eyed her warily.

"Might I inquire if you need some assistance?" Before he could say no, Hannah hurried on. "I can do most anything. I'm quite clever. I'm a fine cook and I've a strong back for cleaning and such, and I also read and do figures. I get along well with most everyone. I helped my mother—"

The baker held up his hand, palm out. "I'm sorry. I wish I could help you, but I've no need. And even if I did, I've not an extra farthing to pay you."

"Of course. I'm sorry to have bothered you." She headed for the door, her eyes lingering on the breads.

Hannah hurried out of the store and walked down the street

toward the river. She stepped onto a bridge and started across. Midway she stopped. She had nowhere to go.

Leaning on the railing, she studied the river as it washed beneath the bridge. Its waters were brown and murky. The cold, dark surge called to her. It could be her way out. She could end her sorrows. All she need do was to step off into the icy waters. It would be over quickly.

Hannah envisioned her mother. She longed to be with her, but Hannah was afraid. If she ended her own life, would she be allowed into heaven? And could God accept her now that she was so badly tarnished? Tears of sorrow trailed down her cheeks.

Hannah stood there for a long while. Hadn't her mum said the Lord accepts all who believe in him—even sinners? Hannah had always thought God loved her. Her mother had told her so. But that was before . . . before she'd been so badly used.

It was not a risk she could take, and so she moved on as darkness settled over the city. It was cold. The wind swirled frigid air beneath her cloak. If only she could warm herself at a fire. She remembered the stove in her cottage and the many times she and her mother had sat quietly in the evenings sipping tea and enjoying the rest. An ache swelled at the base of her throat, and she wondered how far it was to the churchyard where her mother lay.

7

Huddled inside her cloak, Hannah walked for what seemed like hours. The darkness deepened and streetlamps were lit. Strumpets moved onto the streets, lingering along the roadway and leaning against buildings. Some strolled provocatively to better entice clients.

Hannah tried not to look at them as she moved past. A number of the women gave her haughty looks. She hurried on, hoping to find a place to seclude herself. A gentleman dressed in a silk suit approached. He boldly looked her up and down and then stared into her eyes.

"How much for an hour?"

Hannah could not believe what she'd heard. She tried to walk past him, but he stepped in front of her. "Sir, you've made a mistake. I'm not what you think." She glanced at the street-walkers.

"If I may be so bold . . . you look to be in need. And I would be pleased to accommodate that need." He touched a strand of hair that had fallen free of its pins.

"Sir!" Hannah pulled back.

"You're a handsome one. And spirited." A smiled played at his lips. "I'd pay well."

Hannah pressed a hand against her empty stomach; it ached with hunger . . . and she was already tainted. "No. Leave me." Before the need of sustenance made her do something despicable, she stepped around the man and hurried down the street. *Dear Lord, help me*, she prayed. For a moment she'd considered the offer. *I am indecent. No respectable woman would have entertained such an idea.*

She stopped beneath a lantern. Grabbing hold of the pole, she gripped it tightly as if its stability would secure her. *God, can you not see past my shame and provide a way for me?*

Across the street a prostitute sauntered up and down the lane. She rolled her hips back and forth and made no effort to conceal rounded breasts pushing out of a tawdry gown. Her lips were painted red, and she'd piled her hair on top of her head in an effort to look like a lady. The attempt failed.

Rather than being repelled as she had been in the past, Hannah felt ashamed of her previous judgments against such women. She'd always assumed they'd chosen their professions and didn't deserve pity. Only now did she understand how life's circumstances sometimes foisted unseemly choices upon people. Could she make such a choice? There had been a time the answer would have been a fervent no. Today, with hunger gnawing at her, she was no longer certain.

The prostitute leveled a gaze on Hannah. Then with a quick glance up and down the lane, she strode boldly toward her. "On your way. This is me corner. I'll not share it with the likes of you."

"But I'm not—"

"Get. Away with you."

Staring at the cheerless, angry eyes, Hannah knew it would do no good to explain. "I'm sorry," she said and moved on.

She stopped outside a pub and gazed in through a window. It was brightly lit inside and appeared warm. Sounds of laughter and songs rolled out onto the street. She never thought that a pub would entice her, but on this night it seemed welcoming. Taking in a deep breath and letting it out in a puff, she pushed against the door. Just as she did, it shoved back and nearly knocked Hannah off her feet.

A disagreeable-looking man stumbled out and pushed past her. "Out of me way!"

Hannah stared after him, and then gazed inside the crowded inn. It was raucous and smelled of ale and smoke. She didn't belong there. Disheartened, she let the door close and walked away, moving along the shadowy streets, uncertain where to go.

Finally, unable to continue longer, Hannah stepped into the shadow of a doorway. It was a business establishment and not a home, so she was reassured she'd not disturb anyone's sleep. She squatted down and pressed her back against the door. Pulling her cloak tightly about her, she stared out from her tenuous shelter.

Here, the world felt inhospitable and deserted. She cupped her ice-cold hands over her mouth and breathed into them. Her breath steamed the air. Pulling the cloak over her head, she bundled deeply within its folds. The cold crept in, and she shivered.

Perhaps tomorrow will bring good fortune, she thought. Hearing approaching footsteps, she peeked out from beneath the cape and pressed deeper into the shadows. A man walked by without noticing her. How many times had she done the same? The destitute and needy had been invisible to her. *Lord, forgive my indifference*, she prayed and vowed that if ever she found her way out of this horrid predicament, she'd never again overlook the poorest of society.

Exhaustion swamped her. She closed her eyes, hoping for sleep and praying for a miracle. But even as she prayed she didn't believe. God hadn't protected her thus far. Why would he begin now? Perhaps he was done with her.

In her desolation she heard her mother's voice. "God loves all people, especially those without hope. He loved even the lepers." She'd spoken the words during one of their evening chats. Now, Hannah wondered if her mother could have been mistaken. *What if God doesn't love the sullied? If not, then I must be a stench in his nostrils.*

Her mind carried Hannah back to the basement room at the Walker estate. She could feel Charlton Walker's hands on her, and again shame consumed her. Had she tempted him? Could she have fought harder? She stared out at the empty streets, thankful that no one could see her. In the light of day would her shame be evident? Would people know her secret just by looking at her?

Exhaustion finally rescued Hannah from her thoughts, and she slept.

A sharp, cramping pain in the middle of her stomach awakened Hannah. Morning light was beginning to reveal the littered street. The prostitutes and drunkards were gone, but doorways and alcoves housed others like her who had sought shelter.

Shocked anew at her circumstances, reality swept through Hannah. *What am I to do?*

She straightened cramped legs and pushed to her feet. Stretching her arms over her head, she tipped slightly to the side, hoping to work out unyielding muscles.

At least it's not raining, she thought, gazing at the sky. Pink touched the gray canopy. Perhaps today would be sunny and warmer.

Running her hands over tangled hair, she thought, *I must be a sight*. Removing her hair clasps, she worked her fingers through the snarls and then repinned the hair. Opening her cloak, she gazed down at her wrinkled gown and let out a sigh. *How will I ever find work? I look like a vagabond.*

She considered her other dress, but it had been packed in her satchel. Undoubtedly by now it was in worse condition than the one she wore.

Her stomach growled and hunger knifed through her. She needed to eat.

Sunlight brightened a clear sky and cast shadows along the street. With determination, Hannah headed for the market. Maybe she could find work or something to fill her hollow stomach.

A coffee shop door opened just as she approached. A man swept away dirt from his porch and then moved back inside. The smell of coffee and baked goods lingered. Hannah moved to the door and gazed inside, watching while the owner set out a display of sweet rolls. Her mouth watered.

Stepping just inside the doorway, she asked, "Sir. Perchance, do you have need of help? I can do most anything."

The man looked at her, his eyes taking in her disheveled appearance. "I've no need for the likes of you. This is a proper establishment."

"Sir, I am a proper woman. I've only recently fallen on hard times."

He still looked doubtful. Hannah searched for something she could say that would convince him. "I'll do anything."

The man stormed toward her, forcing Hannah to step back onto the porch. "Your kind's not welcome here." He slammed the door shut.

Hannah stared at the door. Tears burned the back of her eyes. She wanted to defend her honor. But what good would it do? And in truth, she had none to defend.

She stepped backward onto the street. The ground beneath her feet shook, and she turned to see a team of horses charging toward her. She leaped away to avoid being trampled, lost her footing, and fell into a mud puddle at the side of the road. The horses and coach flew past. The driver didn't even slow down.

Pushing to her feet, she stared after the carriage. Passersby gaped, but no one offered assistance. Holding muddied hands away from her body, Hannah gazed down at her soiled dress. Now she'd have to use her other gown. She surrendered to hopelessness. How would she convince anyone that she was a decent sort and could be trusted?

She blinked back tears. *Lord, couldn't you spare me a little dignity?*

Three adolescent boys walked up to her. The tallest gawked openly. "Yer a bit old for a mud lark." He pointed at her. "Eh, we got a mud lark, 'ere." He grinned and made a goofy face.

"Mud lark. Mud lark. Mud lark," the boys chanted as they skipped away.

Hannah bit back a retort. She wouldn't resort to fighting with children. And she had to admit that she looked like one of the children who waded in the muck of the Thames, scavenging for pieces of coal and wood and other treasures.

She headed toward the wharf, hoping to find a place where she could exchange her dirty gown for the clean one.

When Hannah came upon a small bridge with a darkened footpath beneath it, she ducked into the shadows. Quickly pulling out her clean dress, she stripped off her soiled one, glancing about to make sure no one would find her in such undress. She stepped into the clean gown and quickly buttoned it. Her hands shook; she didn't know if it was more from cold or hunger.

Trying to keep her mind on practical things, she held up the dirtied dress. "You need a good washing," she said matter-of-factly, as if speaking in an ordinary tone would make life normal. Bundling it beneath one arm, she picked up her satchel and continued on toward the river.

She found a trail that led to the river's edge and followed it. Setting aside her satchel and cloak, she crouched beside the river and pushed her muddied dress into the water. Unspeakable sludge swirled around the gown, but Hannah scrubbed anyway.

When she felt the gown was as clean as she could get it, she wrung out the excess water and then hung it over a tree limb. Brown fog had blocked out the sun, so it would take many hours for the dress to dry. She would have to wait. At any rate, she had nowhere to go.

Pulling her cloak about her, Hannah sat on the bank and watched the river. A flatboat carrying cargo quietly slid past. She wondered where it was headed, and then decided she really didn't care. She was too weary to be concerned about such things.

Bundled inside her cape, she rested against the trunk of a tree. Her eyes felt heavy, but she forced them open and looked about to make sure there were no vagrants nearby. In the end, she decided she didn't care. What did it matter if she were murdered in her sleep? There were worse things than death. Besides, her mother and father awaited her in eternity.

***

Sleep covered Hannah in its safety and she dreamed of better days. She'd been only six when her father was killed in a riding accident, but she remembered him. His eyes radiated joy and contentment. At the end of each day when he'd return home, he'd stride into the house and embrace Hannah's mother and then turn to Hannah and hold out his arms. She could feel joy in his embrace. He tossed her into the air and she squealed with delight.

"Papa," she called. "Papa . . ."

Hannah left her dream and realized she'd been sleeping. She didn't want to awaken. Had she heard something?

Pushing up on one arm, she could still feel the dream and had to force herself to focus on her surroundings. Her eyes went to the tree where she'd hung her dress. The gown was gone. She let out a loud breath. "Oh no. Someone's gone off with it." She looked about. Her satchel was also missing. While she'd slept, someone had relieved her of what few possessions she'd had. Her hand went to her mother's necklace that hung around her neck. She was thankful she'd been wearing it.

Sorrow seeped into Hannah. *Lord, how can you have so completely forsaken me?*

***

Hannah cried until she had no tears left, but pitying herself served no purpose and she forced her mind toward sensible thinking. She must do something to remedy her situation.

She stood, smoothed her gown, and then closed her cloak at the neck and set off for the market. It was the end of the day and someone would need help. Perhaps there would be a generous merchant who would offer leftover produce to the poor.

The marketplace was quiet; most vendors had already closed their stands. Hannah moved toward a man who had a variety of vegetables left. "Sir, I was wondering if you might need someone to cook or to clean for you."

He looked at Hannah and she thought compassion softened his gaze. "Sorry, but I got no need."

Hannah gazed at the carrots and potatoes and considered asking for some. She couldn't bring herself to beg and moved on.

Just beyond, a man sat on the edge of the street, legs crossed and a cup in front of him. When he saw Hannah, he picked up the cup and held it aloft. "Money for the poor," he croaked. "I'm crippled and can't work."

She glanced inside the tin. There were two coppers resting in the bottom. Hannah couldn't bring herself to speak; she simply shook her head and walked on.

She approached a woman loading apples into a cart. "Have you any work for me?" she asked. "I'm strong and will work hard."

"You look puny to me. I need someone with a strong back."

"I'm much stronger than I look."

The woman studied Hannah for a long moment, then said, "Nah. I need someone who can be of real help. Besides, I got no money."

"I . . . I'll take a bit of food in trade."

The woman hesitated, and then shook her head. "No. I can sell these tomorrow." She turned her back on Hannah.

Drawing in a disappointed breath, Hannah's desperation grew. She felt faint with hunger. Her eyes landed on a display of baked goods. There were several loaves of dark bread. She could walk by quickly and grab one and stuff it beneath her cloak. No one would see. *What is one loaf to him, anyway?* she reasoned.

Apprehension grew inside Hannah. She'd never stolen anything before. *What choice have I?*

With her eyes on the prize, she picked up her pace and walked toward the cart. Too frightened to actually take the bread, she walked past and remained empty-handed. She stopped several yards up the street, then turned and looked back. *I must do it.* She closed her eyes and took several deep breaths to build her courage.

Again, she ambled toward the stand. This time when she moved by, she grabbed a loaf and quickly concealed it beneath her cloak. For a moment, she felt triumph. She could nearly taste her prize.

"Thief! Thief!" shouted the vendor. "There! Get her! She's there!"

Hannah didn't think. She ran. Holding the bread against her stomach, she sprinted away. She heard footsteps and shouts of "Stop! Stop!" She glanced over her shoulder and what she saw terrified her. Two constables were chasing her. Where had they been? Why hadn't she seen them? An image of the gallows flashed through her mind. People were sometimes hanged for stealing.

Frantically searching for a way of escape or a place to hide, she ran faster. She gulped in lungfuls of air. A sharp pain cut into her side and her heart hammered. The steps behind her were close!

Someone grabbed her arm. She wrenched free. But the constable managed to seize her cloak. Hannah slipped out of it and kept running. She didn't know what hurt more, her lungs or her legs. She fought for breath.

Lord, save me, she cried desperately and turned into an alley.

"Stop! Stop, I say!"

Hannah kept running, the pounding of boots close behind. Someone grabbed her hair and yanked, wrenching her backward. She fell and her head cracked against the cobblestone street. Dazed, she lay still, sucking air into her lungs. They had her.

"Get up! On your feet!" the constable shouted, dragging her upright.

"Please, sir. I was hungry. I tried to find work, but no one would hire me. I'll return the bread." Her eyes found the dark bread. It had fallen out of her hands and lay in a puddle.

"No one's going to want it now."

"I've never stolen anything before. I'm telling the truth, sir. Please believe me."

"The law's the law." He pushed her toward another constable. "It's prison for ye. The magistrate will decide yer punishment."

"I can't go to prison."

He steered her toward the main street. "Ye should 'ave thought 'bout that before ye pinched the bread."

Ashamed, Hannah walked head down through the market. As they passed the baker, she glanced at him. "I'm sorry. Truly I am."

People stared. Hannah was utterly humiliated. She no longer blamed God for having nothing to do with her. She'd been sullied and now she'd further dishonored herself.

8

Hannah sat in the far corner of a large prison cell. There were bars across the front and a gaoler sat just outside. He never spoke and showed no emotion. She pressed her back against the wall and pulled bent legs close to her chest. Since being arrested she'd kept to herself. No one in this place seemed agreeable to socializing, and that suited her.

The first morning she'd been given a small portion of porridge and water and then stale bread and broth later; it had been the same for three days. Her stomach rumbled with hunger, but at least she was getting something to eat.

She caught the eye of a woman sitting against the opposite wall. The prisoner stared at Hannah through strands of filthy hair and squinty eyes. Frightened, Hannah wondered if she was insane.

Fighting back tears, she considered her mum. She'd be so distressed if she knew of her predicament. For the first time since her mother's death, Hannah was thankful for her absence. At least she couldn't see what had become of her.

Hannah scratched her leg and then studied a red welt. There were dozens just like it covering her body. The prison cell was infested with fleas. Hannah couldn't get away from them. She tried not to scratch, but sometimes the itching was so intense she couldn't refrain. Most of the time she rubbed at the bites with the palm of her hand, but the sores still bled.

She watched a tiny flea burrow into the fold of her elbow. Revolted, she brushed it away, but it simply bounced to another part of her arm. She brushed at it again and then she saw another and another. The little beggars were everywhere, even in her hair. Frantic, she jumped to her feet and slapped at the pests. She ruffled her skirt, hoping to dislodge the insects and then tipped her head upside down and shook her hair. It was more than she could stand. She wanted to scream.

With her arms folded over her chest, she walked the length of the wall, then turned and walked back again. *Lord, help me. Please hear my prayers. Save me from this place.*

She paced for several minutes, then stopped and leaned against the stone wall. The room was crowded with women and children. A couple of women tended to infants. Hannah felt a pang of sympathy. How much more difficult must this be for those with children.

All this for a piece of bread, she thought, feeling more wretched than she'd thought possible. Her mind carried her to the hearing she'd soon face. *Surely the judge will see that I'm innocent of any real crime.*

Even as Hannah tried to quiet her fears, she knew the court's reputation. They rarely displayed mercy. People were often hanged for insignificant offenses. Hannah's pulse quickened and her stomach churned. What kind of penalty would she pay? Uncertainty sent shivers through her. What if she were found guilty and sentenced to the gallows? Feeling sick, she pressed her hand against her stomach.

Perhaps someone would vouch for her. But who? No one who cared about her even knew she was here.

The sound of a door clanging echoed off prison walls. She heard sharp footsteps. And then Ruby emerged from a dark corridor. She stopped at the gaoler's desk and spoke with him.

"Ruby!" Hannah sprinted to the front of the cell.

Her forehead furrowed and eyebrows pinched, Ruby managed to smile. She hurried to Hannah. "Oh my. How distressing to find you here. What happened to you, luv?"

Hannah didn't want to answer. Instead, she asked, "How did you know I was here?"

"I heard just this morning from Mr. Lightner. He saw you arrested three days ago. What happened?"

"Oh Ruby, it was awful." Hannah rubbed her bitten arms. "I was starving and I couldn't find work. . . ." Ashamed, she glanced away. "I couldn't stand the hunger any longer, and I stole bread from a man at the market. He saw me and hollered for help. There were constables nearby. They chased me. . . ." Unable to stop the flow of tears, she sobbed, "I couldn't run fast enough."

"Oh my Lord." Ruby squeezed Hannah's hands. "Why did you leave my house? I would have taken care of ye."

"I know you would have, but I couldn't stay and bring hardship upon you. You've barely enough to care for your own family. And your husband—"

"Tish tosh, my husband. He's too concerned with his own comforts. I tell him how it's going to be."

Hannah knew Ruby spoke the truth. She would stand up to Percy, but then there would be consequences to pay.

A smile played at Ruby's lips as she dug into a pocket. "I

87

brought ye something." She held out an apple and a small loaf of bread. "Figured ye could use it."

"Oh, thank you." Hannah took the food, feeling as if she'd been presented treasure. She pressed the apple to her nose and smelled its sweetness. She bit into it. Juice squirted into her mouth and she closed her eyes to fully take in the pleasure of it. Holding it close so as to discourage anyone from taking it from her, she quickly devoured the fruit, eating even the core.

As Ruby watched Hannah, she couldn't conceal her sorrow. "Wish I could 'ave brought ye more."

Hannah tucked the bread into her pocket and kept her hand pressed over it. "I'll save this for later."

"So, do ye know when yer trial will be?"

"No. No one's said anything."

"I'll vouch for ye. You're a good sort and a kind soul. They'll have to listen, and the judge will be lenient when he hears of your kindly nature and fine character." She smiled. "I got others who'll testify too. But we got to know when the trial is."

"I wish I knew. Perhaps you can go to the courthouse and ask. My name must be on the docket."

"That's a fine idea. I'll see what I can find out." Ruby laid her hand over Hannah's. "Is there anything else I can do for ye?"

"Pray. I need your prayers more than anything. I don't think God is listening to mine anymore."

"Now, listen to yerself," Ruby chided. "Of course he hears ye. He loves ye."

Hannah stared at her hands gripping the bars. "I don't think so . . . not anymore."

"Dearie, ye can't think that way. There's nothing that can keep the Father's love from ye."

"I want to believe you, Ruby, but it seems he's taken his eyes off me." She reached through the bars to grasp her friend's hands. "If I'm found guilty . . . would you please watch over my mother's grave?"

"They'll find ye innocent. They must."

"Please, Ruby."

The kindly woman offered a resigned smile. "Of course, luv. I'll watch over it." She let out a heavy sigh. "Well, I got to go. Percy will be wanting his lunch. I'll come back soon. And by then, I pray we'll know when yer hearing is."

"Thank you. I love you, Ruby."

"You are dear to me, like my own child." She patted Hannah's hand, then turned and walked away.

As Ruby moved toward the passageway, Hannah was overwhelmed at the sense that she'd never again see her friend. She watched until the dark corridor hid her from sight, and then she stood at the bars for a long while. Leaning against them, she tried not to think about what she might be facing. *Mum, I won't shame you anymore,* she promised.

The insistent pleas of a child called her attention back to the cell. She realized the baby had been crying for a long while. Why hadn't its mother quieted it?

The toddler tugged on her mother's arm, then patted her face and finally climbed onto her chest and lay on the sleeping woman. *Surely she must know her baby needs her*, Hannah thought. The child's cries grew louder.

She studied the woman. *She's very still.* Hannah moved closer. She wasn't breathing. Hannah took the last steps cautiously, looking about to see if anyone else had noticed her condition. They looked back at Hannah with knowing eyes, but no one made a move toward the woman.

Hannah knelt beside the young mother and rested her hand on her arm, hoping to shake her awake. Her skin was cold.

"Oh!" Hannah nearly fell backward. "She's dead." Horror stricken, Hannah thought, *Someone should do something!* She looked about. "This woman needs help," she said, then thought, *She's beyond that now.*

A woman with a child of her own spoke to no one in particular. "They don't care. No one cares." Her words carried the weight of her hopelessness.

Hannah turned her attention to the child, and a flood of empathy washed through her. *She's like me. An orphan.* "Come on, luv. I'll take care of you." She scooped the baby into her arms.

Instead of being grateful for salvation, the little girl screamed and threw herself away from Hannah. Close to tears herself, Hannah fought to hang on to her.

"I know. I'm so sorry." She held the little one close and then stood and walked away from the child's mother. She moved to the cell door. "There's a woman here. She's dead."

The gaoler looked up, but he didn't move.

"This child's mother is dead," Hannah repeated.

The gaoler went back to whittling.

Holding the little girl close, Hannah slowly walked back and forth, hoping to quiet her. Finally, the toddler stuck her thumb into her mouth, nestled against Hannah's breast, and closed her eyes.

Several hours later, the woman's body was removed. Although the baby whimpered off and on, she seemed mostly content. When the evening's bread and soup was distributed, Hannah spooned the greasy liquid into the little girl's mouth and dipped the dry bread into the broth, softening it enough so the child could eat it. That night, Hannah slept with the baby in her arms. Both were comforted by the other's presence.

❧

Early the next morning, Hannah's name was called. She searched for someone who could look after the child. Finally an older woman took the toddler. Hannah joined two others at the cell door and the three were hauled out of the cell, chained to one another, and taken to the courthouse.

The courtroom was imposing with its exceptionally tall ceilings. Hannah felt small inside the chamber and wondered if that had been the intent of the architects. The furnishings—two benches along the side walls, two long tables near the front sitting side-by-side, and the judge's bench—were made of heavy, dark wood as were the seats for spectators.

Visitors crowded the chamber. Hannah searched the faces, hoping to see Ruby and her other friends. She recognized no one.

A group of men sat sequestered from the spectators and prisoners. Hannah decided they must be the jury. She studied them, hoping to see kind, sympathetic faces. Most had their jaws and their eyes set, unwilling to reveal their feelings.

Her eyes traveled to the front of the room and an oversized rostrum. A judge wearing a black robe and a white wig moved to the dais. He looked familiar. Taking a seat behind the imposing bench, he looked over the courtroom.

Hannah sucked in a breath. *Mr. Walker!*

She felt her legs go out from beneath her. A guard grabbed her before she fell. The magistrate's eyes met Hannah's; he gazed at her with disdain. He'd known she was going to be here and

91

had anticipated the entertainment. The guard sat her down on a hard bench. Dread filled Hannah. There was no longer any hope of an innocent verdict.

Shackled, she and the other prisoners sat on one side of the courtroom, the jury on the other. Most of the prisoners were men.

Hannah was cold. Keeping her hands clasped tightly, she tried to stop them from shaking. Over and over she prayed, *Lord, have mercy on me.*

The male prisoners were first to face the prosecutor and the judge. Only one man had a barrister to defend him. As it turned out, having representation was of no help. The defendant had stolen jewelry from a wealthy household and now faced the gallows. He was taken away to await execution.

Hannah's heart beat wildly and she breathed in short gasps. She'd only taken a loaf of bread. Certainly she would be released.

The court bailiff called her name. Legs quaking, Hannah made her way to a railing that separated prisoners, prosecutors, and barristers from the Honorable Judge Walker. While a court clerk read the charges, she clutched the handrail and kept her eyes down. She hoped she looked calm.

"Hannah Corinne Talbot, you have been indicted for one count of petty larceny with a second count of grand larceny."

Hannah's eyes widened and she looked at the clerk. "Grand larceny, sir? May I ask why such a charge has been lodged against me?" She looked at the judge. "It's not possible. All I took was a loaf of bread. I was hungry."

The clerk returned to his seat.

Judge Walker looked down on Hannah, his eyes glinting.

A man wearing silk breeches, a knee-length coat, and an embroidered waistcoat strolled toward the front of the courtroom. "A loaf of bread is it?" He smirked. "While in Judge Walker's employ, you left quite suddenly, in the middle of the night in fact. Isn't that correct?"

"Yes . . . but—"

"And you took a silver chalice of fine quality."

"No, sir. That's not true. There's been a mistake. I didn't steal anything from Mr. Walker." Hannah looked squarely at the judge. "I didn't steal from you. Tell them."

"There's no use in denying it," Judge Walker said. "And I wouldn't be surprised if you took other items that simply haven't been discovered as yet."

"I didn't. You know I didn't."

"Are you calling me a liar?" The judge bristled. "You may tell any story you like, but this court will not be fooled."

"I didn't take it," Hannah said in a small voice. She knew that no matter what explanation she gave it would not be heard. She turned to the prosecutor. "You must believe me."

"You expect me to take your word over that of Judge Walker? I think not."

"But, sir—"

"Enough." The judge brought down a gavel and the sound echoed throughout the chamber. "If it were my only task to offer mercy, I would most certainly find you innocent of the charges, but my duty is to serve the law. And that I shall do." He looked at the gallery. "Is there anyone here to speak for this woman?"

Silence.

"Then. You have been accused of larceny, having stolen the said item on the night of 13 March 1804, and the second offense taking place two days after on 15 March 1804."

Hannah couldn't believe what she was hearing. "No," she croaked, her mouth too dry to speak.

The magistrate looked at the jury. "And how do you find for this prisoner?"

The jurors conferred, and then one of them stood and said, "Guilty as charged."

Judge Walker gazed down at Hannah, his eyes like black coals. "You will serve fourteen years transportation, to commence immediately."

"Please, sir. Have mercy. I am innocent of the crimes charged to me."

"Enough!" The judge glared at her. "Careful or your impudence will further extend your punishment."

Hannah closed her mouth. There was nothing she could do or say. Clenching her teeth, she glared at him. She hated him.

A guard grabbed her arm and steered her toward the back of the courtroom. The wagon that had transported her from the prison waited at the bottom of the steps. She was thrust into the back and shackled. There she waited for fate to have its way.

9

As the longboat cut through choppy waters, Hannah kept her manacled hands in her lap. She stared at the convict ship, wishing this were all a nightmare and that she'd wake up.

Sailors brought the boat alongside the ship. The man in charge stood, easily balancing in the pitching vessel. "All right, ladies, one at a time up the ladder."

Hannah stared at a rope ladder hanging over the side. How were they expected to climb such a thing while still in irons? What if someone were to fall?

"I said up! You there," the sailor pointed at an older woman sitting in the middle of the boat. "Up the ladder with you."

She stood and fought to keep her balance in the rocking boat. Unsteadily she moved to the rope and grabbed hold of it with one hand, then the other.

"Hurry up, now. We've not got all day. There are other prisoners on their way."

She glanced at the sailor and then placed a foot in the first loop and pushed up as she grabbed hold of the next handhold. Cautiously she made her way up and finally disappeared over the railing. Hannah let out a relieved breath.

One by one the prisoners negotiated the ladder. When it was Hannah's turn, she took a deep breath and then grabbed hold of a rung while putting her foot in another. When she was nearly half way, the rope swayed wildly and she thought she might fall. She stopped climbing, gripped the heavy ropes, and pressed her body against them.

"Go on!" someone shouted from below.

She glanced down and mistakenly looked at the swells. Dizziness swamped her, but she looked up and kept going. When she reached the deck, she managed to grab hold of rigging and haul herself over the rail. A young woman with vivid green eyes and a look of determination reached out a hand to her.

Grasping it, Hannah swung her legs over and set her feet on the deck. "Thank you."

"Glad to help." The woman turned and waited for the next one up the ladder. Hannah stood with her and together they watched as a mother clutching an infant started up.

"You're doing well," Hannah said. "Come on, then." Although she kept her voice heartening, she was angry. Why wasn't someone allowed to help her?

"Keep on. Yer nearly here," the woman with the green eyes called down.

The woman glanced up and continued to climb.

"Yer movin' too slow. Hurry up," one of the sailors called. He glanced over his shoulder at his mates. "Me grandmother could do better," he said with a chuckle.

"To make sport of her that way is unspeakable evil," said the woman working beside Hannah. "If I could, I'd tear his heart out."

Hannah agreed the man deserved retribution.

The woman and child finally made it up. She was the last of the lot.

Hannah turned to look at the place that would be home for the crossing. Her eyes roamed over the ship. It was a jumble of sails and rigging. The animals on deck were in an uproar. Swine enclosed in a pen snorted and squealed their dismay. Cows corralled beside them seemed unperturbed and calmly chewed their cud. Chickens wandered about, clucking and scratching. The odor on board was rank.

"So we've been brought to a pigsty, eh," said the green-eyed woman. She chuckled.

Hannah couldn't find any humor in it. She looked at the woman, incredulously. "How can you jest about something like this?"

"And what should I do? Whine and wail? That will help, eh?"

"No. But . . . you must agree that this is all quite tragic."

"That it is, but what purpose does grumbling serve?"

Hannah had to admit that complaining altered nothing, but she was still unable to accept the reality of what was happening to her. How could God have allowed it? *This is too difficult a trial, Lord. Pray, have mercy on me.*

Not wanting the daring woman to see her tears, she turned and gazed at London. It was a clear day, very little fog. Smoke belched from chimneys all over the city, staining the unusually blue sky. She felt the tearing of separation. London was the only home she'd known. *I shan't see you again,* she thought, recounting her recent tribulations and all that she'd lost.

A firm hand rested on her shoulder. "Give it no honor. It's a ruthless city."

Hannah looked into kind green eyes.

"Name's Lydia. Yours?"

"Hannah."

"Over 'ere. The lot of ye," shouted a sailor.

The women hurried to obey. They stood in a crowd.

"Line up!"

Scrambling into rows, the women waited while a man dressed in a navy uniform ambled toward them.

"We've a fair number of lydies this trip, sir," the sailor said.

The captain stood quietly, surveying the group. "For the next six to seven months this will be your home. And if you want to live to see New South Wales, you'll follow the rules." He strode to one side. "You'll eat what's given to you without complaint." He moved back to the place he'd started. "There'll be no talking back, no tolerating disrespect, and no fighting between yourselves. You'll be sorry if I hear of any infractions."

A sneer replaced his scowl. "I know you're all innocent as doves. But just in case you're thinking about socializing with the male prisoners, you need to know there's no fraternizing allowed. They're stowed aft and you'll be in the forward hold." His eyes narrowed as he looked from one woman to another. "If I see or hear that any of you have been friendly with a male prisoner . . . you'll wish you hadn't."

He glowered at the women. "I won't heed any complaints against my men. They've been assigned this rotten duty; and from time to time they'll have need of . . . encouragement. So you'll do as they say."

A dark-haired woman who looked terrified whispered to Hannah in a quaking voice, "What do you think he means by that?"

"You'll keep your traps shut when I'm talking!" the captain bellowed. He drew his sword, and in three strides he reached the woman. Pressing the blade against her throat, he asked, "Did you hear me? No talking."

She stared at him, eyes wide.

He pressed the tip of the blade so tightly against her throat that it sliced through her skin. Blood spilled onto the collar of her dress. The captain smirked and then stepped back. "So we have an understanding, then?"

The woman pressed a hand to the wound. "Yes sir. We do."

Swiftly he returned to his place in front of the women. "I won't abide disobedience."

Heads nodded. Hannah's thoughts whirled. She was more afraid than she could ever recall and at the same time furious. He had no right.

A child standing alongside the rail whimpered and pressed in against his mother's skirts.

"And no squalling kids, neither!" His face red, the captain grabbed up the child by one ankle and dangled him upside down over the side.

His mother pressed her hands to her mouth. The boy made no sound, but his eyes were wide and his skin was as pale as the white in the clouds.

"You cry and you'll become fish bait," the captain threatened. "You gonna cry?"

The little boy shook his head back and forth.

The captain held him there a minute longer, then moved him back over the deck and dropped him.

"You mothers take care of your young 'uns. There'll be no sniveling, whining brats disturbing me or my crew."

Women with children pulled the youngsters closer. Hannah's eyes fell upon a little girl with red hair and freckles. Her brown eyes were more defiant than afraid. Still, she stood close to her mother.

"Do as you're told, don't talk back, and keep your mouths shut unless you've got permission to speak. If you do that and don't let the sweating sickness, diphtheria, or ship fever get you, you just might live to see Port Jackson." He smiled sardonically.

A shiver of trepidation moved through Hannah.

"If you brought belongings, leave them here. You'll have no need."

Hannah touched her mother's cross, hoping it wouldn't be taken from her. When the captain looked her way, she immediately dropped her hand.

He walked across the deck and lifted the hatch to the forward hold. "You'll each be given one blanket. Take care of it. You'll not get another."

Two crewmen stood beside the hatch, blankets piled in their arms.

"Down with you."

The women shuffled toward the hatch. Each was given a blanket before descending into the hold.

Hannah was several paces away when the smell of waste and rotting meat hit her. Her stomach churned and she fought to keep from gagging.

A statuesque woman with dark brown hair stopped at the top of the stairs. "How will we manage with these irons on?" she asked, daring to stare directly at the captain.

He met her defiant gaze. "How will you manage?" he mimicked. "The best you can." He laughed and turned away.

"But our shackles." She lifted her hands up in front of her. "Are we to be chained all the way to New South Wales?"

The captain stopped. He stared at her, obviously outraged. "You'll stay in them all the way there and beyond." He rested his hand on his sword.

The woman finally turned and started down the stairs. Hannah wondered when she'd have to face the next dreadful episode.

Lydia moved toward the hatch. She accepted a blanket. "Thank ye," she said blithely and disappeared into the hold.

Hannah took a blanket and followed Lydia. Holding the wool coverlet tightly against her chest, she descended slowly, carefully. A sensation of being swallowed by shadows swept over her as she moved down into the fetid chamber.

Darkness and a horrible stench enveloped her. She swallowed again and again, trying not to vomit. When she stood on the wooden floor, Hannah gazed about the shadowy hold. The only light came from the open hatch. She looked up, fearing the moment it would be shut.

She moved toward a long structure. Three-tiered wooden racks stood in the middle of the room and stretched the length of the space. There were two identical rows. And at one end of the hold there were piles of hay.

Women huddled in the darkness. Some sat on the edge of what was supposed to be a bunk, their face in their hands. Several sobbed while others just stared. The little girl Hannah had noticed earlier sat on a lower bunk beside a gaunt-looking woman who Hannah could only assume was her mother.

She made her way through the dim light, careful not to lose her footing on the slippery wooden floor. She glanced at her feet, wondering what was on the boards that made them so slick, then decided she didn't want to know. She followed Lydia.

A sailor walked behind the last woman to make her way down. The ceiling barely allowed enough room for him to stand upright.

"Find a bunk. I don't want no noise tonight. Mind yer manners and I'll leave ye alone. Cause trouble and ye'll find yourself on the end of this." He moved a bludgeon from one hand to the other. "If yer good, we'll light the lanterns for a while tonight."

Hannah crushed the blanket against her as she watched the sailor climb the steps. The hatch dropped with a thud. Darkness descended. The sound of a wooden bolt being fixed in place sent panic through Hannah. Women and children wept and whimpered.

Still clutching the blanket, Hannah climbed onto a lower berth beside the red-headed little girl and her mother.

"Me name's Lottie," said the girl. "And this is me mum." She rested a hand on the sickly woman beside her. The woman barely managed to nod at Hannah.

"I'm glad to meet you," Hannah managed, preoccupied with her dismal surroundings. When her eyes adjusted to the darkness, she realized that light found its way around the hatch, where the boards didn't fit snugly.

"Up 'ere," said Lydia. "Ye don't want to be on the bottom."

"Why not?" asked Hannah, climbing onto the berth next to Lydia.

"Ye don't want someone puking on ye, do ye?"

"Oh." Reality slammed into Hannah like a fist. This was real and she'd have to endure. She lay on her back. The space was so tight she could touch the ceiling. There was no room to sit up. The prisoners lay side by side like bolts of fabric on a shelf.

The woman the captain had singled out for talking slid in beside Hannah. She lay on her back, staring at the ceiling. "I can't do this," she whimpered. Sobs escaped her lips and she rolled her head back and forth. "I can't stand it here! I mustn't be here! I can't stay!"

"Hush," Lydia said. "Ye'll 'ave the guards down 'ere in a flash." She rolled onto her side and looked at the woman. "What's yer name?"

"Marjorie Dalton. I don't belong here. I'm a gentlewoman, quite wealthy in fact."

"None of us belong 'ere," said someone from the rack below. She climbed out of her bunk and stood up. Her manacles clanked. It was the woman who had challenged the captain. "Me name's Rosalyn. And I guess I do deserve t' be 'ere. I'm no gentlewoman."

Women continued to cry and a little girl, her voice weak and trembling, said, "Mum, I'm scared. And I'm hungry."

"I know, luv," came a soft voice. "Everything will be set right soon."

Hannah rolled onto her side and stared at the light splashing down the stairway. Why couldn't they leave the hatch open?

She closed her eyes, hoping to envision another place, but the darkness swelled and the stench intensified. *How am I to survive months in this hole?*

As if reading her thoughts, Lydia said, "We'll make it. Yer a hardy one; I can see that. And I know I'm strong."

Hannah couldn't think of anything to say, but she was thankful for Lydia.

The ship put to sea under fair skies. The prisoners were glad for calm waters and only a few were sick. That first day, Hannah ate her portion of salted fish and dry bread. She'd decided she would eat no matter the state of her stomach or the condition of the food. She'd need strength to carry her through the months ahead. Hannah downed the last of her water and wished for more to wash away the taste of overripe fish.

"How'd ye come to be here?" Lydia asked.

"It's not very interesting." Hannah didn't want to tell anyone about what had happened to her.

"Maybe not, but we got a lot of time. Might as well get to know each other."

"I was caught stealing bread."

"How long did ye get?"

"Fourteen years."

"Seems a bit much for a piece of bread."

"It was a loaf."

"Still, hardly seems fair."

Memories of the court hearing and the false charges swept over Hannah. "I was also accused of taking a silver chalice from my employer."

"Did ye?"

"No. I've never taken anything that wasn't mine, except for the bread." She rested her head on her bent arm. "I couldn't find work and I was starving."

"Ye don't have to defend yerself to me. I know what it's like to be hungry."

Silence settled over the women.

"Why are you here?" Hannah asked.

"Killed a man."

Startled, Hannah stared at Lydia.

"Don't look so scared. I was only protecting a life. He would have killed her."

"Who?"

"Me mum. It was me stepfather. He come home smelling of ale and dead drunk. He gets mean when he's been at the grog.

He started beatin' me mum. I love her even if she did marry a pig. I couldn't let him kill her." She smiled. "I'm thankful to be on this boat."

"Thankful?"

"Nearly got the gallows. Figure this as a blessing. Course, me mum's alone now." Her voice trailed off.

"I'm sorry."

"No need to feel sorry for me. Figure this is a new start. Ye got to take what comes and make the most of it." Facing Hannah, she pushed up on one arm. "Heard that once we get to Port Jackson there's work in the settlement outside the prison. I figure anything's better than rotting in a London gaol or facing the gallows. And I heard tell that a person can get a ticket of leave."

"How can they do that?"

"Do as yer told, stay out of trouble, and if ye can, be of some help to the governorship. I'm going to do it. Course I got to be better at keeping me mouth shut. It'll take me ten or twelve years because I got a life sentence." She smiled at Hannah. "Yer sentence is shorter, and so's the time 'til ye can qualify."

"I'm serving fourteen years, so . . ."

"Well, best as I understand, ye can apply in six years." Her eyes turned hard and her mouth took on a determined set. "I'm not dyin' on this ship. I'll not give the British courts the satisfaction. Figure to make it home one day, and God willing, me mum will still be there waitin' for me."

Lydia's tone held such conviction, Hannah believed her. Just listening to Lydia gave her courage.

Storms soon pushed away fair weather and the seas turned violent. Waves lifted the ship and then drove it back down. The vessel was picked up and tossed sideways and then rolled, feeling as if it were going to swamp. Most everyone was sick. Cries and groans emanated from all over the hold, and there was the horrible smell of filth and vomit.

Food was still handed out. When the men came down, they held handkerchiefs over their noses. They'd scramble down the steps, hurry from person to person, slopping out rations, and then rush back up the steps and slam the hatch shut.

Although Hannah lost much of what she ate, she forced the food down, hoping that even morsels would help her stay alive. She'd decided to survive and to do whatever it took to do so.

Sick or not, the women had to empty the slop buckets. Like the others, Hannah made her share of trips to the deck. It was a blessing and a curse. If she could get by the men without their noticing her, the time on deck in the fresh air felt like a gift. At other times, she'd have to ignore their taunting and avoid attempts of some to grab her.

<hr />

After days of violent weather, the storm finally relented. One clear, warm afternoon Hannah made a trip up with the bucket. Careful not to look at any of the crew, she moved to the railing and breathed deeply of salt air. A breeze caught at her hair and caressed her face. It was a stolen moment of pleasure.

She couldn't tarry long or someone would notice. When she turned to go back, she saw a man staring at her. He was also a prisoner. Although as filthy as she, there was something about his demeanor and his eyes that moved her. His eyes were the color of honey. They were kind. He smiled, revealing white, unblemished teeth. *He must be someone of distinction*, she thought. Feeling self-conscious, she looked away and descended below decks.

As foolish as it seemed, Hannah's thoughts stayed with the man. She wondered what he had looked like before becoming a convict. The word *convict* didn't suit him. He looked nothing like a criminal.

What had he thought of her? She was a sight—her hair in a tangle and her gown barely more than a rag. She wished he'd seen her properly dressed and clean.

You're a fool. There will be no husband for you. If he knew what happened, he'd not offer any kindness. Her hand rested on her abdomen. She'd missed two menses since that awful night with the judge, and she'd noticed that her breasts were swollen. And recently she'd awakened in the mornings feeling queasy. She was certain she carried Mr. Walker's child.

I can't have a baby. This life is cruel to children. And everyone will know my shame.

Other women had given birth since setting sail. One of the children born hadn't made it through its first night and neither had its mum. Mother and child had been dropped over the side. There would be others born—some would die.

Hannah set down the slop pail. Filled with despair, she leaned against a post. *Lord, I can't have this child.* She knew what she wanted to pray, but was afraid. What she desired was a monstrous sin.

She closed her eyes, her request too horrible to even consider. She was afraid, yet still surrendered to it. *Father, please take this child. I don't want it.*

10

The hatch door flew open, and light and air spilled into the hold. A voice called from above. "Everyone on deck. Time ye had some exercise."

Women clambered from their bunks and made their way toward the steps.

"Praise be!" said Lydia. "I was beginning to think the only way to see daylight was to carry up a slop bucket." She smiled. "I'm in need of a bit of air." She slid off the top bunk to the floor and moved toward the steps. At the bottom of the ladder, she stopped to wait for Hannah. "Come along. Hurry up. We need to make use of every moment away from this hole."

Hannah's feet found the slimy floor. "I'm feeling poorly." Moving carefully, she made her way toward Lydia.

"Seems yer not well a lot of mornings these days." She eyed Hannah. "Ye keeping something from me?"

Hannah couldn't meet Lydia's gaze. "No. Nothing. I'm just not well this morning. I'm in good health most days."

Lydia continued to stare. She lifted an eyebrow. "Nothing, is it? All right, then." With that, she grabbed hold of the railing and started up.

Sunlight and gusting winds greeted Hannah. She squinted against the brightness as she stepped onto the deck. Hands on her hips, she breathed deeply. For a moment she forgot she was a prisoner under the watchful eyes of the crew. She moved to the railing, so flooded with emotions she couldn't speak. The warmth of sunlight, the clean air, and freedom made her feel almost good. She tipped her face up to catch as much of the sun as she could. "How splendid."

"Grand it is," said Lydia, standing at the railing beside Hannah. She leaned way out and peered down at the sea. "Sometimes ye talk high and mighty like someone who's highborn."

Hannah smiled at her. "Me highborn? No. But I did serve upper-class women. My mum was one of the best seamstresses in the city." Hannah gazed out over the waves. "She sent me to school at the church, and she was a stickler for proper diction."

Lydia leaned her back against the railing and gazed up at full sails and a blue sky. "I didn't think ye were one of those types. Yer not fussy enough for that." She smiled and turned to look out over the waves. "Wish we were allowed on deck more." She eyed ogling sailors. "But I could do without them."

Hannah followed Lydia's gaze. "I pray they'll leave us be." She glanced at her rounded abdomen and rested her arms over it, hoping to conceal the child growing inside. Soon she'd not be able to hide her condition.

"How grand it would be to bathe," said Lydia. "Cold salt water thrown at a person isn't a bath."

Her eyes narrowed as they moved from one man to another. "They can all go to the devil as far as I care. Every last one of them. They don't give a whit 'bout us, whether we live or die. We're ill used and they take pleasure in that."

109

Male prisoners emerged from the forward hold. If possible, they looked even filthier than the women and children.

"Must be a work day," Lydia said. "Figured they'd have a reason for letting us on deck."

Watching the men, Hannah tried to imagine what they had once looked like. What had they done that brought them to this detestable place? How many were decent blokes who'd simply had a row with a constable or a judge?

She and Lydia were put to work scouring decks aft. While she pushed the scrub brush over the filthy decking, she allowed her mind to wander back to London and the life she'd known. It hadn't been so long ago, but it felt like forever. The memories were sweet. Had her life truly been ideal? She and her mum had been poor, but even after her father's death her mother had always been a strong presence. Hannah had never gone hungry, and the cottage stayed warm and safe. Tears blurred her vision and she tried to blink them away. Oh how she longed for those days.

"Look!" a woman shouted. "What is it?"

Prisoners and crew crowded the railings.

"It's only a dolphin," one of the sailors said.

Hannah had never seen a dolphin before. She leaned over to have a good look. At first she didn't see anything, then a fin and a glistening silver body broke the surface of the water. An elegant creature leaped from the sea, then dove eagerly, swimming just below the waves, and then leaped again and again as if unable to contain its joy.

Others chased the first. Hannah had never seen anything like it. She too wanted to leap as she watched them dance and move with speed and unrestrained freedom.

"Can I see, mum?" Lottie asked, pressing in beside Hannah.

"Of course." Hannah and the young red-head had forged a friendship since their first encounter, but she'd not seen her recently. "I've missed you, luv. Where have you been?"

"Taking care of me mum," Lottie said, her tone clipped. "With her being sick, we thought she might feel better further up front."

Hannah lifted the youngster, shocked at how little she weighed. She could feel bones protruding beneath her ragged clothes. *Lord, how will she survive?*

Lottie peered at the sea. "Oh, how wonderful they are!"

"They are at that."

"So beautiful!" Lottie leaned farther out.

Hannah tightened her grip. "Careful now. We don't want you falling overboard."

"If only I could ride upon them." Lottie smiled up at Hannah, her brown eyes bright. "It would be lovely, eh?"

"Yes. Lovely." Hannah imagined the joy of being carried over the seas with the wind and spray splashing her. She leaned out, trying to get a better look at the mystical creatures.

"I've never seen such a sight," said Lottie.

She seemed happy. Yet she was one of the mislaid children who would most likely pay with her life. Stirred by compassion, Hannah hugged Lottie. Why would the government send children to prison with their parents? It was the same as throwing them away. "How old are you, dear?" she asked.

"Eight."

She looks much younger. Perhaps because she's so small.

Lottie turned to look at the dancing dolphins. "Me mum would have liked to have seen them dolphins."

"Where is she?"

Lottie's smile faded. "Dead. She died of the fever."

Hannah felt the squeeze of sorrow in her heart. "I'm sorry."

"Died two days ago. I got no one now."

"You haven't anyone at all?"

Lottie shook her head slowly back and forth.

"I'll watch out for you, then. That is, if you don't mind, eh?"

"Oh no. That would be fine."

Hannah hugged her again, smoothing the child's auburn hair. "From now on you'll sleep beside me. We can keep each other warm." She smiled.

"Thank ye, mum." Lottie hugged Hannah about the waist. "I'll move me things there straight away."

She turned and moved toward the hatch leading to the hold. Stopping, she looked at Hannah. "I'll be right back," she said and then continued. The irons around her ankles slowed her steps and made a grating sound as she walked.

Such injustice, Hannah thought, angry. She turned and watched the dolphins. If only she could fly across the waves the way they did, free and oblivious about life's harshness. She leaned against the railing, hoping for a better view. Someone bumped her from behind and Hannah lost her balance. She swung her arms back, reaching for a handhold, and tried to keep from falling. Her momentum was too great and she tumbled over the side. Reaching for anything to hang on to, she only managed to touch the rigging. The cold sea waited. And then her hands found a rope that stretched across the side of the ship. She grabbed hold. Clutching it, she slammed against the side.

There she hung, suspended over the water. "Help! Help me!" She swung her feet toward the ship, searching for a place of leverage. There was nothing. She pressed her body against the side and clung to the rope.

"She's gone overboard!" cried Lydia. "Hannah! Hold fast," she yelled down. "Someone help her!"

Hannah looked up. She didn't think she could hang on much longer. "Hurry!" She flung her manacled feet toward the side of the ship, hoping to find a foothold.

"I'm not puttin' me own life on the line to save her," Hannah heard from above.

No one will help me. I'm going to die.

"Don't let go! I'm coming for you," someone shouted. A rope dropped down, and moments later a man secured by another line was beside her. He quickly made a loop in the rope he'd tossed down and then put an arm about Hannah's waist. "I got you now." He wedged his feet against the side. "Put up one arm, hold on with the other."

"I . . . I can't."

"I won't let you fall."

Hannah managed to look at him. It was the man she'd noticed staring at her when she'd been on deck. The one she thought seemed kindly. She'd never spoken to him, but more than once she'd found him watching her. For reasons she didn't under-stand, she trusted him. She let go with one hand and allowed herself to rest in his grasp, then she slipped her free arm through the loop, and then the other arm.

"Good girl. Hang on, now. I'll climb up and pull you aboard." In spite of his manacles, he managed to use his feet for leverage as he climbed up the side of the ship, hand over hand. When he'd made it back to the deck, he hollered, "You ready?"

"Yes." Hannah tried to do just as he had and use her feet to help propel her upward as he pulled. The irons restraining her ankles made it nearly impossible. Finally the man and Lydia grabbed hold of Hannah and hauled her over the railing and onto the deck.

Hannah shook with fear and exhaustion. Taking a deep breath, she tried to calm herself. She looked into the man's soft hazel eyes, and for a moment she was held captive. Unable to think of what to say, she finally stammered, "Thank you."

"I'm just grateful you're out of harm's way."

"Your kindness will not be forgotten." Hannah lifted the loop of rope over her head and handed it to him.

"Enough theatrics," the captain hollered. "Back to work. All of you."

Hannah moved away from the man.

"Name's John Bradshaw. Yours?"

It didn't seem proper to tell a strange man her name, but he had saved her life. "Hannah Talbot," she said and then hurried aft.

Lydia followed. "He's a fine bloke, that one." When she caught up to Hannah, she asked, "Why ye in such a hurry? Ye running away from him?"

"You heard the captain. Back to work. I'm in no mood for the lash. Are you?"

Lydia smiled. "Ye like him, don't ye?"

"Not like you mean. But of course I like him. He saved my life." Dropping to her hands and knees, she lifted a scrub brush out of the bucket of water and returned to scouring the filthy deck. She glanced back to see if he was still where she'd left him. He was gone.

Lydia stood over Hannah, hands planted on her broad hips and a knowing smile on her lips. "Admit it, yer taken with him."

Hannah didn't want to talk about John. There was no use in it. He was a prisoner just as she was.

"I don't even know him. And unless you've forgotten, we're prisoners and can't be *taken* with anyone. Our lives are not our own."

"Ye can tell yerself that, but it's not true. I've heard tell of prisoners marrying one another. In New South Wales it's allowed." She looked out over the sea. "We have a future. One day we'll have a new life. I'll not let a judge decide my fate."

"He already has."

"You're not scrubbing hard enough," said a grubby-looking sailor with bad teeth. He kicked Hannah hard in the side. The wind went out of her and she clutched her stomach.

The sailor swung around and glared at Lydia. "And what do you think you're doing? Get to work or you'll taste the lash. We'll be porting tomorrow and the captain wants the ship done proper."

"We're porting? Where?" Lydia asked, seemingly unconcerned over the sailor's threat.

"Teneriffe, for the good it'll do ye." He walked away with a swagger.

"Did ye hear that? We'll be porting."

"There's no reason to celebrate, Lydia. All it means is we'll be locked in the hold. That way they won't have to worry about anyone jumping ship."

Lydia sloshed her brush into the bucket and slapped it against the deck. "I wish we could go ashore. I'm about to go mad." She stopped scrubbing. "We've months left, yet." Momentary despair touched Lydia's green eyes. "They'll keep us locked up for sure."

That night Lottie snuggled close to Hannah. As the child fell asleep, Hannah caressed the little girl's hair.

"We have to take our comforts wherever we get them," Lydia whispered. "She's lucky to have ye."

Hannah thought about the child she carried inside her. Soon everyone would know. What would she do? How would Lydia feel about her? Tears burned her eyes and she tried to hold them back, but tonight she couldn't, not tonight.

Lydia's manacles clanked as she moved closer to Hannah. She rested a hand on her friend's shoulder. "What is it?"

Hannah didn't respond right away, but then she rolled over and faced her friend. "I'm going to have a baby," she whispered.

Lydia said nothing for a long while, then in her sensible tone she said, "Well then, we'd best see that ye get an extra portion of bread and meat, eh?"

"The man I worked for in London forced himself on me." The frightful night rushed back at her. "I can't have this child. I'll be forever shamed. And I have nothing to offer it." She glanced at the little girl sleeping beside her. "It's the little ones who suffer the most."

"Children are a blessing from the Lord no matter how they come to be. It will be a hardship, yes, but to have a child—"

"No. Not like this. Not now."

"I'll help watch out for ye. I've attended births before. Ye don't need fear all that."

"I'm not afraid of dying. I'm afraid of living."

Lydia didn't say anything right away, but when she spoke she carefully chose her words. "I know. I can see despair in ye, in all of us. But we have to believe that God wants us to live. And we must."

"Why must we?"

"There's a time to live and a time to die. And while we're living, we should fight for every breath."

"God has no use for me or my life." Hannah bit her lip. Dare she confess the request she'd made to God? As forbearing as Lydia was, Hannah doubted even she could forgive such a thing. "I'm tired," she finally said and rolled onto her other side.

A burning pain cut through Hannah's abdomen and wrenched her from sleep. She breathed slowly and evenly. The pain only intensified. Her stomach muscles felt tight. She clutched her abdomen and tried to silence a groan. *What is this? What is happening?*

The minutes passed and Hannah found no relief. She lay on her back and sweat seeped from her pores, pooling between her shoulders and soaking her dress. Like a poker gouging at her abdomen, the pain continued to assault her. She rolled from side to side and moaned.

"What is it?" Lydia asked. "Are ye sick?"

Hannah knew it was the baby. Her prayer had been answered. How could she tell Lydia about her depraved request? Pain swept through her. "I think it's the baby."

"Oh, Lord. How many months are ye?"

"Only four."

"That's way too early. Ye can't have the child now."

Hannah writhed as a torturous spasm strengthened.

"Mum, ye all right?" asked Lottie, her voice laced with fear.

"She's sick, Lottie," Lydia said. "Ye ought to sleep somewheres else tonight."

"Can't I stay?"

"No. This time ye need to go." Lydia's voice was kind, but firm.

Lottie started to climb down, then she stopped and lay a hand on Hannah's cheek. "Please, mum, don't die."

"I won't. I promise." Hannah rested a hand over Lottie's.

After Lottie had gone, Hannah asked Lydia, "Do you know what to do?"

"This early? No. There's naught can be done, except that ye try to lie quietly. Don't fight the pain. It will only make it worse." She grasped Hannah's hand. "Are ye bleeding?"

"Yes. I think so."

"All right, then." Lydia was quiet for a moment, then in a calm voice she said, "Without light I can't tell how bad it is. But it would be best if ye laid on yer back and tucked yer knees up a bit."

Hannah did her best to obey in the cramped space. She closed her eyes and struggled to keep her cries of suffering to herself. *Lord, I ask for your help,* she prayed. But she knew there would be no comfort from him. This was her doing. She deserved to suffer.

Hannah labored several hours and finally just as daylight touched the gaps around the hatch a tiny, silent infant was born. Lydia helped bring the lifeless child into the world. She held it for a few moments. "It's a little one, a girl."

Hannah could hear the sadness in her friend's voice. She couldn't look. "Please, get rid of it."

"How shall I do that?"

"Take it out in your skirt."

"And what reason have I for going above decks?"

Hannah thought and then she knew the horrible solution. The words came out, hesitant and remorseful. "The . . . slop bucket."

Lydia said nothing, but she climbed down from the bunk, and a moment later Hannah heard the lid to the bucket being lifted off and then set back in place. Lydia quietly moved across the room and climbed the steps. She knocked on the hatch.

"What need have ye?" a voice asked.

"Got to empty the bucket."

"It's early."

"It reeks something fearful," she said.

The hatch lifted and Lydia disappeared into the gray morning. When she returned a few minutes later, she said nothing as she climbed back onto her bunk.

Hannah turned onto her side and pulled her knees up to her chest. She would never forgive herself. Only a contemptible person would do what she'd done. She didn't dare ask for God's forgiveness. Even he couldn't love someone like her.

11

Heavy seas pounded the convict ship, lifting it atop huge swells and then dropping it into deep troughs. Many were sick, yet Hannah was thankful for the storm. It meant she could remain on her bunk without questions.

The physical pain from the previous night's ordeal had decreased, but the ache in her soul had intensified. Again and again, her mind carried her back to the sound of the bucket lid being closed upon an innocent child, one she'd hoped would die.

Unable to look at anyone, even Lydia, she pretended to sleep. Her friend had checked on her twice since daylight, but Hannah only mumbled that she was fine and kept her eyes closed.

Late in the morning, Lottie nudged her. "Are ye still sick, mum?"

Hannah didn't look at her. "Uh-huh. I need to sleep. I'm sure I'll be recovered by tomorrow." Hannah knew another day would not heal what truly ailed her; there were not enough tomorrows to mend that.

"Is there something I can do for ye?" Lottie lay beside Hannah, her face only inches away.

Hannah opened her eyes. She managed to smile. "No. Nothing, luv."

"She'll be better soon," Lydia said, resting a hand on Lottie's back. "She just needs a bit of time."

The day passed and the storm grew more intense. Wind whistled through the rigging, and the ship rolled clumsily in deep swells. *It would serve me well if I were drowned*, Hannah thought. The idea didn't seem so terrible.

"This looks to be a bad one," Lydia said. "Lottie, will ye help me? There are things that will need to be tightened down."

"Course, mum."

Hannah pushed up on one arm. "Can I help?"

Lydia rested a hand on Hannah's cheek. "So good to see ye taking an interest in things." She smiled. "But best ye stay put."

She climbed down, and grabbing handholds as she went, she and Lottie moved about the hold.

Hannah lay back down and wished for sleep. It refused to come as her mind repeatedly returned to her baby and her own hardened heart. How could any decent person wish the death of a child? What had happened to her?

This is no place for children, she told herself. *I was only protecting it from torment and certain death. It is better to never be born than to exist like this.* No matter how sensible the words sounded, they did nothing to alleviate Hannah's guilt and shame.

The ship rose and then rolled as it went over a large wave. They bobbed for a few moments and then swept down the back side of the swell and into what felt to be a bottomless trough. Hannah tensed. They truly could be swamped. The ship wallowed and then was picked up again and thrown upon another wave.

Cries of fear emanated throughout the hold. There were sounds of retching, and the smell of vomit merged with the foul odors that already permeated the prison compartment. Hannah pulled her blanket up under her chin and tried to close out the misery.

Lottie and Lydia returned and climbed in on either side of Hannah. "Things are pretty much secured," Lydia said, her eyes moving over the hold.

Hannah didn't respond.

"Ye need to liven up, luv. Ye can't hang yer head forever."

"Forever? It only happened last night. And you don't understand all there is to know of it."

"I know enough. And life goes on. We've got to endure."

"I don't want to endure," Hannah mumbled.

"Enough of that. I'll not hear that kind of talk."

Lottie smoothed Hannah's damp hair. "Why would ye want to die? Me mum . . . she tried to live. I wanted her to live." Lottie's eyes brimmed with tears. "What would I do if . . . ?"

Fresh guilt swept through Hannah. She was unbelievably selfish. Looking into Lottie's worried brown eyes, she said, "I'm sorry. I didn't mean it. Of course I want to live. And I will." She managed a weak smile. "But for now I need to rest. All right?"

Lottie kissed Hannah's cheek. "I'll keep watch for ye."

"Thank you." An ache squeezed Hannah's heart. She ought to be comforting Lottie, and instead, the little girl was comforting her.

Night fell and darkness enveloped the ship. The storm raged, seemingly angrier than before. Lanterns were lit, and those who weren't sick gathered together. Some prayed and sang hymns, others talked of better times, but nothing shut out the screeching wind and the fear that invaded their souls.

All of a sudden, the ship was lifted high on a cresting wave and then slammed into a deep swell. "Lord, save us," Marjorie cried, her voice quaking as it often did.

"He's not 'ere," a bawdy Rosalyn shouted, tossing long brown hair off her shoulders. "If he was, then none of us would be 'ere either."

"He is here," said Corliss Browning, an elderly woman of faith.

Hannah had great respect for her. It was good to hear her voice.

"He promises to never leave us nor forsake us. And I believe him. We'll not perish. He'll see us through." Barely able to keep her feet under her, she moved to Marjorie, who was crying and huddled on a loose bundle of hay. Sitting beside her, the elderly woman put her arm about the frightened captive.

Hannah wanted to believe as Corliss did. But she couldn't. "Pray for us, Corliss. Please."

"I've been praying."

"It's all a lie," Rosalyn said. "Every bit of it." Keeping a hold of a corner post, she stood beside her bunk. "He's never once come to my aid and I don't expect he will now. He don't see me. Or none of us. We'll be lucky to end up at the bottom of the sea. At least we'll be free of this torment."

Lottie's hand fumbled for Hannah's and gripped it tightly. "Is it true, mum?"

"You need not worry. God loves you," Hannah said.

"Does he love everyone?"

Hannah thought for a moment. What should she say? She believed he only loved some.

123

"Course he loves everyone," Lydia said. "And he's watching over us. I know it."

Lottie was silent for a long while, then she asked, "Why didn't he take care of me mum? She loved him. And she was a good mum."

"Sometimes, God wants the best of us to be with him," Lydia said. "And yer mum is in a better place. This world can be cruel. I'm sure she's happier now."

That seemed to satisfy Lottie. She snuggled closer to Hannah. "I'm hungry. They didn't bring nothin' to eat tonight."

"They're most likely working hard because of the storm," Hannah said. "We'll be fed in the morning. And they might feed us yet. Try to sleep."

"They'll not be down this night," said Marjorie. She looked at the hatch. "They got us locked in. If this ship goes down so do we, drowned like rats."

Lottie whimpered.

Lydia pushed off her cot and stood. "I dare say, that's enough out of the lot of ye. Have ye forgotten there are children 'bout?"

"They might as well know the truth," Rosalyn said.

"Ye wouldn't know the truth if it bit ye," Lydia said. "Now shut yer trap."

Lottie sniffled. "Are we goin' to drown, mum?"

"Of course not." Hannah pulled Lottie closer. "This is a sturdy ship. I'm sure she's seen worse storms than this."

"But the ladies said—"

"They don't know about such things. Now, don't you worry. We'll be fine." Hannah found it ironic that she comforted this child even though she'd thrown away her own. She stroked Lottie's hair and held her protectively. *Lord, why does living have to be so full of trouble?* Her own tears came unbidden.

"Yer cryin' now." Lottie wiped tears from Hannah's cheeks.

"We all cry sometimes." Hannah sniffled. "I'm tired and not well. When I'm feeling poorly, I cry more easily."

"It's that way for the lot of us," said Lydia.

The wind grew stronger and a rumbling sound swept toward them from outside. The ship rolled dangerously and then was thrown upward by a huge wave.

"What is it? What's happening?" cried Marjorie. She fell and sprawled out on the floor.

Shrieks and screams broke out all over the hold. Women were dumped from their beds and others fell as they reached for something to hold on to.

"We're going to swamp!" someone cried.

Hannah pulled Lottie closer.

"Oh, Father in heaven," Lydia prayed.

It felt as if the ship leaped over the top of the wave before it descended the other side. Timbers groaned and buckets tipped. One rolled wildly across the floor. It slammed into a stool holding a burning lantern, knocking the stool and the lantern on their sides. Oil seeped out of the lamp and fire erupted in the hay scattered on the floor. Flames flickered, casting light and shadows.

"Fire!" someone shrieked.

Rosalyn bolted for the ladder. "Let us out!" She climbed the steps and beat her fist against the hatch. Others joined her. "Let us out! We've a fire down here!"

Keeping Lottie close, Hannah climbed down from the bunk.

Lydia scrambled from hers and, grabbing her blanket, headed toward the fire, nearly tripping on her chains. She beat the flames. "Everyone! Help!"

"How?" a voice challenged. "We've nothing."

"Use yer blankets or the slop buckets." Lydia's blanket ignited. She dropped it and stomped out the flames, then picked up a slop bucket. Hannah grabbed another. It was vile, but wet. She dumped the contents on the flames, and a vile stink rose up out of the blaze. Already it had grown too large and the women's efforts had little effect.

"Grab the others," Hannah said, hobbling toward another bucket.

Rosalyn gave up her perch on the ladder and joined the fight.

Others stayed at the hatch, beating the wooden door and pleading for rescue.

The last of the chamber pots were emptied, yet the fire grew. The hold filled with smoke and the stench of burning waste. Hannah choked and coughed.

"Mum, what are we to do?" Lottie gasped.

"We'll get out," Hannah said, grabbing up the child and moving toward the stairway. Black smoke swirled thick and bitter. Hannah struggled to breathe. Every time she inhaled, smoke and heat seared her lungs.

Still holding on to Lottie, she dropped to her knees. There seemed to be more air closer to the floor. They moved carefully, the decking rising and falling beneath them.

Hannah heard the hatch open and the sounds of women scrambling to safety. Crew members descended, handing down buckets of water. Each bucketful tossed on the flames created more smoke. Hannah wheezed, fighting for every breath. Lottie no longer whimpered or coughed. She hung limply in Hannah's arms.

Her eyes burning, Hannah tried to see her through black smoke. "Lottie!" She shook the little girl. "Lottie!"

No response.

"Lord, no. Please don't let her die, not Lottie. Me! Take me!"

All of a sudden strong arms grabbed hold of Hannah. "I've got you," she heard.

It was John. He hefted her and Lottie and carried them both toward the hatch. He was strong and solid. Hannah felt safe.

She tried to take in a breath. There was no oxygen. Her throat constricted. Nothing could save her, not even John.

They broke free of the smoke-filled hold, and wind and rain engulfed Hannah. She sucked in big gulps of air and then coughed in uncontrolled spasms.

John set Hannah and Lottie on the rolling deck. "You all right?"

Hannah managed to nod, barely able to see through the falling rain and spray of the waves. "But . . . she's not. Can . . . you help her?"

Lottie didn't move. She wasn't breathing.

John lifted the little girl and shook her. "Come on, now. Wake up." He slapped his hand against her back. "Take a breath. You can do it."

He laid her over one arm and solidly slapped her back. When she didn't respond, he hit her harder. "Wake up! Breathe!"

All of a sudden, Lottie coughed and then took a wheezing breath. She gagged and choked, but she was breathing.

"The Saints be praised!" John said.

"Thank you, Lord," Hannah said softly.

John set the little girl on the deck beside Hannah. Lottie coughed violently and retched, but she kept breathing. "She'll be all right."

"Because of you," Hannah said. "Why would you risk your life for us?"

127

"I'd be pleased to take credit, but the captain sent us down." He knelt in front of Hannah and took her hands in his. He gazed at her in a way that sent shivers through her. "I would have gone down for you, though. No matter what."

Hannah didn't know how to respond. His look was one of devotion. She glanced at the hatch. "What about the fire? Can they put it out?"

Struggling to keep her feet as the ship continued to roll, Lydia staggered toward them. "Are ye all right?"

"Yes. John saved us."

"The fire's nearly out." Lydia took in a deep breath. "They managed to get enough water on it. But everything's more of a mess than it was before. What little comforts we had are gone."

Hannah pushed to her feet, but her legs were weak and trembling.

John lifted her, setting her on her feet. "You able to stand on your own?"

"I think so." She disengaged herself from his arms. "I can manage. Thank you."

His eyes held hers. "I was exceedingly worried. I should hate myself if something happened to you. I vow to watch over you the rest of the voyage."

For a moment Hannah reveled in the promise, but it was only a moment. Reality prevailed. How could he see to her welfare? "I appreciate what you've done, but how do you propose to watch out for me? We're all at the mercy of the captain and the crew. And once we reach New South Wales we'll be under the Governor's authority." She straightened slightly. His intentions were honorable but imaginary.

Lottie stumbled to her feet, and Hannah lifted the frail girl into her arms. "I thank you for caring, sir," she said and walked away wishing life could be different. John was truly a gentleman. If only she'd known him before.

Before doesn't matter anymore. Life is what it is. There's no room for dreams.

12

John shuffled across the hold. Each step inflicted pain. The irons around his ankles had caused lesions and swelling. They cut into his skin as he moved. Grasping the handrail, he gazed at the hatch, wishing someone would open it from above. He needed to smell the air, to feel a breeze on his face. He'd always taken these simple pleasures for granted. *Never again*, he vowed.

Work offered a reprieve, so he hoped to be ordered to some kind of duty on deck. Even a bone-rattling saltwater dousing was worth time up top.

Thoughts of the life he'd once known reeled through his mind. He could hear his father's voice, see his steady hand at work. He'd stood by John patiently guiding and training him. *I didn't realize the beauty of those days.*

Memories of his mother pressed in. She'd always smelled of soap and of baking. She'd been a woman who stayed busy caring for her family and home. She took pleasure in needle-work and could often be heard humming a hymn while she sewed.

"Mum," he said without realizing he'd spoken out loud.

"What'd ye say?" asked Perry Littrell, one of John's prison mates.

"Nothing."

Perry sat on the bottom step. "I'd give most anything to be on deck. Feels like a fine day, smooth seas."

"It does at that."

Perry scratched at his patchy beard. "Can't get me mind off how I got 'ere." He smoothed his mustache. "What a fool I was."

"You never told me what happened." John had asked before, but Perry avoided the subject. "Can't be so bad you can't tell me, eh?"

Perry stared at him, his blue eyes teasing. "Ye want to know what got me 'ere?" He pushed his short, scrawny self upright. "Stupid beggar I was. That's all there is to it. Me friends were down-and-outs. Knew better." He shook his head. "They pinched some stuff from a high and mighty, and when they got caught, I was with 'em. Had nothing to do with it. Couldn't convince the magistrate of my virtue, though." He grinned.

"Sorry."

"Not like I didn't deserve it. Grew up on the streets. Did a lot to be ashamed of. I earned me place 'ere."

John's anger grew. He'd not earned this penalty. "Wish I hadn't gone to the pub that day. I should have let my cousin solve his own troubles." Hatred burned hot in his gut. "One day he'll know what it means to suffer. I'll see to it."

"Can't say I blame ye for feeling that way. Figure I'd do the same. But ye'd be better served to let it be."

"I want my life back." He smashed a cockroach beneath his boot.

"Revenge won't give it to ye."

131

A man coughed so severely it sounded as if he would hack himself into eternity. John's eyes fell upon the prisoner. "He's not long for this world."

"Heard that sound before. Death is knockin'." Perry shoved his hands in his pockets.

There were a fair number of empty berths, left by those who had died. He was almost used to it, except for the lads. Not even old enough to shave, they'd been rounded up off the streets. Having been shut out of society, they did what they had to do to survive. Many paid dearly.

He looked at Perry. "How did you avoid prison all those years?"

"Lucky, I guess. Nearly got caught a few times. Wasn't all that long ago I decided to become respectable. Seen too many of me mates go to the gallows." He frowned. "Ended up 'ere anyway." Scratching his head, he said, "Could do with a bit of tobacco. I'd love to have a pipeful."

"Heard that in Port Jackson there's work to be done for the landowners and the upper class. They use convicts. Perhaps we'll have proper jobs yet." John offered a sideways grin. "And then maybe you'll get your tobacco."

Perry nudged a chunk of filth up from the floor with the toe of his boot. "How much longer ye think we 'ave?"

"Was told it would take six or seven months. We've five passed already."

"How ye know that?"

"Been keeping a count."

"Figure ye for the kind who would." Perry walked to the nearest row of bunks and leaned against a corner post. "Seen a lot of rat holes in me day, but this is the worst."

Most of the men lay on their bunks, staring at nothing or

sleeping. Some sat on the floor and played cards. They wagered pieces of straw or bet possessions they dreamed of owning some day. There were no books or any other sort of entertainment. Work was the only real distraction for those strong enough to do it.

Every time John was on deck he looked for Hannah. It was a lucky day when they were both there at once. He'd find some way to have a few words with her even though speaking to a prisoner of the female persuasion could bring the lash down on his back.

Although the ravages of the voyage concealed much of Hannah's beauty, he could see she was a handsome woman—compelling brown eyes lined with long lashes, and ivory skin. And her strength of mind couldn't be hidden.

He admired her fortitude. *Even with her courage and strength, she needs someone to watch out for her.* He wanted to be that person. But of course she'd been right when she'd pointed out there was nothing he could do. Although marriages were allowed once in New South Wales, he doubted they'd live near one another. He imagined how she'd look well dressed and clean and then wondered if she ever thought of him.

"What's that swoony look yer wearing?" Perry asked with a grin. "Yer thinking of her. Ye might as well put that pretty lady out of yer head. When we get to Port Jackson, ye'll go yer way and she'll go hers." He flicked a bug off John's jacket pocket. "And I thought ye said something 'bout a wife."

"I *was* married," John said. "She died. May she rot in her grave." He looked down at Perry. "She went off with my cousin. The both of them took my money. No doubt he spent every bit of it."

John clenched his jaws. If he said more, Perry would admon-

133

ish him. He didn't need that today. He had a right to hate Henry and Margaret. They'd done the worst thing a person could do to a man. *One day, God willing, I'll have my revenge.*

"I'm tired." John walked to his bunk. Dropping onto the hard berth, he lay on his back and stared at the bunk above. His mind returned to Hannah. She'd never do what Margaret had. Just the thought of her made him feel somewhat tranquil. He smiled. She was a wisp of a woman, with sad eyes and a quiet way when she wasn't standing up to him.

She's good. Too good for this. She ought to be enjoying tea or going to the opera or the ballet. He didn't know that Hannah had never enjoyed such indulgences except for an occasional quiet evening with her mum over tea.

His sentence was for the remainder of his life, but he'd heard of some who were given a ticket of leave. Perhaps he'd be one of the lucky few. Course he'd have to serve at least another eight years and probably more. *I'm twenty-six now plus eight years. That'll make me thirty-four—nearly an old man.* He almost groaned.

He assumed Hannah was younger than him. He heard she'd been sentenced to fourteen years. She was refined and would certainly get a ticket of leave in as little as six years. She'd still be young enough to marry and have children. *She'd be foolish to wait for me.* He rolled onto his side. *You're acting like an old duffer already. She's got no reason to wait in any case. I'll most likely serve out the entire length of my sentence.*

He stared at the bulkhead.

―――

Hannah lay beside Lottie. Resting on one elbow, she studied the little girl and smoothed her hot brow. She'd been sick for days, and each hour she seemed to grow weaker. Hannah guessed it to be ship fever, which had already taken a number of lives. *God, she can't die. Please let her live. I know I'm unworthy to ask you for anything, but she's a bright little thing with a kind heart.*

Lottie's eyes fluttered open. "Me head hurts, mum. And I'm cold."

"I know, luv. You'll be better soon."

Lottie closed her eyes as if to gather strength and then looked up again at Hannah. "If it's me time to die, it's all right. I'll see me mum, then."

"You'll not be dying today. You're too strong for that." Hannah held back tears. "You're needed here. I need you."

Lottie smiled. "I need ye too. I'd say yer very near to being me own mum."

Hannah caressed the little girl's freckled cheek. She was so pale it frightened her. Holding a tin of water to the child's lips, she said, "Have a drink, eh." She lifted Lottie up slightly so she could sip from the cup. After taking a drink, Lottie lay back down with a heavy breath.

Clanking irons announced Lydia's arrival. She stood beside the berth. Leaning on the bunk, she studied Lottie and then looked at Hannah. "Ye need time to yerself. I'll watch over her."

Hannah looked down at the youngster. She was already asleep. "I'm afraid I'll look away and then she'll be gone." She closed her eyes and gave herself permission to cry. "It's not right. None of this is right. Why would God allow so much suffering, especially for someone like her?"

Lydia laid a hand on Hannah's arm. "We can't know God's mind." She squeezed Hannah's arm. "Shame on ye for givin' up on her. She's not one to quit. She's a vigorous little un, and she'll get well." She met Hannah's gaze. "In the end, she'll be stronger for this. Strength will serve her well."

"Right you are." Hannah climbed down from the bunk and moved toward a group of women who sat together. They picked insects from each other's scalps.

Corliss looked up from tending a fiery red lesion on a woman's leg. The entire calf was swollen. "You in need of company, dear?"

"I don't truly know what I'm in need of."

"Perhaps you'd like to join us?"

"Thank you, no." Hannah had seen enough of weeping sores, and she'd nursed too many with the flux, ship fever, and sweating sickness. Today she had no more to give. She moved toward the stairway. *If only it were wash day*, she thought. The cold water made her hands ache and she detested the foul odor of the crew's clothes, but she relished the time on deck.

She gazed at the hatch and wondered if the sun was shining. Light blinked in around the edges of the door; it seemed bright. Forcing her mind from the stench of sickness and filth, she imagined fresh sea air and a breeze.

Corliss Browning hobbled toward her. "How are you today, luv?" The elderly woman smiled and her face became a patchwork of lines. "You seem troubled."

"Of course I'm troubled. I'm imprisoned here."

"I mean more distressed than usual." Corliss smiled.

She always knows, thought Hannah. She loved this woman who never seemed to lose heart. Her faith remained intact no matter how dreadful the circumstances.

"I must admit to being disheartened." She glanced at Lottie.

"She's so ill. Part of the time she's not in her right mind. I'm afraid."

Corliss looked at Lottie. "She is a dear one. But her fate is in the Lord's hands. He knows her better than you or I. She's his child."

"I wouldn't do something like this to a child of mine," Hannah said, but before the sentence was complete, she was struck by a horrible truth. She'd done worse—she'd wished her own child dead. The room lurched and bile rose in her throat. She gripped the ladder.

"Are you all right, dear?"

Hannah nodded. "I'm worried about her. That's all."

"Ship fever kills. But not this child. She's strong."

"I pray you're right." Hannah choked back tears and tried to focus on Corliss. "How are you faring?"

"Good for an old woman." She smiled. "I've a bit of rheumatism, but I'm well enough. The Lord has been good to me."

"Good to you? What could someone like you have done that deserves this sort of treatment?"

"I am innocent of crimes against the King, but I'm a sinner all the same and do not deserve God's grace. I deserve destruction." Gratitude touched her eyes. "Instead, God blessed me, and he has all of my life. When I was growing up, I never knew a day of hunger. And I was loved by my family. I have much to be thankful for."

"But all of that's gone now. You live in this fetid hole and you've no hope for freedom when we arrive in Port Jackson. How can you be thankful?"

"Even here my life has value. And I'm fed and housed." She glanced about. "Perhaps not in the way I'm accustomed. I admit this would not be my choice of accommodation." Gentle eyes

137

returned to Hannah's. "I'm certain of my Lord's presence. He takes this journey with me." Tears washed into her eyes. "He suffered so much more than I can imagine. Because he loves me."

"I wish I could believe as you do," said Hannah. "To have unyielding faith is surely a comfort. I have so little faith."

"The Lord has given you all the faith you need. It's there." She pressed her palm against Hannah's chest. "Inside. You just need to believe it."

Hannah shook her head. "No. It's not there. God doesn't love me."

"Of course he loves you."

"You can't know the depth of my sin. You've surely never known such an offense." Hannah wiped at her tears. "God can never forgive me."

"There's nothing he cannot forgive, except the sin of not believing in his Son."

"I do believe. But . . ." Hannah needed badly to unburden herself, but she couldn't bear to have anyone know how she'd wished away her child.

Corliss rested a hand on Hannah's arm. "The Scriptures say that he loves us even while we are sinners."

Hannah wanted to believe Corliss's comforting words, but she knew she was forever tainted.

<hr/>

That night when the lanterns were lit, several sailors descended into the hold. "What a stink!" one of them said. "My gal will need a bath before she lies with me." He stood at the bottom of the stairway and looked about.

Another one said, "Just keep yer nose pinched closed." He laughed.

Hannah knew what was coming. She tried to be invisible, lying flat on her bunk. It had been many days since the men had come for the women. She'd hoped they'd never return. *Lord, protect me*, she prayed, unable to keep from quaking.

A sailor moved to a berth and grabbed a woman, dragging her off the bunk. It was Elizabeth. She was young and unmarried.

Lottie was still fevered and delirious. Hannah moved close to her and pretended to be asleep.

Rosalyn stood with her chest thrown out and her hips set in a provocative pose. "I can show ye a fine time. And I don't ask for much." She smiled. Three sailors moved toward her. "I'll only go with one of ye."

"Me. It'll be me," said the larger of the three. "I've a bit of brandy to share."

"Brandy, is that all? Ye have no pretty things? Something a woman might like, eh?"

"I've a brooch, with fine gems," another man said.

Rosalyn moved toward him. "I dare say, I'd like to see that." She linked arms with him. "Do ye think ye could remove these irons?"

He looked at her manacles. "Can't. Captain would flog me for sure." He lifted her in his arms. "They'll be no trouble." With a chuckle, he carried her out of the hold.

Some of the women were like Rosalyn, hoping for favors from the men, but several were dragged from their beds, crying for mercy. Hannah closed her eyes and pressed her hands over her ears. Her blanket was thrown off and someone grabbed her. Hannah gasped.

139

"Awake with ye now." A sailor with the smell of spirits on his breath studied her and grinned. "Ye'll do just fine."

Hannah huddled closer to Lottie. "Leave me. I'm not well."

The sailor's eyes wandered to Lottie. "I'll take the girl, then."

"She's got ship fever," Hannah said.

He reached for Lottie anyway.

"No. Please, sir, don't." Hannah took a deep breath. "I'll go with you."

He straightened.

"Ye've no right to take any of us," Lydia said. "Prisoners we be, but still citizens of the King." She pushed off her bunk and stood with her hands on her hips. "I'll report ye. When the King finds out, ye'll be sorely punished."

"Got the captain's permission. Figure that's all I need." He grabbed for Hannah. "Come on, then." He yanked her from the bed.

"Leave her be. She's a gentlewoman and deserves better than you."

"No such thing as a gentlewoman on this ship," the sailor jeered. He eyed Lydia. "One's the same as another, though. How 'bout ye go in her stead?"

"I'll not go anywhere with the likes of ye." Lydia defiantly met his gaze.

"Ye'll do as yer told." He dropped Hannah and grabbed for Lydia. She ducked out of his reach. Angry, he leaped toward her, and when Lydia evaded him again, he grabbed her hair and held it fast, yanking her toward him. Grabbing at her hair, Lydia shrieked.

The sailor held her up in front of him. "Ye'll do just fine. I like a wench with a little fire in her." He grinned and pulled her along with him.

Hannah watched, horror spreading through her. She was certain her friend was still innocent. "I'll go with you," she shouted at the man.

The sailor stopped and looked at Hannah, studying her up and down. "Yer a bit scrawny. I like sturdier women." He grinned at Lydia and kept moving.

Lydia pummeled the man with her fists. Finally, the sailor threw her over his shoulder and hauled her up the stairs. The hatch slammed shut.

Hannah stared at it, sick at what had happened. It was her fault.

Lottie pushed up on one arm. "Mum, is Lydia coming back?"

"Yes. She'll be back. You sleep now." She gently pressed Lottie down and covered her with a blanket, then moved to the bottom of the stairs where she waited.

13

Weak from months at sea and too little food, Hannah slowly climbed the stairs and stepped onto the deck. Perhaps the sunshine would fortify her. Today she and several others would wash the crew's clothing. She looked down at her own dress, tattered and filthy, and wondered if it would hold together were it given a proper cleaning.

Her eyes immediately found the sea, searching for signs of land. There was naught but ocean all around. Several times in recent weeks, she'd heard cries of "Land ho!" She hungered to place her feet on solid earth, to see a tree or a bush, even a building. For too long she'd known only the confines of the ship and the endless roll of waves. Each time the ship ported, Hannah could only listen to the sounds of foreign seaports. Prisoners were not allowed on deck.

Today the seas were calm, glistening beneath a brilliant sun. The air felt hot and humid, and there was little wind to fill the sails. Without heavier breezes, they'd not put in to Port Jackson anytime soon. They'd already been at sea a month longer than expected.

Disheartened, she moved toward the front of the ship. Her

eyes searched for a speck of ground in the distance. A sudden burst of wind caught the sails and lifted Hannah's hair away from her face. It was cooling and reassured her that life could be pleasant.

Lottie skipped across the deck. Although dreadfully thin, she seemed in good condition. It was grand to see her so active and good to see her free of shackles. The captain had relented and allowed those who had shown themselves trustworthy to go without restraints. Hannah was also one of the lucky ones who'd been relieved of her irons.

Although thankful her shackles had been removed, Hannah couldn't quell her anger. Why had they been forced to spend so many months fettered? What did the captain think might happen if prisoners could move about freely? The women were certainly no danger to him or his crew.

Lottie moved to the railing and peered over the side. "Look! Fish! Loads of them."

Hannah joined her young friend and gazed down at the sea. "I've never seen so many." The clear waters were alive with brightly colored fish. "That's what we must have been getting in our stew."

"I like it. Didn't used to, but I'd say it's one of me favorites these days." Lottie smiled, her brown eyes looking like crescents surrounded by a palette of freckles.

How lovely she is, thought Hannah.

"Do ye think we'll see John about?" Lottie looked toward the men's hatch, then to the back of the ship.

"I doubt we'll see him. It's wash day. Men don't help with that." Hannah turned and faced the wind. Closing her eyes, she relished its touch as it brushed her cheeks and eyelashes. Even the dampness in the air was something to be appreciated.

143

Perhaps there would be rain and fresh water. The water coming from the ship's casks had become brackish.

"It feels like a perfect day," said Lottie.

Hannah opened her eyes. "It's certainly a fine day." Batches of white clouds hung in the blue sky. "A day to be thankful for."

Lydia stepped out of the hatch and onto the deck. She sauntered toward Hannah and Lottie. "I'm grateful to be free of that place, even for just a bit." She took a deep breath. "Fresh air—a true blessing." She smiled and then looked about just as Hannah had done. "I was hoping we'd see land today. I've heard them calling out sightings. How long do ye think before we port?"

"Soon I hope. I can scarcely imagine how wondrous it will be to walk on solid ground again."

"I hope there are trees where we're going." Lydia gazed out over the water. "They would be grand, eh?"

"It would be lovely to walk among trees." Hannah smiled. "Do you think we shall be allowed to?"

Lydia shrugged. "We'll not be free in Port Jackson any more than we are here even if we be on solid ground." Lydia grabbed the bodice of her dress and pulled it away from her, fanning it in and out. "I sweat and sweat." She wiped perspiration from her forehead. "I thought the cold was appalling, but this heat is worse. The bugs are everywhere. I can barely sleep at night for the scratching and swatting."

Hannah didn't want to talk about the ugliness of life. Today she'd think only of blue sky and swimming fish in a calm sea.

A door leading to the officer's quarters opened and Rosalyn stepped out. She glanced at Hannah and Lydia, but she didn't stop.

"She's hoping one of the officers will give her a ticket of leave or maybe a pardon." Lydia frowned. "It's a hard way to earn yer freedom."

"A lot of the women are doing it. But I've no confidence it will help at all."

Sadness touched Lydia's green eyes. "Don't want to think on it."

Hannah could feel a knot tighten in her gut. When Lydia had been taken by the crewman, Hannah had waited at the bottom of the steps until she returned. Her friend had said nothing then, nor since, about what happened.

Lydia glanced toward the hold. "Corliss is sicker than before. I fear she'll not live to see Port Jackson."

"Oh, but she must." Hannah moved toward the hatch. "I'll see to her."

"Land ho!" called a sailor from a lookout on the main mast.

Sailors and prisoners crowded the railing. "Where? Where is it?" Lydia sounded exultant. She leaned way over the rail.

Hannah hurried to the balustrade. She grabbed the back of Lydia's gown. "Be careful. John's nowhere about to rescue you if you fall."

"Indeed, I need me own champion." Lydia's eyes shimmered with merriment.

Hannah searched the deck, wishing John could be with her. It was a notable moment and one she wanted to share with him.

In the many months they'd sailed, they had managed few exchanges, yet she was drawn to him. His handsome face and his kindness had made the long days and nights more bearable.

Her eyes followed the gentle rising and falling of the waves. *What shall become of me?* she wondered, suddenly afraid. For

145

so long the future had stretched out, far from her reach. Now it loomed close. What would it bring?

She gripped the railing and cautioned herself against hopes for a better life. Sadness crept inside as she realized John would no longer be even a small part of her life.

"I can barely wait. Do ye figure we'll see land soon?" asked Lydia.

"There's no need for excitement," Hannah said. "There's nothing good waiting for us."

"Nothing, mum?" asked Lottie, sounding crestfallen.

Hannah had spoken carelessly, forgetting about the dreams of little girls. "What I meant is that we don't know what our future holds. We ought not be overly stimulated."

"One never knows what will come," said Lydia. "I've heard stories. We can and should expect good fortune. Upright conduct can bring shorter sentences."

"Always the optimist, aren't you," Hannah said quietly, wondering how someone like Lydia, who'd been given a life sentence, could feel hopeful.

"No other way to be." Lydia leaned far out and gazed down at a sea of plenty. "I'm hoping for a big chunk of fish in me soup tonight."

Hannah felt a hand on her shoulder. She turned to see a white-faced Marjorie. "Corliss is doing poorly. She's asked for you."

"How bad is she?"

"Quite stricken I fear. She's insistent you come right away."

<hr />

Hannah descended the stairs, returning to the fetid hold. In all these months, she'd yet to become accustomed to the stink. She held her breath momentarily but finally had to let it out and breathe in.

Corliss lay on a lower bunk. Even in the dimness, Hannah could see the pallor of her skin and the dark smudges beneath her eyes. High cheekbones that had once been attractive now added to her skeletal appearance. Hannah squatted beside the berth and rested her arms on the edge of the bunk. She grasped one of Corliss's hands. "Marjorie said you wanted to speak to me?"

Corliss nodded.

"Would you like a drink?" Hannah lifted a tin half filled with water. Corliss struggled to push up on quaking arms. Hannah put her free arm about the elderly woman, assisting her, and held the tin to her lips.

After a few sips Corliss lay down and struggled to catch her breath. "This earthly body has failed me."

"We're nearly to Sydney Cove. After we get there and you're off this ship, you'll feel better."

"No, child. I won't." Corliss smiled. "And that's all right. I quite agree with the apostle Paul when he said, 'To live is Christ and to die is gain.'" She squeezed Hannah's hand. "I'm ready to be with my Lord." Her eyes warmed. "I wanted you to know that."

Hannah felt a flush of fear. "What shall we do without you?"

"You'll do fine." Corliss wheezed in a breath. "You and Lydia have each other and dear Lottie. The Lord will see to you, all of you."

"He's not done well so far."

"He surely has. You're not perceiving the truth, luv." Even in such a state of frailty, Corliss's eyes were lit with passion. "Our Lord sees with eyes of wisdom and knowledge. He knows the beginning and the end." She rested a hand on Hannah's. "Trust him. Know that he is God. And that you're never alone."

Hannah wanted to believe. But she didn't. He'd abandoned her and rightly so. Still, she didn't want to cause this fine lady distress, so she lied and said, "I believe you."

A knowing look touched Corliss's pale blue eyes. "You don't. Not yet. But you will." Her lids closed and she let out a whispered sigh. Again looking at Hannah, she said, "Do not mourn me or my life. I've had a goodly number of years, many fine days. Even this journey has blessed me. The Lord intended me to take it."

She looked up and beyond Hannah. As if she were seeing someone. Her expression was expectant. Then she gazed at Hannah. "Now, you go and enjoy the fresh air and beauty of God's creation."

"No. I'll stay."

"I thank you for your tender heart, dear, but I'm weary and think I'll sleep."

"All right, then. But I'll be back to check on you when I come down again."

<hr>

When Hannah returned to the railing, she stood beside Lydia and Lottie. Leaning on the balustrade, she gazed across open water. Where was the land? She so wanted to see it. The need was nearly as intense as the hunger that gnawed at her belly.

"How is she, then?" asked Lydia.

"She's dying."

"Miss Corliss?" asked Lottie.

"Uh-huh."

"She told me she's going t' see Jesus." Lottie placed her hands on the railing in front of her and rested her chin on her hands. "She wants us to be happy for her." She looked up at Hannah. "But I'm not."

"I know what ye mean," said Lydia. "I want her to stay too."

"Land ho!" came a shout from above.

Hannah glanced up at the platform above and then gazed across the water in the direction the sailor had been looking. Just as before, she couldn't see anything. And then through the haze, white cliffs appeared tall and straight, looking as if they'd shot straight up out of the blue sea. "There!" she shouted. "There it is! Do you see?"

"I do!" shouted Lottie. She jumped up and down. "Are we there, mum?"

"We certainly must be close."

Shouts went up all over the ship. Even prisoners who knew that land simply meant being moved from one prison to another cheered. At least they'd be free of the foul ship and of the sea.

Was it possible that life would be better in New South Wales? Hannah looked down at Lottie. What if they were separated? She couldn't bear it. The little girl felt like her own. And who would look out for her? Hannah rested her hand on the child's head. Lottie looked up and smiled, her freckles more pronounced than usual.

The sails were full and the ship moved swiftly north and west. While the women laundered, they kept watch. After a time, golden beaches with foaming surf appeared and there were trees beyond, crowding hillsides. Cliffs grew taller and steeper and became a reddish yellow.

The women moved to the railing. The crew didn't seem to care. It had been so long since Hannah had seen land. Looking upon the wild shoreline felt like sustenance. She was enthralled.

Hannah became aware of a presence beside her. Looking up, she saw it was John. Hazel eyes met hers and Hannah's heart speeded up. "The guards let you out?"

"We drew straws for who got to bring up the slop bucket. I won." He glanced at a sailor whose attention was on the sights rather than on the prisoners. "And I'm glad for the crew's distraction."

Hannah turned back to look at the view. "It's wonderful, isn't it?"

"That it is." For a moment, he kept his eyes on hers, and then the cliffs and beaches drew his attention. "Our journey is nearly ended."

"No. It's only just begun," Hannah said, unable to keep the despair out of her voice. She looked at a sailor who still paid them no mind. "They'll order us back to our labors any moment. I can scarcely believe we've been permitted this much time away from our work." She glanced at the washtubs.

"Perhaps they've forgotten. The crew must be impatient to see the end of their journey as well." John smiled and his angled face softened.

Hannah wanted to lean against him, to feel his strength. She didn't dare.

"I hope we'll not have to say good-bye," he said.

"But of course we will. Prison awaits us, Mr. Bradshaw. Have no expectations."

"Perhaps we'll see each other. Port Jackson can't be so substantial as all that. And I've heard prisoners sometimes work for landowners and businesses 'round about."

Hannah dared not allow longings to lift her hopes. "Alas, I wish you were speaking the truth, but I'm certain that what awaits us is not favorable to our friendship." She stepped away from the rail. "It's been a pleasure to know you, sir, but I'm sure that once we port we'll not see each other again." She moved away and then glanced back. "I wish you well."

"Hannah, I pray this is not good-bye." John smiled, his eyes touched by a hint of mischief. "I have intentions as far as you're concerned. And I believe there will come a time . . . a time for us."

Hannah felt a blush heat her face. "You are quite bold, sir."

John smiled. "That I am. In London I'd never dared be so brash, but I've learned that sometimes there is no room for caution in such matters." The teasing tone became earnest. "Please understand . . . my feelings are not platonic."

Hannah didn't know how to reply. She wasn't at all displeased, but didn't dare encourage the man. "We shall see, then."

"Will ye look at that!" someone shouted.

Hannah turned to see imposing cliffs on either side of the ship. A mile or so of ocean lay between them. Like grand gates, the four-hundred-foot rock faces welcomed the ship and its cargo into an enormous bay. The ocean was the color of blue sapphires.

Hannah returned to the rail. "It's magnificent."

John stood beside her. "We *have* come to paradise, then?"

"If only it were true. But we dare not claim paradise, for it's prison that awaits us." Yet even as Hannah tried to push down hope, she couldn't quiet the stirring dreams.

She remembered Corliss. And knew the dear woman had gone to her Father's arms. *Lord, carry her into heaven with you.*

Tears blurred Hannah's vision as she gazed at the expansive bay with its golden beaches. She wiped her eyes clear. There were all kinds of trees beyond the shore, some large and impressive although a bit peculiar with their heavy limbs all askew. And there were tall, straight cedars too, standing like guardians.

Hannah took in a deep breath. Was it possible that happiness waited for her here?

14

Hannah listened to the shuffling steps of male prisoners as they were transported to longboats and their new quarters in Port Jackson. Maybe now it would be the women's turn. The ship had set anchor in Sydney Harbour the previous day, and instead of being transported, the women had been locked into leg irons. Still they waited.

Rosalyn and some of the others who had bartered their bodies for tickets of leave paced in spite of their manacles. They'd been given no assurances of freedom, yet couldn't quell their hope. No one came for them.

Hannah and Rosalyn couldn't have been more different, yet Hannah felt a connection with the brash woman. They both knew what it was like to be alone and to be a captive. Now that it was nearly time to disembark, Rosalyn expected a ticket of leave. Hannah was almost certain it wouldn't happen. She approached her.

Rosalyn shot Hannah a defiant look. "I don't need yer sympathy."

"And I can't help but offer it." Hannah tried to think of the right words. "I have sympathy even for myself." She glanced around the hold. "For all of us." She took in a breath. "What's happened to us is grim. And for many it's been a great injustice, but there's nothing to be done about it. We simply must endure."

"I'll do better than endure. I'll be free. Ye'll see. I'll have me ticket of leave." Rosalyn set her jaw.

"I pray you'll be rewarded with freedom. But you know it's unlikely."

"Ye may have given up hope, but not me." She folded her arms over her chest. "Ye'll see yer wrong."

"I hope I am," Hannah said, for Rosalyn had paid dearly for her expectations.

That night seemed especially dark and unbearably long. Hannah couldn't sleep. Finally when the first light splintered through gaps around the hatch, the door was flung open and the women were ordered above decks.

With Lottie's hand in hers, Hannah took the steps steadily and as quickly as her shackles would allow. She didn't look back. The hold was a place she never wanted to see again. Yet, she knew memories of the miserable days would go with her.

Thirty-five of the original fifty-six women who'd been transported from London remained. They were weak and many were sick, but they managed the climb down the rope ladder to waiting longboats. Hannah, Lydia, and Lottie settled onto bench seats.

Acting brave for her eight years, Lottie sat with her spine straight and her hands tightly clasped in her lap. She kept her eyes on the ship as they moved away. When they'd made it nearly halfway, she grasped Hannah's hand.

Hannah couldn't take her eyes from the vessel. It looked ugly, its rigging disorderly. The hideous craft had been home for months, and as wretched as it was, it felt peculiar to be free of it.

Hannah glanced at the dock where three soldiers waited.

She suddenly felt afraid. What was to become of them now? Rumors were that treatment at Port Jackson could be worse than what they'd experienced on the ship.

"Look, mum," Lottie said, standing up.

"Sit down! Yer 'bout t' tip us," a sailor snapped.

Sitting, she leaned close to Hannah and whispered, "There's a town. A real town."

Hannah gazed at the colony. Port Jackson was more than she'd expected. A sizable settlement huddled along the bay and spread out and up along bordering hillsides. Businesses sat at the edge of the harbor. There were houses just beyond. What looked to be government buildings stood farther back, and on the hill there was a cluster of huts and a sandstone building. She guessed that to be the gaol.

She looked back at the bay. Although she'd longed to escape the sea, she'd become accustomed to it. Waves bucked the boats and a breeze cooled her sun-heated skin. Port Jackson would now be her home.

There were trees covering nearby hills. She liked that. During the long months at sea, she'd dreamed of trees. She breathed deeply, hoping to smell vegetation, but the pungent odor of the harbor overwhelmed everything else.

"Will ye look at that," Lydia said. "Those men are black and nearly naked."

A group of black men stood on an outcropping. They watched the approaching boats. Hannah wondered if they were friendly.

"I never seen anyone like that before," Lottie said. "Do ye know what they are?"

"People, of course," Rosalyn said.

"I know they're people. But what kind?"

155

"The black kind," Rosalyn teased.

Lottie leaned close to Hannah. "Will they hurt us?"

"Certainly not. If they were hostile, I'm positive they wouldn't be standing in the open that way. They look quite peaceable."

"Them's Aborigines," a sailor said. "And ye can't trust 'em. Ye'd be wise t' keep yer distance. They been known to snatch whites." His eyes were alight, almost feverish. "And they eat captives."

He laughed at the gasps of horror and then added, "Ye best watch yer backs."

"Port Jackson looks like a fine place," said Lydia. "It might even be better than where we come from."

"It's tolerable as long as yer not staying too long," another sailor said. "And it's a wild place that don't take kindly to convicts."

Hannah tried to ignore the man's comments. Life here had to be better than the ship's hold. But even as she told herself this, the strangeness of the place felt powerful. It was nothing like England. The air was hot and damp, the trees looked peculiar, and the beaches with their golden sands were nothing like the ones she'd seen at home. She watched the Aborigines and her trepidation intensified. They looked so strange and terrifying. Would the soldiers protect them from the natives?

"How grand to be part of a small township." Lydia's green eyes held delight. "And look there toward the mountains. The air is blue. Have ye ever seen the like?"

"No, I haven't. I prefer the London fog." Marjorie Dalton's chin quivered with emotion. "I adore London."

No one commented. What could be said? London was home, this was not.

When the boat reached the dock, one of the sailors tossed a line to a soldier who secured the craft. Holding their muskets across their chests, the soldiers eyed the women suspiciously.

A shiver of fear coursed through Hannah. She stood in the rocking boat, her legs quaking. *Calm yourself.* She tried not to look at the soldiers.

Lydia was one of the first to disembark. She offered Lottie and then Hannah a hand.

After all the boats reached shore, the prisoners stood on the dock. The women huddled together, uneasy. Those who had hopes of freedom seemed especially edgy. When nothing was said about their being released, Rosalyn said, "I'm expecting a ticket of leave or perhaps a pardon."

The sailors chuckled.

"I was promised."

"Ye really believed that, eh?" one sailor taunted.

Rosalyn planted her hands on her hips and looked him square in the face. "I'll not take a step until I speak to Lieutenant Brown."

Hannah cringed inside. This is what she'd expected. *Poor Rosalyn.*

"You'll do as yer told," the sailor said. He looked at the soldiers. "She and the rest of these whores are yer problem now. Do with them as ye like." He grinned. "There's plenty of good fun to be had if ye've a mind."

All but one of the soldiers seemed indifferent to the woman's plight. He wore a hateful look. "Move on!"

"I'm not going," Rosalyn stated.

The women standing close to her edged away. Looking fierce, the soldier strode up to Rosalyn. "You'll go where I say and when I say." He grabbed her hair and jerked her head back, then bellowed in her face, "You'll do exactly as you're told."

She glared at him, but said nothing more.

The women were herded away from the port. Many walked with a clumsy sway.

Sick over what she'd just witnessed, Hannah did her best to follow. She was dizzy and the ground felt peculiar. It pitched back and forth. It simply wouldn't remain still.

"What's wrong with this place? The earth is tipping," a woman said.

One of the soldiers grinned. "You've got sea legs; you'll be getting your land legs soon enough."

Giving no mind to the women's difficulty, the soldiers kept a rapid pace and allowed no lagging. They moved up a hill toward the huts.

Most of the time Hannah kept her eyes on the ground, but when she chanced a glance at the soldier who had been so rough with Rosalyn, she could see he was studying her and the others with lecherous eyes. She trembled inside. During the voyage she'd managed to avoid the sailors' advances. Would she now be forced to submit? What of Lottie and Lydia? She couldn't bear the thought of their being so ill used.

Out of the corner of her eye, Hannah saw something move alongside the trail. At the same moment one of the women screamed. A black striped lizard stood its ground in front of the women. It stuck out a blue tongue, flattened itself against the ground, and hissed.

"My Lord, what is that?" asked Lydia. Even she sounded unnerved.

Hannah's pulse jumped. *What kind of place is this? Blue air and blue-tongued lizards?* Involuntarily, she glanced back at the ship. Had she been better off on board?

"Step lively," a soldier ordered, ignoring the reptile.

When they reached the sandstone building Hannah had

seen from the quay, they stopped. "Right then, off with your clothes," the lead soldier said with a grin.

Hannah couldn't believe what she'd heard. He couldn't possibly expect the women to disrobe in front of him and the other men.

"Do as you're told or I'll lay a bludgeon across your skull."

The soldiers shifted their muskets uneasily. One young man couldn't even look at the women.

A rotund woman stepped out of a nearby building. "Enough of that. You blackguards. I'll have ye reported. Yer to offer them some discretion and ye know it."

The one in charge glared at the woman, but lowered his musket.

The woman marched up to the prisoners. "I'm Matilda," she said as she removed the women's leg irons. "Ye 'ave a need, ye ask for me." After unlocking the last manacle, she straightened. "Now, inside with ye. Yer badly in need of a bath."

She followed the women inside the building. "Take off those rags and wash yerselves. Make sure to use soap." She wrinkled up her nose. "Yer not fit for decent company."

The women moved into a washroom. There were barrels of clean water, bar soap, and towels.

For a moment, the women eyed each other, suddenly shy over exposing themselves.

"Well, I got nothing to be embarrassed about," said Rosalyn, stripping.

The others followed suit. The idea of being clean overriding inhibitions, Hannah gladly shimmied out of her dress.

She washed her hair and then scrubbed every curve and crevice of her body, breathing in the scent of soap. As the filth fell away, she felt renewed.

159

Lottie needed help getting the soap out of her hair, but otherwise she was quite adept at washing herself.

"There are dresses for ye," said Matilda. "Ye'll each have two. Every week ye'll wash the dirty one and put on the clean." She pulled sacklike dresses out of a bag, handing one to each woman. "Not fancy, mind ye, but clean."

"Thank you," Hannah said, accepting hers. She pulled one over her head and pushed her arms into the sleeves. The material was coarse and the dress hung loosely, but Hannah didn't mind. It was clean. She combed the tangles out of her hair with her fingers.

"Mum, ye look pretty." Lottie smiled at Hannah.

"So do you." Hannah tweaked the little girl's nose.

Matilda hustled the women into an adjoining room. "Ye'll wait 'ere for the surgeon."

Hannah, Lottie, and Lydia sat together, leaning against a wall. The solid floor still tipped and rocked, but not as badly as before. Hannah stared at the windows. She hadn't seen any in so long. They allowed air and light inside. Such a little thing, yet it meant so much.

Clasping her hands in front of her, Marjorie joined them. "Do you think they'll have us put back in irons?"

Lydia shrugged. "Why? Where would we go?"

Marjorie held her shift away from her. "This dress is utterly impossible. It has no style whatsoever."

Lydia closed her eyes in an exaggerated way. "That's the least of our worries."

A small man with a tiny mustache and a stern expression stepped into the room. "Everyone stand in a line." Hands clasped behind his back, he waited while the women did as instructed.

When the last woman found her place, he stepped to the first. "You have any complaints?"

She shook her head no.

"Bend forward." She did as told and he examined her scalp. "Straighten up. Open your mouth." He examined the inside of her mouth, her throat, and her teeth. After that, he palpated her neck and then said, "Cough." He checked the skin on her arms and legs then moved on.

Most of the women were emaciated from lack of proper nutrition and illness. Some had oozing sores about their ankles from the irons and a myriad of other skin infections. Many had rasping coughs.

As the surgeon moved along, he took notes and offered ointments or liniments to some. A few he separated from the group, asking them to stand by the door.

Keeping hold of Lottie's hand, Hannah waited her turn and wished there were some way to avoid the degrading examinations. But of course there wasn't.

When he'd examined each one, he looked at Matilda. Nodding at the women he'd set aside, he said, "See they get to the infirmary." Without another word he walked out.

A few moments later, soldiers appeared and marched those deemed healthy out of the building. The women were steered toward derelict huts. Several were ordered into each. Still holding Lottie's hand, Hannah prayed they'd stay together.

The one in charge pointed at Hannah, Lottie, Lydia, Marjorie, and Rosalyn. "You five! In here!" He grabbed Rosalyn's arm and shoved her toward the door. She shrugged him off. Instantaneously, he backhanded her across the face. "I know your kind. If you want to live, you better smarten up."

Rosalyn didn't look at him. Holding her body erect and without saying a word, she stepped into the hut. Hannah followed her, wondering why she insisted on being so pigheaded.

161

The hut had a dirt floor, five woven rope hammocks, and a chamber pot. Its two redeeming qualities were a door that could be left open and a window.

"This isn't so bad," said Lydia. "It's better than the hold of the ship, I'd say."

Rosalyn dropped into a hammock. She touched her cheek. It was already bruising.

Lottie crossed to her. "Are ye all right?"

"Yeah. He didn't hurt me."

"He will," said Lydia. "Ye bring trouble on yerself and on the rest of us."

"What's that?" shrieked Marjorie, her eyes fixed on a corner of the room.

A huge brown spider as large as a woman's hand was fastened to the wall.

"It looks like a sea crab." Marjorie stepped backward as far from it as she could get. When she backed into the opposite wall, she startled.

Lottie huddled close to Hannah. "I never seen a spider that big."

"It's easily taken care of." Rosalyn swung out of her hammock, walked up to it, and removed a shoe. With a swift blow, she smashed it. "No matter how big it is, it's still just a spider." She ignored the mashed remains on the wall and returned her shoe to her foot.

"Aren't you going to clean it up?" Marjorie asked.

"Must I do everything?" Rosalyn eased into her hammock, folded her arms behind her head, and closed her eyes.

"But it's ghastly."

Wearing a smirk, Rosalyn looked at Marjorie. "Then I'd say ye ought to get rid of it."

162

"Oh!" Marjorie exploded.

Lydia picked up a stone from the floor and scraped the remains off the wall, then tossed the rock out the door. "If we're to be housemates, we'd best learn to get along."

Lottie fell into a hammock. Wearing a smile, she pushed one foot against the floor and swung back and forth. "This is fun."

Although feeling like a lost soul, Hannah offered the little girl a smile. Weariness enveloping her, she took the hammock next to Lottie. She closed her eyes and sleep quickly overtook her.

15

Marjorie scooped out the last of her porridge with her fingers. "The very least they could do is give us proper utensils. They make us eat like animals."

"We don't need yer complaining today," Rosalyn said.

"At least we've something to eat," Lydia said in her usual cheery voice.

Hannah dropped the last bite of biscuit into her mouth. It was dry, but filling.

"Do ye think we'll work for the Browns again today?" Lottie asked.

"I should think so. We've been there a week now. Mrs. Brown seems well pleased with us."

Hannah was happy to work for Mrs. Brown. She and Lottie scrubbed floors, washed clothes, and helped with other household chores. None of it was overly taxing, and working helped the days go by. She'd also been asked to do some sewing, which Hannah thoroughly enjoyed.

"I rather like it there." Lottie smiled. "Mrs. Brown's nice. Sometimes she gives me treats."

"She is nice," Hannah said, thankful that she and Lottie had been assigned to someone who treated them with courtesy. Mrs. Brown had married a soldier who'd been assigned to Port Jackson. She'd decided to accompany her husband rather than wait for him in England.

The Browns had three children, a set of twin boys and an infant. The boys were lively, and Mrs. Brown had her hands full trying to keep up with them and her new daughter, which is why Hannah and Lottie had been assigned to her.

Lydia hadn't been so lucky. She worked for a family who lived on the outskirts of Port Jackson, and it seemed they had little respect for convicts. They threatened to beat poor Lydia over the least infraction and worked her so hard that at the end of each day she dragged in exhausted with barely enough energy to eat. She'd fall asleep immediately after her evening meal.

Marjorie and Rosalyn had both been assigned to local businesses where they sorted and packed goods and kept the establishments clean. They were treated decently enough, but of course Marjorie managed to find reason to complain.

"It's time we were off," Hannah said to Lottie. She settled her eyes on Lydia. "I'll keep you in my prayers today."

Lydia smiled. "Thank ye. I'll be fine. A bit of hard work never hurt anyone, I always say."

Hannah and Lottie didn't have far to walk. The Browns' home was less than a mile from the gaol. Hannah still worried, though, about hazards and would keep watch for any kind of threat, especially Aborigines. She'd seen a few about town but had never had an encounter. There were other dangers as well. More than once she and Lottie had come across snakes warming themselves in the midst of the path, and there were a number of different kinds of lizards. Hannah didn't like snakes or lizards.

165

"What do ye think we'll see today?" Lottie asked, adventure in her tone.

"I can't imagine."

"I liked the bird we saw yesterday. I never seen one like that before—all white with yellow feathers on its head. It was pretty."

"It was at that," Hannah said. "Rosalyn told me they're called cockatoos."

"That's a funny name." Lottie kicked a stone into the brush.

Hannah watched it fly. It landed at the feet of a black man. She gasped and instinctively caught hold of Lottie.

The man, though small, stood with a spear at his side and looked fierce. Matted hair stuck out from his head, exaggerating his square black face. He stared at them from dark eyes; even the whites looked brown.

Hannah barely breathed. What should she do? If she ignored him and kept walking, would he attack them? Should she try to communicate? She decided it would be best to act cordial. Smiling, she said, "I'm Hannah." She glanced at Lottie. "And this is Lottie."

The Aborigine looked from one to the other and then said something in a foreign language.

"I'm sorry, but I don't understand." Hannah was perplexed at what to do next.

The man spoke again and then walked away, seemingly indifferent to Hannah's mistrust and fear.

"I never seen one of 'em up close like that," Lottie said when he'd gone. "I was afraid he'd steal us away and eat us."

Hannah laughed nervously and stared at the place she'd last seen him. "Of course he's not going to eat us. He meant no harm."

"But that sailor said—"

166

"He was only trying to scare us," Hannah said. "Obviously that man was harmless." But she wasn't at all certain that was true. She'd heard stories of Aborigines attacking whites.

"Mrs. Brown will be waiting for us," she said in a matter-of-fact tone, hoping to conceal her own apprehension. Grasping Lottie's hand, she hurried on.

Whenever Hannah was out and about, she watched for John. Several times she'd caught a glimpse of him, but always from a distance. She'd heard that he'd been assigned to a road crew and could be away for days at a time. Once, he'd spotted her at the same time she'd seen him. He'd waved, but then had been forced to move on.

Hannah thought about him often and wished there were some way to find quiet moments together. But each time her mind went to that place, she'd force it back to reality. There was no reason to associate with John. He was serving a life sentence, and she fourteen years. There could never be a time for them. She might as well get used to living as a convict in this inhospitable land.

New South Wales was nothing like England. Although Hannah found it tolerable, it took some getting used to. There were some things about the country that she actually preferred over what she'd experienced in London or aboard ship. The temperatures could be hot, but the air was cleaner than London. And although conditions in the huts were deplorable, they were still better than the hold of the ship. She struggled most with the hungry bugs, especially mosquitoes. They could make nights torturous and sleep elusive.

Soldiers still made visits to the ladies' huts, but there were enough women who were willing to exchange their favors for small extravagances that those who weren't so inclined were left alone. Hannah was thankful she, Lydia, and Lottie had not been bothered.

A camaraderie of sorts developed between Hannah and her roommates. Rosalyn mostly kept to herself, but often shared rewards from her nighttime rendezvous, bringing home blankets, drink, and food. Once she was given a comb, a prized possession in this place.

Marjorie could be sanctimonious and sometimes hurled barbed comments, mostly at Rosalyn, but she also helped with the work and on occasion tended to Lottie's needs. She was, however, often frightened and always bitter.

On a Sunday morning, their only day to rest, Rosalyn woke late. She immediately dug into her bag. "I've something better than that salt beef and dry bread we get." She smiled mischievously. "Chocolate." She held up a hunk of the confection. Dividing it, she gave a piece to Lottie. "There you go, luv. It's a bit soft, but still good."

Eyes aglow, Lottie bit into it and chewed. "Mmm."

"Hannah. Lydia. There's some for you too." She handed them each a piece.

"Thank ye." Lydia immediately popped hers into her mouth. She closed her eyes as she chewed. "It's grand."

Hannah accepted hers. "Thank you." She looked at the gift. "Rosalyn, this isn't worth what you do." Gently she added, "We don't need it."

Rosalyn tilted up her chin and narrowed her eyes. "Just because those blokes lock me up in a hovel doesn't mean I'm going to live like a savage. I want some of the finer things. And

168

I'll have them." She walked to the doorway and looked outside. "One day, I'll find one to marry." Her words were confident, but not her tone. She looked at Marjorie. "Ye want a piece?"

"From you? No."

"Ye think yer so much better than me . . . than all of us. Well, yer not. Yer stuck here just like us."

"I'm innocent of the charges. My brother-in-law's lies put me here."

"Yer not the only innocent 'round 'ere." Leaning against the doorframe, Rosalyn gazed out. "I'm going for a walk."

"Please don't go," said Lydia.

"I'm not meeting anyone. Just need some fresh air." She glared at Marjorie.

The sun had gone down and the staccato buzzing of cicadas filled the night air. The mosquitoes were especially voracious and Hannah couldn't sleep. Moonlight spilled in through the hut window, pushing back the darkness.

A hammock creaked and someone moved across the room. Rosalyn. She went to the door, hesitated a moment, and then stepped outside.

Hannah propelled herself out of her hammock and followed. "Rosalyn," she whispered loudly. "Rosalyn."

The tall, dark-haired woman stopped and looked at Hannah. "What do ye want?"

"Where are you going?"

"I don't like using the chamber pot. I prefer me privacy."

Hannah stared at her. "I don't believe you. You're meeting someone, aren't you?"

169

"What is it to you?"

"I know you don't want this—"

"Have I a choice?" Rosalyn whispered back vehemently.

"Yes."

Rosalyn folded her arms over her chest and stared at the bay where moonlight shimmered. "I can't live out me life as a prisoner. If I'm not free, I shall die."

Hannah remembered when she'd considered trading her body for food. The shame she'd felt then rushed at her anew. "I know what it's like to feel you have no choice. But you do."

"Go back to your bed."

Hannah tried a different tact. "It's not safe. There've been attacks by Aborigines. I saw one myself a few days ago."

"I'm meeting a guard. He'll see to me safety."

"Please don't go."

Rosalyn glared at Hannah. "Why do ye care?"

"You have value, Rosalyn. We all do."

Rosalyn stared out into the darkness and then turned to Hannah. "What I do has nothing to do with ye. Just because we're forced to live in the same hut doesn't mean we're friends."

Rosalyn's words hurt. "I just thought—"

"Don't waste time on me." Rosalyn's voice had lost its hard edge. "I'm not worth it." She moved on.

Hannah watched her disappear into the darkness. *I'm really no different from her*, she thought, regret engulfing her.

She wasn't sneaking off to meet men, but she felt as much a prostitute as Rosalyn. They all were—doing whatever it took to survive, groveling and doing as they were told. And worse than Rosalyn, she'd traded the life of her baby for so-called respectability. She could nearly understand Rosalyn's actions. Perhaps she was right—why bother with decency?

170

Late in the afternoon the following day, a genteel lady came to the hut. Hannah had seen her before, but she'd never met her. The stout, kindly looking woman held a large satchel and stood just outside the doorway. "Might I come in?" she asked, her blue eyes gentle.

"Yer welcome to," said Lydia. She stood and offered her stool to the visitor.

Moving gracefully, the woman crossed the room and sat. "I'm Mrs. Atherton. I live a little way from here. I visit occasionally to see what I can do to help. I know a bit about doctoring."

"No one here needs anything from ye," Rosalyn said.

Mrs. Atherton's eyes moved about the room. "Are you all in agreement?" Her gaze settled on Marjorie. "How about you?"

"I've some complaints, but there's nothing can be done about them. And I'd never consider allowing anyone but a real surgeon see to my needs."

"I understand your concerns, but there's only one surgeon and so many prisoners. Most likely you shan't see him." Her eyes went to Marjorie's hand. "You've a cut that needs tending."

"Do you think it's serious?" Marjorie asked, seeming to have forgotten her resolve about professional doctoring.

"Might I have a look at it?"

"I suppose it would be all right." Marjorie held out her hand. The edges of the wound were fiery red, the center puckered with infection.

"It must be painful." Mrs. Atherton cleaned the cut, applied salve, and bandaged it. "Clean it every day. I'll leave bandages and some of the ointment."

171

Marjorie held the hand close to her abdomen. "Thank you."

Next Mrs. Atherton moved to Lottie. "And how are you?"

"Good, mum, just a little hungry. Wish I got more to eat."

Mrs. Atherton smiled, but her eyes looked sad. "Perhaps I can help with that." She reached into a satchel and retrieved a small bag tied shut. Untying the string, she asked, "Would you like a sweet?"

"Yes, mum." Lottie's eyes were bright with anticipation.

"There's enough for all of you." Mrs. Atherton gave a piece to each of the women.

Lottie had eaten half of hers when she said through a mouthful, "This is good." She leaned against Mrs. Atherton. "You're a fine lady."

"Thank you, child." She looked at Hannah. "Is this your daughter?"

"No. Her mother died during the crossing." Hannah rested a hand on Lottie's shoulder. "We found each other."

"You're a pretty little thing. What's your name?"

"Charlotte, but everyone calls me Lottie."

Mrs. Atherton dug into her bag. "I think I have a dress here that might fit you." She lifted out a small pink gown.

Lottie sucked in a breath. "It's beautiful. I've never had such a fine dress."

"I think the pink will go nicely with your freckles," said Mrs. Atherton. "I've other dresses too. Each of you may have one. They're in the large satchel."

The women descended on the bag, except for Rosalyn. They each found dresses—Hannah a white linen, Lydia a green one, and white for Marjorie. Reluctantly, Rosalyn chose a pink gown.

"It's been a long while since I've had anything nice," Lydia said. "Thank ye." She held the dress up against her.

172

"I'll visit again." Mrs. Atherton's eyes settled on Lottie. "There's a family I know who would love it if a pretty little girl like you went to live with them." She looked at Hannah. "They're a fine family. Would it be all right if I inquired?"

Hannah felt the instant sting of tears. She adored Lottie. How could she let her go?

"Of course," she said. "This is no place for a child." She smiled at Lottie. "Imagine having a real family." She tried to keep her tone light.

Lottie frowned and said nothing.

"Good then." Mrs. Atherton stood. "I'm sure I'll be back soon. Good day to you."

16

John and the crew ambled up the road to a waiting wagon. Fatigue had fixed itself in his very bones. He wasn't sure his legs would carry him. Glancing at blistered, bloody hands, he kept walking.

When he reached the wagon, John climbed into the back and sat, leaning against a side rail. He closed his eyes and allowed his mind to rest. Another man's misfortune had provided the entire crew with a day's respite, for they were required to return to the prison.

Kian Murphy, an Irishman, had tried to escape. He'd been hunted down, put in irons, and marched back to Port Jackson where he awaited punishment. John didn't want to think about what that could mean for Kian.

"Right poor reason for a day off," Perry said, sitting beside John.

"You're right there." John let out a haggard breath. "Poor Kian."

"Wouldn't want to be him, that's for sure." Perry rested his arms on bent legs. "Living on the streets I had some bad days, but nothing like he's gonna have. The gallows would be better."

He was quiet for a moment. "Wish there was some way to save the poor bloke."

John only nodded. There was nothing to be said and he didn't want to talk about it. Exhausted, he closed his eyes and tried to sleep, but his mind remained with Kian and he could find no rest. At the end of this day, Kian would most likely be dead. John didn't know the young man well, but he seemed pleasant enough and not the type to run off. Why had he tried? It was common knowledge there was no escape, not overland anyway.

On the trip back to the gaol, the men were silent. Even Perry turned uncharacteristically quiet.

At the prison John hobbled to his hut and dropped into his hammock. It was the first time in three weeks he hadn't slept on rocky ground. Longing for sleep, he closed his eyes, but an image of Hannah intruded. He wanted to see her. Was she still at the prison or had she been moved? He'd heard that several women had been transferred to the Female Factory in Parramatta. If she'd gone with them, he'd likely never see her again.

Sleep, he told himself. *Don't think.*

"In the yard! Everyone in the yard!" a soldier bellowed as he walked along the row of huts.

John groaned and rolled to his side, dropping his feet to the floor.

"That'll be Kian," Perry said. "Poor beggar." He walked to the door and looked outside.

John pushed out of the hammock. "He'll be made an example of. It'll go hard on him."

"It's depraved, but yer quite right." Perry remained in the doorway. "Don't guess there's a way to escape this, eh?" Stuffing his hands into his pockets, he shuffled outside.

175

"Hope he makes it through." John followed, resigned to witnessing a flogging.

John worked alongside Perry. Sweat dripped into his eyes and ran down his back, soaking his shirt. His muscles quaked at the stress laid upon them. Still he continued to swing his pick, digging out rock and earth.

Perhaps if he worked hard enough he could erase the images of poor Kian. The prisoners had been called into the main yard and forced to watch while the young man had endured one hundred lashes with a cat-o'-nine-tails. John could still hear the sound of the leather strap whir as it snaked through the air and the drumbeats that counted off each stroke.

Hannah had been there. She'd looked pale, but with tear-filled eyes and her jaw set she'd watched, as ordered. Pride stirred in John. Hannah had been courageous.

He drove his pick into the hard ground. Why force the women to watch? What purpose did that serve? He wanted to protect Hannah from the miseries of this place, but there was nothing he could do. His frustration was so intense it burned in the center of his gut.

Kian had survived the flogging, but just barely. The memory of it made John's stomach turn, and it angered him. Flogging a man to that degree was unpardonable. There was no justification for such punishment, especially not for a man like Kian who, like so many others, didn't belong in Port Jackson. He'd been arrested as a subversive. Simply being an Irishman offered so-called proof of wrongdoing, and he'd been transported.

176

John's mind turned to his own injustice and to those who'd served it to him—Margaret and Henry. Fierce bitterness raised up in him. His mind filled with thoughts of what he'd do if he ever saw Henry again. *No use thinking about that. There's nothing served in such musings.*

He straightened and rested the shank of his pick against his leg. Taking a handkerchief from his back pocket, he wiped away the sweat and dirt from his face and eyes. Kian had been an example of what happened to anyone foolish enough to try escaping. The only safety lay beyond the Blue Mountains, and no white man had ever crossed them. John's eyes rested on the mountain range, and a longing for freedom welled up inside. But there was no escape. The few prisoners who had escaped were never seen again; but it was said that the bones of many had been found scattered north and south along the New South Wales coast.

Perry glanced at John and flashed him a smile. The man was an enigma, always seeming to find reason for cheerfulness. There seemed to be nothing that could be thrown at him that he didn't manage to come back at it boldly.

Still smiling, he said, "Breaking a good sweat today."

"That I am." John stuffed his handkerchief back into his pocket. "But better this than lying about at the prison."

"Right you are. A life sentence would be hard to face with nothing to do."

A guard approached John. "There's a gent wants to talk to you." He nodded at a carriage parked alongside the road.

John's gut tightened. This couldn't be good. He walked toward the carriage. A tall, slender man with graying hair stood alongside one of the horses. He was well dressed and clearly an aristocrat.

"Sir, you wanted to speak to me?" John asked as he approached.

"John Bradshaw?"

"Yes. That's me."

"I'm William Atherton." He shook John's hand. His grip was sturdy. "I was told you know something of toolmaking."

"That I do. My father owned a tool manufacturing company. I was raised in the business and apprenticed as a young man. When my father died, I took over the company."

"You're just the man I need, then. I own a timber company and live on a farm west of here in Parramatta. I've need of a toolmaker. British merchants can't get tools to me quickly enough." His gaze moved to the road crew. "Your talents are wasted here. You'll come to work for me."

Relief and jubilation spread through John. "I'd be glad to, sir." He barely managed to conceal his excitement. It wasn't always wise to give away too much of one's feelings.

"Splendid. I'll see to it that you're transported to Parramatta. A man will come for you."

Although unwise to press a new employer, John didn't want to leave Perry behind. He feared that working on the road crew would eventually kill his friend. "Sir, have you need for more workers? Tool men?"

"Indeed I do."

"I know a man. He's a fine chap and a hard worker. Name's Perry Littrell."

"You're recommending him?"

"That I am, sir."

"All right, then. I'll transfer him as well." Mr. Atherton climbed into his carriage, and the driver set off.

Wanting to shout his exultation, John managed to control

178

his emotions and returned to his pick. No longer feeling his pain, he labored beside Perry and quietly said, "Got us a job. A good one."

"Both of us?"

"Right. We'll be working for a William Atherton. He lives in Parramatta. Says he needs tool men."

"I know nothin' 'bout tools."

"No. But I do. I'll teach you."

"So, ye lied to him?"

"Not completely."

Perry shook his head, but he was grinning. "Hope yer stretching the truth don't come down on our heads."

❦

As promised, John and Perry were transferred to the Atherton farm. It was a fine place and Mr. Atherton seemed a fair and honorable man. He raised cattle and sheep and an assortment of other farm animals, just enough for food. He also harvested feed for the stock plus managed to grow a large garden. Mr. Atherton dealt mostly in timber, an emerging commodity in New South Wales. He'd done well since immigrating nine years previously.

The tool shop was more than John could have hoped for. Well stocked, it had every convenience, including a large fire hearth and billows for founding. He and Perry set to work immediately. Perry learned quickly, not only because he was a dedicated pupil, but also because he had a natural bent for toolmaking.

Life was good, considering—except for James Lewis, the overseer who had an unreasonable dislike for John. James had little integrity, and making John miserable seemed to give him pleasure. He was forever complaining about John's work, requiring him to rebuild and reassemble tools unnecessarily. And he seemed incapable of giving an order without bellowing.

John could do nothing to please James, and he finally quit trying. He decided to do his work, keep to his tasks, and pay no mind to the overseer. In time, Mr. Atherton would see he did superior work.

One afternoon James ambled into the shop. As usual, he looked surly. Lifting his hat, he wiped wetness from his forehead with the back of his hand. Sweat mixed with dirt became a mud smear. He swiped back thinning hair and replaced the hat. "Ye get that work done I give ye?"

"It's done," John said, keeping his eyes on a chisel he was making. "Finished it more than an hour ago."

"Ye act pleased with that." James strode up to John. "I wanted that auger and bits two days ago. There's a ship in Sydney Harbour ready to sail, except they can't because they're waitin' on ye. They got repairs to make. I told ye!" His skin flushed red and sweat trailed down his face. "I've had enough of yer loafing." He crossed to the workbench. "Show them to me. Where are they?"

"Where they always are." John nodded toward a workbench on the far side of the room.

James stormed across the shop. He picked up the auger and studied it. "Shoddy work this is. It'll not last. I've a mind to send ye packing."

Anger seething just beneath the surface, John moved to the bench. "Those are good, solid tools." He stared at the auger in James's hand. "Let me have a look at it."

The foreman slapped the tool into John's upturned palm.

John tried it out and then studied it from every angle. "There's nothing wrong with it. It's fine."

"Don't get high-and-mighty with me." James's cheeks puffed out and his eyes bulged. "I've had enough of yer insolence. Get yer things!" He stormed out of the shop and headed for the main house.

Stunned, John stared after him. "So that's it, then."

"Guess the both of us will be packin' up," Perry said. "Kind of liked it 'ere."

John and Perry walked to their quarters where they packed their belongings and then sat at a table to wait. They played a game of cards.

"I call," John said. "Let me see what you have."

Perry frowned and set a pair of threes faceup in front of him.

"That's it?" John laid down two nines.

"Nines are so much better than threes, eh?"

"Still beat you." John scooped up the six straws that had been set out as a wager. He shuffled the cards from one hand to the other. "Hate working on the road crew. That kind of labor can kill a man."

"Right, but it can make ye strong too. And in this place a man needs to be strong." Perry grinned. "We'll do all right."

John looked at his friend. He didn't figure he'd last long building roads. He was small and skinny.

Perry stared at John. "Don't worry 'bout me. I'll be fine. I might be puny, but that don't make me weak. I lost me mum when I was young, but I still remember her sayin' I was scrappy. Bein' tough helped keep me alive. Counts for a lot."

John dealt the cards. "True. You're a hardy one at that. You may outlast me." He knew it was unlikely, but he wasn't about to steal his friend's hope. And he had to admit that Perry had more spunk than most. He just might make it.

It was several hours before anyone came for them. It was Mr. Atherton. John and Perry were sitting on the porch when he walked up. They both stood.

"Afternoon, sir," John said.

Perry nodded and tipped his hat.

"Afternoon to you." A pipe rested on Atherton's lower lip. He took it out of his mouth and studied the bowl for a moment, replaced it, and then turned his gaze on John. "James came to me today. Said he's unhappy with your work."

"I know he feels that way, sir."

"It's not true," Perry said. "John does first-rate work."

"That so?" Mr. Atherton spoke in clipped tones.

John looked directly at his employer. "Yes. I'm good at what I do."

Mr. Atherton puffed on his pipe. "I had a look at the records. Your production is good. Also examined some of the tools. They were fine. Seems you're highly thought of 'round here as well." He put a foot on the bottom porch step. "So Lewis has been giving you a hard time?"

"That's true," Perry said. "He's been real hard on John, from the beginning."

"That right?"

"Yes, sir."

"Lewis has been with me a long while." He studied his pipe a moment. "But he's wrong about you and your work." He smiled. "I decided it'll be Mr. Lewis who'll be moving on."

Perry's eyes widened, but he kept quiet.

"What are you saying, sir?" John asked.

"Lewis has a bad history. I don't need his kind here." He

182

leveled serious eyes on John. "I grew up a poor relation to a wealthy family. Because of that I was offered a first-rate education and the finer things in life, but in the end I still had to make my own way. And I did." He turned his pipe over and tapped out the burned tobacco. "I've a good eye for people. You're a good sort, hard worker, dependable, and a fine toolmaker. I want you to stay."

"Thank you, sir." John could have cheered, but he remained steady.

"You've run a business of your own, and I need someone who knows how to deal with people, someone who's levelheaded." He smiled. "With Lewis gone, I'll be needing someone to take on his job. You think you could do it and still keep up with the tooling?"

"Yes. But I'll need another man here at the shop."

"I can do that for you."

Mr. Atherton set his pale blue eyes on John. "Why were you transported?"

John's stomach tightened. He considered lying. Instead, he met his employer's gaze. "I killed a man."

"Tell me about it."

John explained how he'd gone to the pub with his cousin, how he'd tried to defend Henry, and in the end, how he'd killed Langdon Hayes.

Atherton tucked his pipe into his front pocket. "I'll need you to start right away. And I'll see what I can do about getting you another man."

"Right." John couldn't believe his good luck.

"Good, then." Mr. Atherton's eyes fell upon Perry. "Seems John here oversold your experience." His gaze moved to John.

"I only said that he was a good sort and trustworthy, sir."

183

Mr. Atherton smiled. "Right you are. You did. And how is he doing as a toolmaker?"

"Right well. He has a knack for it."

"Good."

Perry straightened. "I won't disappoint ye, sir."

Mr. Atherton glanced at the main house. "That's it, then. I've got other business to attend to." He grimaced. "My wife's maid Lucinda is returning to Port Jackson. So Catharine has need of a new housemaid. I've got to see about finding one."

"A housemaid, sir?" John ventured. "I don't wish to be presumptuous, but I know a woman who would make a fine housemaid."

"And how do you know this person?"

"She came over on the ship with me. She's genteel and educated, and doesn't mind hard work."

"Do you know where I might find her?"

"Yes, sir. She's in Port Jackson . . . at the gaol."

"Her name?"

"Hannah Talbot, sir."

"I'll tell my wife about her."

John's spirits lifted even more. It would be grand if Hannah came to work for the Athertons—better than he could have hoped for. *Lord, can you make it so?*

17

Hannah dipped the last bite of stale bread into her broth, then popped the soggy crust into her mouth. She chewed slowly, extending her meager meal.

A guard stepped into the doorway. "Lottie Smith?"

Lottie slurped her broth and stood. Her brown eyes wide, she stared at the guard. "I'm Lottie. I've done nothing wrong, sir."

Every eye in the room focused on the guard. Hannah automatically moved closer to Lottie and circled an arm about the girl.

The guard stepped aside and a woman walked in. She had a gentle quality about her, and sad blue eyes. She looked at Lottie. "Of course you've done nothing wrong." She crossed the room and knelt in front of Lottie. Cupping the girl's chin in her hand, she said, "You're a lovely child. Catharine said you were."

Lottie withdrew and huddled close to Hannah.

A stout man with a hat tucked under his arm stepped into the hut. He stood beside the woman. He seemed a friendly sort. When he smiled at Lottie, his round face plumped even more.

They seemed to be refined people, but Hannah couldn't quiet her suspicions. Why the interest in Lottie? "Might I ask who you are and why you're here?" she said, trying to keep her tone compliant.

"My apologies. I should have introduced myself right off. I'm Grace Parnell and this is my husband Charles." Charles offered a nod. "We're here because of Catharine. The woman who visited you recently. She told us about Lottie."

"Mrs. Atherton?"

"Yes. She explained that Lottie didn't have a mother and that she was living here at the prison."

Tightness settled like a lump in Hannah's chest. She remembered that Catharine Atherton had mentioned the possibility of a family for Lottie. Of course it would be best for Lottie. Yet, Hannah couldn't do away with her longing to hang on to her.

Grace straightened. "Catharine said that Lottie was being well cared for by one of the inmates. Would that be you?" She offered a gentle smile.

"Yes. After Lottie's mother died, she and I became like family. We've been very close."

Grace's eyes traveled from Lottie to her husband and then back to Lottie. "We had two little girls. But they live in heaven now." She looked at Hannah. "They died of cholera. There've been no more children." Her eyes glistened. "We were hoping Lottie might like to come live with us."

"That's kind of ye, mum," Lottie said, "but I want to stay with Hannah."

Hannah wished Lottie *could* remain with her, but it wouldn't be right. She needed a proper home. "Do you live near here?"

"Not so far. In Parramatta. Our farm is about fifteen miles inland."

"Mind you, it's not a fancy place but we do all right," Mr. Parnell said. "She'd have a proper upbringing."

"We attend services every Sunday and we'd see that she's educated."

The Parnells could take Lottie if they liked. They didn't need Hannah's permission. "It's kind of you to ask." Hannah took Lottie's hand and glanced at the Parnells. "Can we have a moment?"

"Of course."

Hannah led Lottie outside. They walked toward a eucalypt grove. The pungent scent of the trees seemed stronger than usual.

"Do I have to go, mum?"

"Don't you want to?"

"I want to stay with ye."

Hannah looked about the encampment. There was nothing here for a child, only desperation and suffering. "I would love that too, but this isn't a proper place for a little girl. Wouldn't it be nice to have a mum and dad and live in a real home where you can sleep in a fine bed and never again have to go hungry?"

"I'd like that, but I want ye to come too. Do ye think they'd let ye come along with us?"

"Oh no. I can't. Remember I have a sentence to serve." She looked toward the west. "Parramatta isn't far. Perhaps Mrs. Parnell will bring you for a visit now and again, eh?" Hannah managed to smile. "I'd miss you, but I'd also be very happy to know that you've a family to take proper care of you."

Lottie looked back at the hut. Mr. and Mrs. Parnell stood just outside the doorway. "They seem nice." Her bottom lip pushed up in a pout as tears filled her eyes.

"Your mum would be very happy to know that you've a home with a mother and father." Hannah fought her own tears.

Lottie nodded and wiped at her eyes. "I guess I could go." She sniffled. "But only if they'll let me come see ye."

"That's right." Hannah knelt in front of Lottie and hugged her, knowing the Parnells would not bring Lottie for visits.

The little girl wrapped her arms about Hannah's neck and squeezed hard. "I love ye, mum."

"I love you too." Hannah pressed her cheek against Lottie's and smoothed her auburn hair. "Well then, we best tell the Parnells." She straightened, took Lottie's hand, and walked back to the hut.

"She's decided to go with you," Hannah said.

Mrs. Parnell pressed a palm against her chest. "Wonderful." She reached out a hand to Lottie. "Shall we go, then?"

"I want to live with ye, but only if ye let me come see Hannah."

"Of course you may. We'll see to it." Mrs. Parnell glanced at Hannah with a look of apology for her untruth. They both knew it would be best for Lottie to forget what had happened in this place.

"All right, then." Lottie crossed to Lydia and hugged her. "I'll miss ye."

She gave Marjorie and Rosalyn a hug too, then moved to Hannah. She pressed her cheek against the scratchy fabric of Hannah's skirt. Hannah circled her arm about the child.

"I won't forget ye. And how ye took care of me," Lottie said, chin trembling and eyes shimmering. Then she broke away, took Mrs. Parnell's hand, and allowed the woman to lead her outside.

Hannah moved to the door and watched Lottie walk away.

When she was out of sight, she retreated to her hammock. With tears sliding down her cheeks, she stared at the ceiling.

"It's a blessing from God," Lydia said. Her eyes brimmed with tears. "Ye did the right thing by her."

Hannah nodded. "She deserves a home and a good life."

The women were quiet that night and went to their beds early. Hannah wished for sleep, but it wouldn't come. She'd likely never see Lottie again. She'd lost her. God couldn't entrust a child to her. She was unfit to mother anyone.

Two days later, Hannah and several other women from Port Jackson were transferred to the Female Factory at Parramatta. They were loaded onto a barge and slowly moved up the broad Parramatta River.

While men thrust long poles into the water and propelled them forward, Hannah settled her back against a bag that held her few belongings. She was curious and fearful about the factory. She'd heard it was a harsh place.

Lydia sat beside her. "I like this, floatin' on the river. It's nice."

"Almost peaceful," Hannah said.

As they made their way upriver, the Parramatta narrowed and began to wind. Its banks were crowded with lush green plants and trees. Hannah especially liked the eucalypt trees with their white bark and slender, spinning leaves. Bushes crowded for space among the trees; some were heavy with yellow flowers. When they passed a small tree decorated with large red blossoms, Hannah wished she could stop and pick them. That wouldn't happen. She was a prisoner and she'd never have the freedom to do as she liked.

"They're wonderful!" Lydia said. "One day I'll pick a whole armload."

Hannah leaned back and wished she could enjoy the March sunshine. If only she had Lydia's positive outlook. She decided not to think about what awaited her and allowed her thoughts to wander to Lottie. Living at the factory, she'd be closer to her young friend, but Lottie wouldn't know she was there. Hannah's heart was heavy. She'd never believed Lottie would visit her, and now she was more certain than ever.

A cloud of green swept toward them from upriver. A whirring sound filled the air.

"What is it?" Marjorie asked, her voice laced with fear.

Hannah sat upright, staring at the approaching green and blue swirl. "It's birds! There are so many of them."

"Ah, them's just rosellas," one of the crew said. He stared at the mass of fluttering color. "Ye best get used to them."

Hannah was enthralled at the sight. The birds weren't very large. They had red heads with white faces and vibrant green and blue feathers, and she thought them delightful.

"They're grand," said Rosalyn.

"They're a nuisance." The guard pointed his musket at the colorful cloud, but he didn't fire.

The birds disappeared into the forest, and Hannah settled back against her bag. The woods were alive with all kinds of fowl, flitting back and forth among the trees. There were large, brightly colored squawking birds and small, trilling ones. The concoction of sound and sight was soothing. Hannah tried to imagine what it would be like to be free and to float upon the river any time she liked. She decided it would be incredibly pleasant. *When I'm free, I'll be sure to float the river again.* She

190

tried not to think about the number of years she still had left to serve. It was too dreadful.

They hadn't traveled far when the first farms appeared. Broad fields of wheat surrounded some; others had pastures speckled with grazing sheep. There were small properties as well, with homes and garden patches. Hannah wished that one day she could reside in such a fine place. She wondered if Lottie lived in one of the houses. Perhaps the barge had floated past her home.

⬤

The men with the poles pushed the barge toward a dock at the edge of a small hamlet. *This must be Parramatta*, Hannah thought. It seemed a nice settlement. Homes and businesses were huddled among rolling hillsides, open fields, and clusters of trees. On the uppermost hill there stood a building of significance.

"What is that place?" Rosalyn asked.

"Government House. And you'd best keep your distance. Government business goes on there. No need for whores."

Rosalyn eyed the building. "There's always a need for whores," she said with a smirk.

"Out with you," the guard ordered the women, keeping his musket ready in case of attempted escape.

Hannah joined the others on the dock. She wanted to stay on the barge. It had felt safe. Now she'd have to face the factory and her future.

⬤

Hannah stared at the two-story structure called the Female Factory, which measured approximately twenty by sixty feet. They were ordered inside to the cells. It was utter squalor, and

191

the stink of the privies assaulted her. The bedding consisted of filthy, bug-infested piles of wool. Hannah was nearly convinced the hold on board ship had been better.

There was no kitchen, only a single open hearth. Hannah guessed it was used for cooking and heat. She doubted it would be of much help during the winter months.

"These are your quarters," a guard said. "Upstairs is the factory. You'll be spending most of your time there."

Hannah held her bag against her stomach. It contained folded dresses and her blanket. She moved to her wool bed.

Lydia sat on one next to Hannah's. "Pretty fancy, eh?" she teased.

"No talking! Upstairs!"

The women followed the guard up a narrow flight of steps that led to the second floor. The factory was nothing more than an open loft with floorboards so warped it was difficult to walk. The room stank of sheep and filth and sweat. Women worked at long benches carding wool or weaving yarn into coarse material. Some made rope. Others sat at spindles.

"This'll be home to you now," a guard said with a smirk. "Get to work. The others will show you what to do."

Hannah and Lydia squeezed into spaces at the workbench. "I thank the Lord Lottie's not here," whispered Hannah.

"It's a blessing for sure."

Hannah glanced at the nearby hillsides. "At least there's countryside about."

"Too bad it's as much inside as out," Rosalyn snapped, sitting across from Hannah.

Marjorie stood alongside the bench, hugging her waist and watching the others. "I don't belong here," she murmured.

"None of us do," a tall, angular-looking woman replied. "Name's

Abigail. Sit down. Figure you can twist these into rope. Like this," she said and showed the women how to transform twine into sturdy ropes. "If you're here as long as me, you'll get good at it." She smiled. "It's better than carding wool. Can't abide the stink."

"How long ye been 'ere?" Lydia asked.

"Four years." Her jaw tightened.

Hannah suddenly felt sick. She couldn't imagine spending four years or more in this place.

"All you do is make rope?" asked Lydia.

"No. We share the work. Today I make rope, tomorrow I card wool. We do some sewing too." Her eyes moved over the newcomers and stopped at Hannah. "You'll likely not be here long. You're comely. You'll find a husband. The men come by and choose wives. The lucky ones get picked."

"I'll choose me own husband, thank ye," Lydia said.

"You'll see," said the woman. "Soon enough you'll be praying to be chosen and you'll be willing to go with anyone." She held up cracked and callused hands. "It's worse in the winter. You never get warm. A lot of us die." She squared her jaw. "Never been picked. Figure I'll finish out my days here."

Hannah couldn't imagine being forced to become someone's wife. "If you're chosen, must you go?"

"Depends on who's doing the choosing. Some of 'em won't take no for an answer."

Hannah felt flushed and thought for a moment that she might be sick. How had her life come to this?

⬥

The days stretched out, long and tedious. At night the cells were hot and stifling, the ticks relentless, and the irritation and stink of sheep dung in their beds pervasive. Hannah preferred working. In the loft, air flowed and helped cool hot skin. However, her thoughts often went to the approaching winter. She wondered how difficult conditions became in the winter months. Here there was little protection from the cold.

She spent most of her days sewing coarse clothing worn by prisoners. Since she was a good seamstress, she was allowed to work at the sewing table much of the time. Lydia preferred making ropes, and so did Rosalyn. Marjorie, who didn't like doing any kind of work, insisted she'd been raised too genteel to lower herself to such tasks. Lydia had little patience for the woman, nor did the other prisoners. Hannah tried to be tolerant.

She often thought of John, but the idea of never seeing him again hurt too much, so she'd force him from her mind, hoping that one day she'd truly forget him.

And what of Lottie? What was she doing, where was she living, was she happy? She prayed for her every day and longed to see the freckle-faced little girl. She'd look out at the surrounding countryside and wonder which house she lived in.

The men came on a Saturday—farmers, laborers, and even some who looked like gentlemen. Most were ill-mannered and common. Hannah, Lydia, and Marjorie hung back while Rosalyn walked right up to the men, moving provocatively. *What decent man would want a wife who behaves in such a disgraceful manner?* Hannah wondered.

"Rosalyn," Lydia whispered. Rosalyn either didn't hear or decided to ignore her. Lydia said her name louder. "Rosalyn."

She looked back and then sauntered toward her. "What is it?" She folded her arms over her chest. "I don't want to miss me chance."

"Yer chance for what?" Lydia rolled her eyes. "Be sensible. Working here is not as bad as becoming a slave to some foul-mouthed, foul-smelling bloke."

"She's right," Hannah said. "You shouldn't go."

Rosalyn lifted her chin. "I'm getting out of this place. Being a wife to any one of these gents is better than slaving 'ere." She strutted away, moving toward the men who openly ogled the women, especially Rosalyn.

"All of you, line up," a guard ordered. "Let the men have a look."

Humiliated and angry, Hannah joined the others. She kept her eyes straight ahead and prayed that none of them would want her.

"For those who are new here, it works like this—when a gent fancies you, he'll drop his scarf or handkerchief at your feet. If you pick up the scarf, you've accepted his offer."

There were a few minutes of quiet while the men considered the women. Finally one of them moved toward Rosalyn. And then another man. They hurried toward her, both dropping a handkerchief at her feet.

One of the fellows looked like a decent sort, but was rather unattractive with an overly large nose and close-set eyes. The other behaved boldly, was brawny and good-looking. Rosalyn sized them both up and then chose the handkerchief of the bold gent.

He raised a fist in triumph and lifted her into his arms. "I got me a wife," he said, carrying her away.

Hannah felt the sting of tears. What would become of

Rosalyn? *Lord, watch over her*, she prayed, fearing Rosalyn would end up paying dearly for her transgressions. Her mind turned toward her own lot, and Hannah pleaded with God, asking that no one come for her. She took a step backward, hoping she'd not be noticed.

A young man approached Lydia. She met his gaze. He looked boyish and carried himself with a swagger. He dropped his handkerchief at her feet, but she ignored it and instead stared at the man. Finally, he snatched it up off the floor and chose another.

Marjorie quaked. Her face looked pinched. Hannah feared she'd collapse. Although attractive, Marjorie was older than most of the women. No one chose her.

One of the last men walked toward Hannah. He was tall with a broad chest and a full beard and long hair. He tried to smile, but by the look of him Hannah guessed he was bad-tempered. He dropped his handkerchief at her feet. She didn't look at it.

He stood directly in front of her for a good while, then finally demanded, "Aren't ye gonna pick it up?"

"No." Hannah tried to appear indifferent.

"Pick it up, I say." Dark eyes bore into hers.

"I shan't."

Finally, he snatched it up. "I'll be back. After ye've been here awhile ye'll be beggin' me to take ye with me."

That will never happen.

The men left and the remaining women went to their beds. Some were distressed at not being chosen, others were grateful. Although the sun blazed and heat permeated the cells, Marjorie went to her bed and shivered.

Hannah sat beside her and rested a hand on her back. Lydia sat on the opposite side of the makeshift bed.

Through tears, Marjorie looked at Hannah. "How can this be happening to me? How could my brother-in-law have done this to me? I'll die here. I know it."

In spite of Marjorie's snobbishness and her complaining ways, Hannah felt sorry for her. "Hush, now. It will all turn out right in the end."

Marjorie pushed up on one arm. "It won't." She stared at the cell bars for a long while and then said, "I'd rather be dead than live like this."

Lydia grasped Marjorie's hand. "Come on, now. It's bad, I can't deny that, but we'll get out one day. It's been a year since we left London."

"One year gone and six left." Marjorie's voice sounded empty. "I can't bear it." She lay on her side and pulled her legs up against her chest. She stayed like that, eyes closed and silent.

Hannah thought about what Marjorie had said. She was having trouble facing six years and Hannah had another thirteen to serve. *How shall I bear it?* she wondered, momentarily allowing herself to look at the painful, empty years stretching out before her.

She and Lydia moved across to the other side of the large cell. They sat on the floor, their backs pressed against the wall. "This place is despicable," Lydia said. "She has a right to be distressed."

Hannah watched the fragile woman. "I'm worried about her."

"As ye should be. Ye ought to be worried 'bout the whole lot of us."

That night was dreadfully hot. Doors and windows were left open to let in more air, but mostly all it did was allow in flying pests. Hannah tried unsuccessfully to find a comfortable position. She considered the floor; it would be cooler, but it was too filthy to even contemplate. She heard someone get up and go outside. When they didn't return, she thought it strange, but fatigue finally dragged her into sleep and its blessed oblivion.

⚬

The following morning, Hannah awoke, still sweating. "I thought March was supposed to bring cooler weather," she complained.

"One never knows," Abigail said.

A shriek came from outside. A woman ran into the building, hands pressed against her face. "She's dead! She's dead!"

"Who's dead?" Hannah asked.

"That friend of yours. She's out there. Hangin' from a tree."

Hannah and Lydia sprinted outside. Marjorie's body hung from a tree limb several paces from the building. "Oh, Marjorie. No . . ." Hannah pressed her hands to her mouth.

"Oh luv. Why'd ye do it?" Lydia moved toward the dead woman and grabbed hold of her body. "Someone cut her down!"

A guard ambled toward the tree. "Fool woman," he muttered as he sawed through the rope and then lowered her to the ground.

Lydia gently brushed the hair off Marjorie's face. "I'm sorry. So sorry."

Hannah stared at Marjorie, her anger growing. "This didn't have to happen." Her vision blurred by tears, she stared at the dead woman. "She shouldn't have been transported."

"Hannah, ye all right?" Lydia asked. She stood and grasped Hannah's arm.

"No. I'm not all right!" She wrenched her arm away. "She

198

didn't have to die." Hannah whirled around and faced the guards. "This is your fault, you and your kind. You did this!" Hands in fists, she stormed at them. "You humiliate and torture and use us until there's nothing left! You've no right to treat us like dogs!"

"Shut your mouth!" one of the guards hollered. He brandished a sword.

Lydia grabbed Hannah. "She's distraught. Pay her no mind." She held Hannah close to her and whispered, "Stop now. Or you'll be dead too." Out loud, she said, "Come on, now. Ye'll be fine. Work will help." She steered Hannah inside.

Hannah sat on her bed of sheep's wool. "I can't do this. Not anymore."

"Ye can and ye will. I'll not listen to that kind of talk."

"But—"

"It's sniveling and pathetic. And what ye did out there was foolish. Ye want to give those monsters cause to kill ye?"

Hannah stared at Lydia. "There's no way we can prevail."

"Yes, there is. We survive. There's honor in it."

"I have no honor."

Lydia grasped Hannah's upper arms. "Ye have to fight. Trust in the Almighty. He's greater than them."

She met Lydia's gaze. "But he doesn't care about me. He's given up on me."

"That's foolish talk." Lydia straightened. "Yer only defeated if ye believe ye are. Fight, Hannah. If not, then ye will die."

18

Hannah twisted and then pulled the twine. "Ouch," she gasped as it cut into her skin. She grasped her finger and waited until the sting eased. Turning her palms up, she studied raw, blistered skin. *They'll never heal.*

Before returning to her work, she glanced at the other women at the table. Every one of them looked haggard. Some were incredibly thin. Days of sitting at this table, lack of proper nourishment and sleep, bouts of sickness, loss of hope—all of these worked together to sap a person's spirit and strength.

Hannah's back ached from long hours at the bench. Straightening her spine, she rubbed tired muscles. Today, despair threatened to overwhelm her. A sharp wind cut through the loft, and she was cold. Gazing out at the countryside, she longed to look at someplace beyond here. She couldn't see far, only the nearby hillsides, which were mostly bare and dotted with tree stumps and an occasional farmhouse. It didn't look as lovely as when she'd first arrived.

Lydia elbowed her in the side. "The guard's coming," she whispered. "Ye don't want to be caught idle. Especially after what ye said to him, he'll be looking for a reason to punish ye."

Hannah focused on her work.

The guard's boots echoed on the wooden floor. He walked toward the back of the loft in Hannah's direction, then stopped beside her and stood silently for a long moment.

She kept at her work without looking up.

The guard remained silent, then in a booming voice, he said, "Hannah Talbot."

She jumped and then set her work down and looked at the man. *Lord, I pray for your protection.* The guard glared back at her. *If it's the lash, then let it be. They'll not destroy me.*

"Sir," she said and stood.

"Someone here to see you." He gestured toward the stairs. "See to it."

Hannah's first thought was of Lottie. Had she come? *Of course not. I'd not be called away from work to see a little girl.* She hurried down the rotting stairs, wondering if this were all just a ploy so the guard could get her alone. *There's no reason for that. He can do whatever he likes anyway.*

She stepped outside. A man she'd not seen before stood beside a handsome chestnut stallion. He was tall with graying hair and looked a bit imposing but not threatening.

Hannah moved toward him. "Sir, I was told you wished to speak to me?"

The man smiled. "Yes. That is, if you're Hannah Talbot."

"That I am."

"I'm William Atherton. I had a time finding you. Heard you were at Port Jackson, but once I got there I was told you'd been transferred here."

"I've been here more than two months now." His name sounded familiar. And then Hannah remembered. It was a Mrs. Atherton who had visited at the gaol in Port Jackson.

"Yes. Well, I'm in need of a new housemaid, and I was told you'd make a fine one. Is that true?"

Hannah's pulse picked up. "Yes, sir. It is." Her mind swam with thoughts. Was Mrs. Atherton his wife and had she been the one who'd spoken to him about her?

"You're small and a bit frail-looking."

"I've always been small, but never frail. I'm strong. And when I've had enough to eat, I'm actually quite robust."

His smile was caught up in his gray-blue eyes. "I can assure you those who work for me are properly fed."

The guard took a step closer to Hannah and Mr. Atherton. "Sir, she's a troublesome one. Don't figure you'd want the likes of her working for you. Can't be trusted."

"Is that true?" Mr. Atherton asked Hannah.

"No, sir. I'm quite reliable and I'll give you no trouble."

"I consider myself a good judge of character." He studied Hannah a moment longer. "I think you'll do nicely." He turned to the guard. "Have her papers drawn up. She'll be working for me now." He looked back at Hannah. "That is, of course, if she'd like to. I have a farm near here and I own a logging company. The house is large but not tremendously so."

Mr. Atherton seemed a good sort. Could she trust him? *He's my escape from here.* She eyed him a moment longer. Was he being honest about what he wanted from her? Glancing at the guard, she knew it mattered little. She couldn't stay. He would find a way to punish her for her outburst the day Marjorie died. "I'd be pleased to go with you, sir."

The guard glowered. "I'll be back with the papers." He stomped off.

"I'll send someone 'round to fetch you," Mr. Atherton said.

"And I'll have a word with that guard before I go." He tipped his hat. "Good day."

Hannah sat in the back of a wagon, hands clasped in her lap. Traveling through the countryside was exhilarating. She could hardly believe she was free of the factory except she hated saying farewell to Lydia. They'd both cried, but Lydia was quick to hearten her. They were the best kind of friends. Finally with well wishes and congratulations Lydia waved good-bye. Hannah knew it wasn't the end of their friendship. They'd see each other again.

Her thoughts turned to the Athertons. Did they have children? Mr. Atherton hadn't mentioned any. Apprehension threatened her good mood, but she pushed it aside and concentrated on the beauty of her surroundings.

The wagon rolled over a single dirt lane filled with potholes and mud. It tipped, dropped, and bucked. But the rough ride couldn't distract Hannah from the pleasure she felt as they moved through forests of eucalypts, cedars, and acacias. Occasionally she'd spot the Parramatta River, which flowed lazily from the west. She imagined picnicking along its shores.

I'm not free, she reminded herself. *I'm still a convict. Certainly there'll be no opportunities for picnicking.*

The wagon slowed and turned onto a long drive. Hannah could see a house nestled among trees. It had two stories and was somewhat sprawling, but not intimidating. Several chimneys jutted up from the roof, reassuring Hannah that the winter chill was not allowed to settle too severely indoors.

There were a number of outbuildings. Some looked like cottages. She guessed the others to be shops or storage sheds. Not far from the house stood a large barn with a corral housing a mare and her foal.

Hannah was pleased to see rows of fruit trees and a vegetable garden on the north side of the home. An assortment of farm animals ranged about—pigs, cows, sheep, and fowl.

The driver steered the wagon to the back of the house where he stopped. He jumped out and opened the back. Hannah climbed down and grabbed her bag.

"Mrs. Atherton will be waiting for you." Without another word, the driver climbed back onto the front seat, slapped the reins across the horses' backsides, and headed down the drive away from the house.

Hannah stared at the back entrance of the home. She wasn't afraid, but she was nervous. She didn't want to do anything that would upset Mrs. Atherton. At her discretion her employer could send her back to the factory. *I'm capable and hardworking,* she told herself. *I'll just do my best.*

Taking a deep breath, she walked up the steps and opened a door, which led to an enclosed porch. Uncertain just what to do, she moved into a kitchen that smelled of freshly baked bread. She breathed deeply. Her mouth watered and she realized she was hungry.

A stout, no-nonsense-type woman appeared. "Are you the new maid?" she asked, wiping her hands on an apron.

"Yes. The driver told me to come in. And so I have."

"Wait here. I'll let Mrs. Atherton know you've arrived." The woman disappeared and a few moments later returned. "You're to meet with her in the study." Her eyes lingered on Hannah. "Best leave the bag here."

Hannah was keenly aware of her unkempt appearance. She

set down the bag and tried to smooth her soiled dress. "I would have bathed if I could have and combed my hair some. I'm straight from the factory."

"Yes, of course." The woman walked toward the interior of the house.

Hannah followed. While hurrying after her, Hannah nervously brushed at her skirt; the grime clung tenaciously.

The woman opened a door and stepped inside.

Hannah hung back.

"Come in. Mrs. Atherton can't speak to you out in the hallway." Her voice was sharp.

Hannah swallowed hard and walked into a large study. The walls were lined with crowded bookshelves. The furniture was stout and dark, and a grand fireplace took up a large portion of the opposite wall. Mrs. Atherton sat behind a substantial-sized desk. She *was* the woman who had visited the gaol in Port Jackson.

Mrs. Atherton stood. "Hannah. How nice to see you again."

"I wondered if it was you," Hannah said, her spirits lifting.

"And I wasn't certain you were the young woman from Port Jackson. I thought possibly." She smiled. "I'm sure you'll be glad to know that Lottie is doing quite nicely at the Parnells."

"I'm pleased to hear that. I think of her often." Hannah wondered how far away the Parnells lived. Would it be possible for her to see Lottie? "They seemed like fine people," she said.

"They are, indeed." Mrs. Atherton sat. "As you've been told, I'm in need of a housemaid. And you've come highly recommended."

If it wasn't Mrs. Atherton who recommended me, then who was it? Hannah wondered, then decided all that mattered was that she was here. "It will be a pleasure to work for you, Mrs. Atherton."

205

"We'll get you settled." She scrutinized Hannah. "Of course you'll need more appropriate attire. And a bath will do nicely, I should think. I'll have a gown brought over."

"I am a sight," Hannah said, looking down at herself. "I apologize, but we weren't allowed to bathe but twice a year."

"Here you'll bathe every week. And you'll have a cottage of your own."

A cottage of my own? Hannah could barely imagine such a luxury.

"The housemaid is often called out at unexpected times," Mrs. Atherton continued. "It's a position with a good deal of responsibility. You'll be in charge of overseeing the proper upkeep of the entire house, including cleaning and laundry. And if we have guests, it will be your task to see they are made comfortable and that all their needs are seen to." She settled more deeply into her chair. "Do you think you can do that?"

"Of course. It will be a privilege."

Mrs. Atherton smiled. "Well, I think it best that you get yourself settled, then. You'll begin tomorrow."

Hannah fit in nicely at the Atherton estate. The work was not difficult, and once her experience as a seamstress was discovered, she took on responsibilities in that area as well. It was pure delight to bathe regularly and to wear clean clothing. When she burned her prison rags, it felt like a celebration.

The house servants shared most of their meals, although Hannah was allowed to eat in her cottage when she chose to. She enjoyed gathering around the kitchen table with the others who worked in the house. She liked them all quite well, even the woman she'd met her first day. Elvine could be a bit brusque, but she was fair-minded and, as it turned out, good company. Gwen, the scullery maid, was young and pleasant to be around. Like Hannah, she'd come from the factory. Hannah enjoyed her lively antics and youthful outlook. The houseman, Dalton Keen, could be a bit intimidating. He was tall and quiet. But all in all a pleasant fellow.

Hannah's first meal there was more than she could have hoped for. When a thick mutton stew with fresh bread was set on the table, she thought that perhaps God hadn't forgotten her after all. She spooned up a bite of the stew enjoying the mix of flavors—vegetables with lots of meat. "I had no notion that stew could taste so delicious."

Elvine tried not to smile. "I pride myself on my cooking. It's not always easy here at the end of the world. I sometimes have to make do with what's handy."

Hannah took a bite of bread. It was fresh and soft. "I doubt I've ever tasted bread this good." She took another bite.

"I dare say, there's lots of bread just like it round about. I imagine your exuberance comes from having so little during your captivity." She eyed Hannah. "You could use a bit more meat on your bones."

"I'm quite willing to do all that is required to accomplish that." Hannah smiled and then settled down to her meal, eating every bite. When she left the table she was overly full. That night for the first time in many months, she went to bed without feeling hungry. She snuggled down on a cushioned bed beneath plentiful blankets and slept soundly. When she awoke the next morning, she forgot for a moment where she was. When she remembered how her life had changed, she was eager for the day.

This was wash day, and Hannah helped Gwen with the laundry. There was a pile the size of a small mountain. They were responsible for washing bedding, towels, and all the clothing for those who lived and worked on the premises.

"It's a terrible lot," Gwen said. "Can't imagine how much there would be if the Athertons had children."

"They don't have any?"

"Not a one."

"Do you know why?"

"No. No one ever said. But I'm certain Mrs. Atherton would have made a fine mother."

"I agree. She's very kindhearted and she's helped orphans at the gaol find homes. In fact, a little girl I knew . . ." Hannah stopped, for the thought of Lottie raised a lump in her throat. Swallowing away the hurt, she continued. "Mrs. Atherton helped her find a home." She dropped a sheet into a basket. "I wonder why she never adopted any herself."

"Can't say."

Hannah was still puzzling over that question when she headed outside with a basket of clothes. She set the basket on the ground and then straightened, breathing in the country air. It was comfortably warm. A breeze caught at the eucalypt trees, stirring up their sharp fragrance.

Hannah moved along the clothesline, taking pins from her pocket and securing items. While hanging one of Elvine's aprons, she heard someone walking through the dry grass behind her.

"Hannah?"

She looked over her shoulder and then turned to stare at the man approaching. Was it John? He looked quite different—well dressed, clean shaven, and his dark hair cut and pulled back away from his face. It was him. She gasped. "John?" Quickly

208

pinning the apron, she turned to face him. "It can't be you. I don't believe my eyes."

He smiled broadly and moved toward her. "It's me all right." He reached for Hannah, lifted her, and held her in his arms. "I thought it was you, but I wasn't sure." He set her back on her feet.

Hannah smoothed her skirt and her hair, uncertain just what to do. It was inappropriate for him to embrace her in such a fashion.

"I'm sorry for my enthusiasm." He gazed at her, adoration lighting his hazel eyes. "I just couldn't believe it was you. I told Mr. Atherton about you, but he never said that you'd been put to work here."

"I wondered who'd told him about me. Mrs. Atherton said I'd come highly recommended." She barely managed to keep her smile modest. "Thank you kindly for rescuing me from the factory."

"That's where you ended up, then? I'm sorry. Heard it's a dreadful place."

"That it is. Lydia's still there. I've been hoping to find a way to rescue her. It really is horrible."

"Perhaps there'll be need for more help here."

"Perhaps." Hannah studied John's angular face. "I've never seen you cleaned up."

"Better?"

"Yes. Much."

"And I've never seen you looking quite so beautiful." He couldn't conceal his admiration.

Hannah felt her face redden. "How is it that you came to work here?"

"Mr. Atherton heard about my tooling skills. He needed a

man and hired me off a road crew. I'm overseeing the toolmaking as well as taking care of some other business responsibilities."

"You've done well then since I last saw you." She folded her arms over her chest. "I'm happy for you."

"God has been good to me. Life's not so bad after all, eh?"

"Not so bad," she said, though she hadn't forgotten how ugly and cruel it could be. And might be again. If she made a mistake or if the Athertons discovered the secret of how despicable she really was, she could end up back at the factory. "I best get to my work. It's wash day and the pile of clothes is tremendous."

"Right. Of course." John remained where he was. "So I'll see you about, then?"

"I should think so." Remembering that John didn't know how wicked she could be, she felt an inexplicable malaise.

He lingered. "Would you consider taking a walk with me tonight after dinner?"

"Is that allowed?"

"We're permitted to move about freely. Mr. Atherton has no fear that we'll run off. Where would we go, after all? And he's good to us. A man would be a fool to leave."

"All right. I'll walk with you."

"After dinner, then." John moved away, then stopped and waved.

Hannah waved back. The old fears and self-loathing threatened to strangle her joy. She refused to allow it. This was a moment to be savored.

19

Pulling a shawl around her shoulders, Hannah hurried to the main house. She stepped carefully to avoid puddles from the previous night's rain. Guests were expected four days hence, and a long list of duties awaited her; the flatware and silver needed polishing and Mrs. Atherton's gown still waited for final touches. There were also the daily chores that must be completed, including preparation of the guest rooms.

When she stepped onto the back porch, she stumbled into Elvine who was leaning over a basket of clothing. "Forgive me," Hannah said. "I'm in a rush."

"No harm done." She folded a dress and laid it in the basket.

Gwen set an empty basket on a table. "Why in such a hurry?"

"I've a great deal to do before the guests arrive."

"We've all a lot to do." Gwen smiled. "It's always this way when the Athertons host an event."

Elvine brushed back graying hair and studied a shelf piled with clothing. "I've got pies and cakes to bake. Plus I need to sort through these dresses. There are more than usual this time 'round—for the ladies."

"More than usual? For what?"

"Mrs. Atherton is going to the Female Factory today. She drops in from time to time, seeing to the needs of the prisoners."

"Yes, of course. I first met her at the gaol in Port Jackson."

Elvine glanced outside at the dark sky. "I'm glad she's going no farther than the factory today. The weather's looking dreadful."

"Do you think she needs help?"

"Certainly." She eyed Hannah. "You thinking of going, eh?"

"Possibly."

"And what about your duties, then?"

"I'll work later tonight and start earlier tomorrow." Hannah needed to go. If Lydia was still there, this was an opportunity to see her.

"I don't think it wise for anyone to go out there. Heard they've an outbreak of sweating sickness."

"Disease is part of a convict's life. It'd be difficult to find a time when there wasn't an outbreak of some sort."

"I'll never set foot in that place again," Gwen said. "It was a horrible time I had there. And I don't need to be reminded of them days."

"I understand, but I've a friend still there," Hannah said, moving toward the kitchen. "I'll speak to Mrs. Atherton and see if I can be of assistance. Do you know where she is?"

"In the study. I believe she's looking for books to take with her."

Hannah hurried to the study where she found Mrs. Atherton standing on a chair and reaching for a book on a top shelf. It seemed a precarious position for one of her age and plump figure. "Do be careful." She moved toward her mistress.

"I've got it." Mrs. Atherton grasped a book and held it against

212

her chest. With one hand on the back of the chair, she gingerly climbed down. Blowing on the cover, she said, "Dusty on the top shelves."

"Sorry, mum. I'll make sure it's taken care of."

"I'm sure you will." She smiled. "You look in good humor this morning. Did you sleep well?"

"I did, indeed."

"Good." She added the book to an already full crate and then stooped to lift the box.

"I'll carry it," Hannah offered.

"Thank you, dear. I'm not quite as robust as I once was." She stepped back as Hannah hefted the box. "Can you take it to the back porch? I'll have Mr. Keen load it into the carriage."

The box pressed against her abdomen, Hannah headed for the porch. Mrs. Atherton followed.

"Elvine said you're going to the Female Factory today."

"I am."

"Could you use some assistance? I'd be honored to accompany you. I know some of the ladies and could be of service to you there."

"I suppose that's true."

Hannah stepped into the kitchen. "It's charitable of you to assist the ladies." She pushed against the door leading to the porch and set the box on a table. "I remember when you came to Port Jackson. I was much encouraged by your visit. . . ." Her voice caught. "Knowing that someone cared meant a lot."

"I feel badly for the women and especially the children. So many were transported without just cause. I do very little for them, but I pray my presence brings a bit of pleasure into their dismal lives."

She peered out the porch door. "It would be best to take the

213

carriage. It's miserable weather. I do hope the rain holds off." Mrs. Atherton glanced back at Hannah. "Having your company will be an added blessing today."

Hannah's stomach churned. She tried to maintain a calm exterior, but the closer they came to the factory, the more distressed she felt. Like Gwen had said, it held memories best forgotten.

Mrs. Atherton had been quiet, mostly watching the countryside pass by the window. "It seems the weather is improving. Dalton is a skilled driver. I trust him no matter what the weather."

Hannah glanced outside. Sunshine peeked through heavy clouds. "It may turn out to be a fine day after all."

Mrs. Atherton settled a sympathetic gaze on Hannah. "I've often wondered what it is that troubles you, dear."

"Troubles me?" Hannah felt a knot of fear in her stomach. "Nothing's troubling me. I'm quite content."

Mrs. Atherton's eyes seemed even more gentle. "I've been thinking about Lottie and how much she must have meant to you." She rested a hand on an open window. "I do hope my finding a home for her wasn't too painful for you."

"No. Of course not. Certainly, I've missed her, but I'm thankful she has a good home and a family."

"Good, I was just wondering. You seem to carry a burden, and I wondered if that might be it."

"We all have our burdens," Hannah said, hoping her tone didn't give away her alarm. She didn't want Mrs. Atherton to know about her past. She changed the subject and asked, "I've wondered why you never adopted. You've helped others."

Her mistress didn't answer right away, and Hannah feared she'd crossed the line of propriety.

Then Mrs. Atherton smiled. "I don't believe anyone has posed that question to me before."

"I apologize. I shouldn't have asked. Forgive me."

"No." Mrs. Atherton sighed. "I don't mind, truly." Her eyes took on a faraway look. "When William and I first married, we planned on a family. We believed it would simply happen. But the years passed and there were no babies. I kept believing God would bless us with children of our own, but it didn't happen.

"In his younger years William was quite an adventurer." Her eyes sparkled at the memory. "He'd accomplished a great deal in England, but when he heard about this place with so many opportunities, he decided we should move here." She smiled. "That's my William." She let out a soft breath. "So we came. It was a wild place in those days."

Her eyes turned sad. "We were no longer young and we were still childless. I must admit that I wallowed in my sorrow. By the time I saw beyond my own need, it was too late. I was too far advanced in years. Taking care of a child requires more stamina than I have." She pressed her fingertips to her lips and then continued. "I always watch for the little ones, and if I know of a good home, I see to it that they have a chance at being part of a family."

Hannah's heart ached at Mrs. Atherton's sorrow. "I'm so sorry, mum."

"No. No. Don't be. God has blessed me in ways I'd never counted on. I couldn't do what I do if I'd children of my own to look after." Lifting her eyebrows slightly, she added, "Sometimes I feel like a mother to the suffering women in the gaols and a grandmother to their little ones."

As the carriage approached the Female Factory, Hannah tensed and her stomach ached. At the Athertons, her old wretched life seemed like someone else's. Now, it came rushing back—real and ghastly.

The carriage stopped. Dalton opened the door and assisted Mrs. Atherton as she stepped out. She looked back. "Hannah, dear, can you bring the dresses?"

Hannah remained tucked safely inside the carriage. She stared at the building, picturing the pitiful conditions inside. Maybe it had been a mistake to come. Then she remembered Lydia.

She grabbed the bag of clothing and moved to the door. When she stepped out, she immediately came face-to-face with a familiar and malicious guard. Wearing a scowl, he stared at her.

Hannah held his gaze. She stood erect and defiant. *He'll not intimidate me.*

Mrs. Atherton glanced at the driver. "Pierce, could you please carry in the box of books?"

"Glad to, mum." He lifted the box off the floor of the carriage.

Stepping around a large puddle, Mrs. Atherton smiled pleasantly as she approached the guard. "Good day, young man. I'm here to—"

"Right, I know, to offer these poor women a bit of solace." His tone was sarcastic.

"Indeed." Mrs. Atherton remained unruffled. "And I might add the Governor has been quite pleased to hear of my visits. I'm certain he'd also be interested to know how I've been received."

A puzzled expression touched the guard's face, and then grudgingly his demeanor softened. "Go on in." He stood aside.

"Thank you." Mrs. Atherton moved indoors and then up the stairs. She glanced back at Hannah. "Come along, dear."

Hannah didn't try to conceal her satisfied smile as she followed her mistress. Her satisfaction, however, quickly faded as she moved through the downstairs quarters. They were just as awful as she remembered, only now they were also damp and cold. The hearth contained no fire, and the stink was worse than before.

Upstairs in the loft, women sat as they always did on the benches, twisting rope twine and carding wool. There were new faces, including children she'd not seen before. She thought of Lottie and thanked the Lord that she'd been adopted. The Parnells were good people and fine parents. Since arriving at the Athertons, she'd hoped to see Lottie in church, but heard that the Parnells had been on holiday. *Maybe soon we'll become reacquainted.*

Without warning, Hannah's mind carried her to her dead child. It would have been happy and well cared for at the Athertons. *If she'd survived, we could have shared a life.* She tried to focus on the women.

Abigail, the first woman Hannah had met at the factory, was still there. She looked thinner. She stood. "Mrs. Atherton. Grand t' see ye."

"Hello, Abigail. I have gifts for the ladies." Mrs. Atherton sat on a bench.

"Abigail," Hannah said. "Do you remember me?"

"Hannah?" Abigail smiled. "Ye don't look the same."

Hannah glanced down at her simple but fine-quality frock. "The Athertons have been good to me. Are you well?"

217

"Good as a soul can be in a place like this." She managed to smile, her big teeth showing their lack of care. "Yer lookin' real fine. Like a lady."

"Thank you."

"Hannah? Hannah!" a familiar voice cried.

"Lydia," Hannah said, turning to see her friend running to her.

"I was out back. Heard someone, but never expected ye." She threw her arms about Hannah and hugged her tightly. "Ye've been on me mind every day since ye left. Wondering how ye are." She stepped back. "And look at ye. Yer a grand lady now."

"Just a housemaid," Hannah said with a laugh. It was so good to see her friend. She was a bit thinner and pale, but she was the same Lydia—her red hair falling down around her shoulders and her green eyes steady.

Lydia hugged her again then stepped back. "Oh dear, I'm going to get ye dirty." Staring at Hannah, she smiled broadly. "It's truly grand to see ye."

"I've thought about you every day." Hannah stepped aside and glanced at Mrs. Atherton. "This is my employer, Mrs. Atherton. Mrs. Atherton, this is my good friend Lydia."

Lydia nodded slightly. "I remember meeting ye at Port Jackson. Ye come by with some pretty dresses and sweet treats."

"Oh yes. It's been some time ago. As soon as the weather improves, I'll be on my way to Port Jackson again." With a smile, she hoisted a basket. "I've brought cakes."

The women crowded around the visitors, and Mrs. Atherton distributed the sweets. "I've also brought some gowns for you." She turned to Hannah. "Could you and your friend Lydia match up the ladies with the right dresses?"

"Absolutely." Hannah hefted the bag of gowns.

"I've books as well," Mrs. Atherton said. "I'll leave them here and you can share them."

The women chatted excitedly while they sorted through the dresses and tried them on. There were exclamations of delight and even some prancing as they showed off their new gowns.

Mrs. Atherton walked among the women, asking questions about their health and their troubles. Some needed doctoring and she did what she could for them.

One woman had a terribly infected foot. There was little to be done, but Mrs. Atherton cleaned it and applied liniment and a bandage. "Make sure to change that every day and wash it."

"We're only allowed to bathe twice a year, mum."

Mrs. Atherton looked at the man standing guard. She chewed her lip as she studied him. "I'll ask if you can wash every day until it heals."

"Thank ye, mum. Don't know what I'd do without ye."

Mrs. Atherton rested a hand on the woman's arm. "I can do little. Lean on Jesus, dear. Find strength in him."

"Yes, mum," the woman said, sounding unconvinced.

Lydia walked toward Hannah. She hadn't put on her dress.

"Why aren't you wearing your new gown?"

"Figure I'll wait until I bathe. Don't want to ruin it."

Suddenly Hannah was angry. It wasn't right that someone like Lydia lived such a cruel existence. She studied her friend. She looked gaunt and weary. *Quiet yourself. Being angry won't help.* She took a steadying breath and asked, "Have you been well?"

"I'm all right. I had the fever, but I'm better now." Lydia sat on the bench beside Hannah. "Tell me 'bout life at the estate. Is it grand?"

"It's good. The Athertons are kind and generous. John works there too."

"John? Really?"

Hannah nodded. "He's even more handsome cleaned up. And he's a fine man."

Lydia grinned. "Has he asked ye to marry him yet?"

"No. You know that can never be. If he knew . . ."

"It won't matter to him, not if he loves ye."

"I can't tell him. And I won't deceive him." Hannah changed the subject. "There seems to be several new women. Any of the others come back?"

"There's lots of new ladies. They come and go. The gents still show up lookin' for wives." She glanced at her dirty hands. "That man who took Rosalyn . . . he was back last week. Said he needed a new wife."

"What happened to Rosalyn?"

"I guess she went with another man." Lydia's eyes turned hard. "So he killed her. He was braggin' 'bout how he done it. Said he wanted the rest of us to know what we'd get if we dared look at another man."

"Poor Rosalyn." Hannah had known she'd end up badly. The blood thundered through her head. Things like this shouldn't happen.

She couldn't talk about it. She took Lydia's hand. "I miss you. I think about you and pray you'll find a better life."

Lydia smiled. "Thank ye."

"Are you really all right?"

Lydia averted her eyes, then looked at Hannah. "I need yer prayers. I'm not so strong anymore. It's gettin' harder to believe there'll be something better. Months go by and I'm still 'ere, not knowing if I'll ever get home. I think of me mum and wonder if she's all right. I pray for her."

In all the months at sea and the days in the gaol at Port

Jackson, Hannah had never heard Lydia so disheartened. "I wish there was something I could do." She pressed Lydia's hands between hers. "I will pray."

Lydia smiled softly. "This world comes with peril and hardships. The Lord says we'll know tribulation. Figure there's no reason I be spared." She smiled.

Hannah shook her head. "It's wrong that you're here."

"I hang on to my Savior." She closed her eyes and took a deep breath and then said, "Even if his will is that I die, then I say yes, make it so."

Hannah remembered Corliss from the ship and how she'd been ready for heaven, but this was different. This was Lydia. She looked her friend straight in the eye. "You can't give up. You mustn't. You've many years left to you. I know it." She gripped Lydia's shoulders. "Don't surrender. Remember when you told me you wouldn't die on that ship. If you let go now, those blokes from the ship, the soldiers at Port Jackson, and the guards here will win."

"I know, but I'm tired." Lydia stared at the floor, then looked at Hannah through tears. "Sometimes it's hard to fight."

The guard stepped into the workroom. "All right, back to work with you."

His eyes went to Hannah. She could feel his loathing. He was the type who took pleasure in meting out pain. Why did God give him authority over these women? They didn't deserve it. Especially Lydia. *God, be merciful. Deliver her from this place. I beg you.*

"I hope to see ye again," Lydia said.

"You will. I'll return. I promise." Hannah rested her hands on her friend's shoulders. "Don't give up."

Lydia nodded.

Hannah hugged her.

"On your way," the guard shouted.

<hr />

As the coach bounced over the rough road, Hannah's mind remained at the factory. Even Mrs. Atherton was quiet and thoughtful.

Finally she asked, "Are you all right, Hannah? You've said almost nothing since we left."

"I guess I don't have anything to say."

Mrs. Atherton reached across and rested a hand on Hannah's. "It's never easy to watch the suffering of others. But we must trust in the Lord. He has a way of working these things out."

Hannah looked at Mrs. Atherton's hands. Her touch was gentle and kind, yet Hannah dare not speak her mind.

"What is it, dear? Please, tell me."

Hannah looked up at Mrs. Atherton. "I used to believe that, but I don't anymore."

"You don't believe in God?"

"I believe in him, but I don't see him as just. What I see in this world is the strong beating down the weak." *And God as a liar*, she thought, knowing to speak of such a thing would be blasphemous. "My mum used to read the Scriptures to me. And she told me God is loving and kind, and that he watches over his children. But he doesn't. Instead, he stands back and watches while they suffer and die."

"Indeed, it does appear that way at times, but he isn't the one who brings calamity. He created perfection for us. It was mankind who rejected his gift. We yearned for our own desires and did exactly what God told us not to do. Yet he still loves us, so much so that he sent his Son to redeem us."

Mrs. Atherton settled back more comfortably in her seat. "It is evil in this world that kills and destroys. Not God. He offers us his presence and his peace. Even when we suffer we can trust in him. He sees it all and promises to reward those who endure."

Hannah didn't know how to respond. She'd heard similar words from her mother. After all that had happened to her and to those she loved, how could she believe in a benevolent God? What had he given her other than sorrow and heartache? She could hear Lydia's reproof. "Ye've been given so much. Be thankful." *And she's right*, Hannah thought. *When I look at how Lydia lives, I am truly blessed.*

"I've been thinking," Mrs. Atherton said, cutting into Hannah's thoughts. "I need quite a bit of sewing done. Most of the gowns that have been donated for the women are gone. I'll need more. You're a fine seamstress. Perhaps you could make some for me?"

"I'd like that."

"I'm also considering making some alterations in the house. I'll need new draperies. Would you mind taking care of that for me as well?"

"Not at all, but what of my other duties?"

"You'll need help, of course. Another housemaid could see to some of your present duties." She folded her hands neatly in her lap. "Do you know anyone who would be right for the position?" Her eyes gleamed with mischief.

Joy crept into the dark places inside Hannah. "What about Lydia?"

"The young woman you were speaking with today?"

"Yes. She's a fine person. I've never seen anyone work as hard as she. And she's absolutely honorable."

Mrs. Atherton smiled. "You're quite sure of this woman?"

"I am."

"Well then, I shall have her transferred."

Hannah brought her hands together. "You mean it?"

"Of course I do." Mrs. Atherton smiled.

"Thank you, mum. You can't imagine what this means to me and to Lydia."

"I'm pleased to do it." She glanced out the window. "Now then, we have someone to visit before we go home."

The carriage turned onto an unfamiliar drive and stopped in front of a modest home. Chickens roamed about a small garden, pecking at the ground, and a cow stood in a corral chewing hay.

A woman stepped onto the front porch. She looked familiar.

"Mrs. Parnell!" Hannah exclaimed. A little girl wearing a green dress skipped onto the porch, her red ringlets bouncing. "Lottie?" Hannah could barely wait to get out of the carriage. Her eyes brimming with tears, she looked at Mrs. Atherton. "Thank you," was all she could manage to say.

Mrs. Atherton patted her arm and with the driver's assistance stepped out of the carriage. Hannah followed.

Mrs. Parnell approached them. "What a pleasant surprise." She held out a hand to Mrs. Atherton.

Wearing a smile, Mrs. Atherton grasped her hand. "I hope it's not an imposition. I made the decision to stop on impulse." She turned to Hannah. "I've brought a guest."

"Mum!" Lottie cried and ran to Hannah. Throwing her arms about Hannah's waist she said, "I can't believe it's you." She squeezed Hannah tightly and then stepped back. "Ye look so fine."

Hannah felt as if her heart would burst with joy. She knelt in front of Lottie and, holding the little girl's face in her hands, said, "You look wonderful too. I had no notion just how beautiful you are." She hugged the little girl.

Mrs. Atherton turned to Hannah. "I thought that if it's all right with Mrs. Parnell, perhaps you and Lottie could have a visit while we chat."

"That's a lovely idea." Mrs. Parnell turned to Lottie. "Would you like that?"

"Yes, mum."

"Well, then I'll make us all some sandwiches. You and Hannah can have a picnic."

Hannah and Lottie settled in a grassy spot beneath a tree. Lottie played hostess and offered Hannah half a chicken sandwich. "They're very good. Me mum made them."

Hearing Lottie refer to Mrs. Parnell as Mum reassured Hannah that she'd done the right thing by sending her to live with the Parnells. She accepted the sandwich. "It looks good." Taking a bite, she said, "You seem happy, luv."

"I am. It's grand here. My new mum and dad are splendid people." Her eyes lit on a nearby corral where a small brown pony stood munching hay. "I've a pony. His name is Champion." She grinned.

"How wonderful. He looks like a fine pony too."

"He is. We have great fun together." Lottie bit into her sandwich. "Mum's teaching me to read. I'm getting quite good. And I'm learning to cipher too."

Still holding her sandwich, she let her hands rest in her lap. "I've missed ye. I wanted to go and see ye, but Port Jackson was too far, and when we found ye were at the factory, Mum said it wouldn't be proper for me to go there."

"I absolutely agree. It's a horrible place, not suitable for fine young ladies."

Hannah's answer seemed to satisfy Lottie. "I'm so glad ye came to see me," she said, leaning against Hannah.

The afternoon passed too quickly, and soon it was time for Hannah and Mrs. Atherton to leave. With hugs and promises of more visits, Hannah stepped into the carriage and settled on the seat opposite Mrs. Atherton.

"I'll be at church next Sunday," Lottie said. "Will ye be there?"

Hannah rested an arm on the window. "Absolutely. I wouldn't miss. I've been hoping to see you there."

"We were out of town and then I was ill," Mrs. Parnell explained, "but we'll be there this week, allowing there are no new difficulties."

"I'll look forward to seeing you," Mrs. Atherton said.

When the carriage pulled away, Hannah waved at Lottie and then settled back in her seat. She felt content.

Was it possible that God had forgiven her? *Thank you, Lord, for this day.*

20

Hannah added a piece of cedar to the morning's fire. "That ought to help ward off the chill."

Lydia stood in front of the hearth. "I still can't believe I'm here. I keep thinking I'm going to wake up from a dream."

"It's wonderful good fortune," Hannah said, setting another chunk of wood in the flames. "I'm still stunned." She smiled at Lydia. "It's grand that we get to share the cottage." She crossed the room, opened a bureau drawer, and took out a pair of stockings. "When we left London on that dreadful ship, I couldn't imagine anything good would come of my future."

"From the start I knew it would turn out well." Lydia's smile warmed the entire room.

"You never lost hope?" Hannah sat and pulled on her stockings.

"I knew God would see me through." She compressed her lips. "That's not completely true. I must admit that before Mrs. Atherton freed me from the factory, I was feeling rather low. Ye know that. Ye were there." She smiled. "I don't believe yer coming when ye did was an accident. It was the Lord."

She reached for a gown hanging in the closet and held it against her. "But this . . . I couldn't imagine—three dresses."

She flashed Hannah a mischievous smile and whirled away from the closet, holding the dress in front of her. "And good shoes too. And undergarments." She stopped her frolicking. "I'm grateful to ye and to Mrs. Atherton."

"Mrs. Atherton knew we were good friends. She's wonderfully kind. And it is true; I do need help. There's so much to be done, especially now with the additional sewing."

Lydia returned the dress to the closet and took out one made of green linen. "Did ye make this one?"

"I did."

Lydia smoothed the material and pressed down the collar. "It must cost Mrs. Atherton a goodly amount—buying fabric for so many gowns. I can't imagine."

"Their business is prospering. They have two enterprises actually. Mr. Atherton sells tools, but most of the earnings come from timber. He ships logs and cut lumber, some of it out of the country. My understanding is that he was once quite adventurous, and I'd say he's still rather daring."

"He's quite good-looking, for an elderly gent, that is." Lydia grinned.

"He is, but I think it's his heart that makes him so. He treats everyone kindly and fairly." Hannah studied her friend. "You ought to wear the green for services this morning. It's lovely with your eyes."

"The one I have on is fetching too, don't ye think?"

"It is."

Lydia pressed a hand to her abdomen and took in a deep breath. "All of this and church too." She shook her head. "I'm absolutely giddy." She returned the gown to the closet. "Will John be going?"

"He rarely misses, especially since it's required that prison-

228

ers attend." Hannah sat on the bed. "From time to time Mr. Atherton sends him out of town, so of course he can't make it then. But I'm sure I saw him about yesterday, so he ought to be joining us this morning."

Hannah's mind turned to John. Each morning he was her first thought and the last before falling asleep at night. During the day she often found herself seeking him out. Just being near him made her feel more content. Was it possible she was in love with him? *No. I can't be. And if I am, I simply won't allow it.*

Loving John would only bring about more sorrow. If he knew of her dishonor and her sin, he'd not spend another moment with her.

"Do ye think the two of ye will marry?" Lydia asked.

"I told you I couldn't marry him."

"He's a fine gentleman and—"

"And I don't want to speak of it." Hannah stood. "We've little time before we have to leave. I'll see if Mrs. Atherton needs me for anything before we go."

"Hannah, I think ye ought to consider marriage."

"I don't want to talk about it."

Lydia nodded in resignation. "I'll be praying about it, then."

"Do as you see fit."

Lydia smiled. "Is there anything I ought to be doing?"

"I don't believe so. Mr. and Mrs. Atherton ride to church in the carriage. The servants use the wagon. The stable man will bring it to the back of the house when it's time to go." She glanced out the window. "I'm glad for good weather." She moved to the door and stepped outside.

John and Perry were on the walkway and she nearly collided with them. Discomfited by John's presence since she'd just been speaking about him, Hannah found it difficult to meet his eyes.

He smiled. "You're in quite a hurry."

"I was just on my way to see if Mrs. Atherton needs anything."

"Are you all right?"

"Fine, thank you." *I can't allow anything even slightly romantic,* Hannah told herself, profoundly aware of John's good looks.

"I heard Lydia's been transferred from the factory and is working here. Is that true?"

"Yes. As a matter of fact, she'll be going to church with us. She's not quite ready yet."

"I was just wanting to say hello, but we'll wait and see her on the way, then." He flashed Perry a knowing look.

"Are you two up to something?" Hannah asked.

"No. Why do you ask?"

Hannah glanced from John to Perry. Truth struck her. "You can't seriously be thinking—"

"We're not thinking anything in particular," John said. "Just wanted to introduce Perry."

"John told me she's a fine woman, and 'round 'ere there's not many of them to be had."

"Did John also tell you she's a mind of her own?"

"Yeah, I heard, but figured she might be interested." Perry grinned. "And she's not the only one with a mind of her own. I've been known to be a bit determined meself."

"Belligerent is more like it," Hannah teased. "I've work to do," she said and headed for the house, but she couldn't keep from smiling. Perry sometimes behaved insufferably, but he was a good sort and she liked him. Still, she couldn't imagine him and Lydia ever pairing off.

Crowded with employees and servants, the wagon pulled away from the Atherton farm. Hannah and Lydia sat next to each other on a bench that ran along the side of the wagon bed. Elvine had taken a place next to them. John sat across from Hannah, his arm slung across the top of a side rail. Beside John, Perry leaned forward, resting his forearms on his thighs. A roustabout shared the front seat with the driver and another sat in the back behind the driver's seat. His wife and son were with him.

"It's a shame Gwen's unable to join us today," Elvine said.

"Is she ill?" Hannah asked.

"Oh, just a case of the sniffles. I dare say that most likely she's enjoying a morning of leisure."

"I'm thankful to be allowed to attend. Whilst living in London, Sunday services were mostly for the royals and the well-born. Me mum tried attending a few times, but people made it clear we weren't welcome. After that, we had our own services at home. We'd sing hymns and read from the Holy Book."

"I'm sorry to say I never gave the lower class's condition much thought," John said. "But now that you mention it, I don't remember anyone in church who wasn't upper crust. These days I'd certainly be turned away." He grinned.

Perry kept looking at Lydia. Hannah smiled inwardly. He obviously wanted to become acquainted.

"Eh, would ye put yer eyes back in yer head." Lydia threw one leg over the other and turned away from Perry.

"What? Me?" Perry asked.

"Who else would I be talkin' to?" Lydia turned her gaze toward the hillsides.

"I wasn't starin' at ye."

Lydia didn't look at him. "Ye weren't, eh?" A smile played at her lips.

Hannah glanced at John. Their eyes met and held for a moment, and then she looked away. Hannah knew his intentions, but he'd not said anything. *If he does, I'll be forced to refuse him.*

She needed to keep distance between them. Nothing could come of a friendship. She couldn't possibly tell him of her past, and she wouldn't marry him under false pretenses. *I'll remain a spinster. It's the only prudent thing to do.*

The driver pulled the horses to a stop beneath a tree, alongside the Atherton coach. Dalton helped Mr. and Mrs. Atherton disembark, and then closed the coach door and joined the other servants.

Thankful to be free of the close quarters, Hannah moved to the rear of the wagon. John propelled himself over the side and held out a hand to assist her.

She stared at it, then accepting the offer she stepped down. He held her hand for a moment longer than need be. Hannah liked the feel of it. His grip was strong and his palm callused. Reluctantly she pulled her hand free. "Thank you." She moved toward the church steps.

Lydia walked beside her. "He's quite taken with ye," she whispered, glancing over her shoulder at John.

"Matters little to me." Hannah could still feel the strength in his hands.

Reverend Taylor stood at the door where he greeted parishioners. When Mr. and Mrs. Atherton approached, he grasped

Mr. Atherton's hand. "William. Catharine. Good morning. Fine day, isn't it?"

"That it is," Mr. Atherton said. "A fine day for church." He smiled. "Always look forward to your sermons, Reverend."

Mrs. Atherton extended her gloved hand to the minister. "We could do with a bit of sunshine. There's been far too much rain."

"I'll be glad for summer." The minister smiled. "Always did enjoy the heat."

The Athertons stepped through the front door of the church.

Hannah and Lydia approached the reverend. He smiled at them both. "Welcome. Good to see you again, Hannah."

"I'm pleased to be here, Reverend. And eager to hear what you have to share with us today." Hannah turned to Lydia. "May I introduce my good friend, Lydia Madoc. She's just come to work for the Athertons."

"Welcome." He smiled warmly.

"It's a pleasure," Lydia said, doing a little dip as if meeting royalty.

Reverend Taylor laughed. "None of that is necessary here."

As Hannah moved inside, Lottie spotted her. She ran up the aisle and hugged Hannah about the waist.

"Good morning, luv."

"Good morning." She smiled up at Hannah.

"I so enjoyed our picnic. Perhaps you can come to my house one day soon." Hannah turned to Lydia. "You remember Lydia, don't you?"

"Course I do. Grand to see ye. How'd ye come to be 'ere?"

"Mrs. Atherton has put me to work as a housemaid."

"How grand." Lottie smiled broadly. "Ye look right elegant."

"Thank you. So do you." Lydia squatted and gave Lottie a hug.

"It's wonderful to see ye again." She held her at arm's length. "I swear ye've grown six inches since I last saw ye."

"Really? Ye think so?"

"I do. And ye look well. Ye happy?"

"Oh yes. Me new mum and dad are fine people." She glanced at them. They'd already found seats. "I better go." She hugged Lydia and Hannah once more and then skipped toward the front of the church, red curls bouncing.

"I can hardly believe my eyes," Lydia whispered. "She looks like a different child—healthy, her skin all rosy."

"Good food and love can do wonders. I could barely believe it when I saw her last week. I'm grateful to the Parnells for all they've done."

Still thinking about how grand it was to actually be neighbors with Lottie, Hannah walked down the center aisle. She liked being in church. It was small and unadorned, nothing like the elaborate churches in London. The sanctuary was divided into two sections of wooden pews, and the floors were made of cedar planks that had been polished to a high sheen. They gleamed beneath morning sunlight spilling in through the windows. White walls made the room look bright.

As a hush settled over the congregation, Hannah sat in a pew near the back of the sanctuary. If she'd wanted, she could join the Athertons, but it seemed bold of a servant to do so. To be allowed to worship here was enough.

As often happened on Sundays, Hannah was troubled by doubts and questions. She'd been accepted by these people; why didn't she feel God's acceptance? *He knows my secrets. They do not,* she decided. *If they knew, they would be appalled.*

Mrs. Sullivan, a frail young woman, moved to the piano. She played for all the services. Her fingers moved lithely over the keys. Occasionally she would glance at the front row where her husband and four children sat; she'd smile and return to the music.

When the last chord was played, Reverend Taylor stepped to the front of the church and led the congregation in singing a hymn. Hannah enjoyed worship. The music had the power to carry her above her troubles. She looked at Lydia. Her green eyes shown with delight, and she smiled as she sang. *Thank you, Lord, for Lydia.*

The song ended and Hannah glanced at John. He looked her way and smiled, devotion in his eyes. She turned her attention to the minister. She mustn't encourage his attentions. Yet her mind stayed with him, wishing things could be different between them. When she allowed herself the freedom to dream, it was always John she imagined as her husband.

Reverend Taylor leaned on the lectern. The gesture was so like Judge Walker's the day he'd falsely accused Hannah that a flash of fear and loathing exploded inside her. She worked hard to focus on what the minister was saying.

He's not Judge Walker, she told herself.

The reverend was a small man with gray hair and blue eyes. His face was deeply lined, especially around his eyes and mouth. Hannah thought it must be because he smiled a lot. He was dedicated to the Scriptures and severe in his personal disciplines of God's Word, yet he always seemed friendly and benevolent.

The minister looked out over the congregation. "Motherhood." He said the word as if it were a statement. "How often do we diminish the value of mothers? We all have mothers, or have had. None of us would be here otherwise." He smiled. "And wasn't it our mothers who cooed over us as infants, who loved and cared for us through fevers and injuries? Weren't they our first spiritual teachers?"

Hannah thought of her mother. She missed her so badly. If only she could talk to her and tell her that all was well. *Perhaps she knows.*

"Mothers deserve our gratitude and our thanks," the reverend continued. "Our Lord had a mother. We speak of our heavenly Father, and so we should. But what of our Lord's mother?"

He glanced down at his Bible. "When the angel Gabriel came to Mary and told her she would bear a son, the Savior of the world, she accepted God's calling without question. And she knew it could cost her life."

Condemnation buried Hannah. Feeling as if she were suffocating in it, she looked at her hands clasped tightly in her lap. A groan thundered deep inside her. She'd not thanked God for her child. She'd rejected it and prayed for its death. *Lord, forgive me. I'm wicked beyond comprehension.*

"You mothers and fathers must never take lightly the gift of your children," Reverend Taylor continued. "The Lord has plainly said children are a blessing from God. And I say amen to that." He seemed to look directly at Hannah.

She felt a sudden panic under his gaze. Did he know? Could he see her heart? Her palms were wet. She felt flushed. The room was stifling hot. She needed air. She needed to get out.

The morning that she lost the child rushed back at Hannah. She could hear the sound of the bucket lid closing and Lydia walking up the steps. The darkness, the fetid odor was all around her.

I should have wanted it. I should have loved it.

Feeling as if she might faint, she gripped the pew in front of her. "I . . . I'm not feeling well," she whispered to Lydia. "I'm going home." She stood, made her way to the aisle, and then rushed to the back of the church. She stepped outside so quickly she nearly fell onto the porch. Hurrying down the steps, she headed for the road.

"Forgive me. Forgive me," she cried as she stumbled toward home.

"Hannah," someone called.

She looked over her shoulder. *John. I can't speak to him. Not now.* She kept moving.

"Hannah," he called again.

She heard his steps as he ran to catch up to her. She kept walking. Wiping away tears, she tried to compose herself.

When he caught up to her, he asked, "Didn't you hear me?"

"Please, leave me alone. I'm going home."

"What is it? Are you all right?"

"I'm not feeling well."

"Then all the more reason I should accompany you." He gently grasped her arm. "You're not ill. It's something else."

"Leave me be. I can't talk about it." Hannah kept walking. "I'm quite all right. Go back to church."

"I can't do that." His voice was tender. "It's not safe for a woman to be on the road alone."

"Fine then, but please don't speak."

They walked for a long while, silently. The only sound was the soft buzzing of insects and an occasional call of a bird.

"Why can't you tell me what's troubling you?" John finally asked. "Perhaps it will help to speak of it."

"No. It won't." Hannah stopped abruptly and faced him. "Why are you here? I don't want your company."

"I'm worried about you. You're distressed."

"Yes. I am. And when I'm troubled, I prefer to be alone."

Hurt touched his eyes. "I'm sorry. You're right. I shouldn't have bothered you. But I'll not let you walk alone. I'll stay behind where you can't see me."

Hannah stared at him. Why did he insist on being so gallant? She'd given him no cause. And she certainly didn't deserve it.

"Go on ahead," he urged. "I'll follow."

Hannah's resolve collapsed. It would be ridiculous to make him follow behind her. "No. It's all right. You can walk with me." She moved on, only more slowly. "Thank you for your kindness."

"Quite all right."

Hannah felt drained of energy. All she could think of was lying on her bed, closing her eyes, and seeking refuge in sleep.

"So, can you tell me what it is that's bothering you?" John inquired gently.

Hannah didn't answer for a long moment and then she said, "Honestly, John, I would if I could. But it's not possible. There are some things best left unsaid."

"And then there are things that must be said." John stopped walking.

Hannah kept moving until she realized he'd stopped. Turning to look at him, she asked, "What is it?"

"I must tell you how I feel."

Hannah was terrified at what he might say. "I think it best we talk about it another time."

"Now is a good time." John moved toward her. He was broad shouldered and several inches taller than Hannah. When he looked down on her, she felt enveloped by him. His expression was tender, and she felt passion and need sweep over her.

"When I first saw you . . . I knew."

Hannah turned her head. She wanted to hear but didn't dare.

"I love you, Hannah." He took her hands in his. "I want to marry you."

Hannah wanted to love him. She did love him.

Staring at her hands, she longed to let him love her, to look after her, to hold her. She looked up at him. Somehow she managed to remain calm. "John, you're a fine man. But . . . I don't love you. I'll never love you. Not that way. Please don't love me." She gently extricated her hands, turned, and walked away.

Hannah managed to hold back her tears until she reached the cottage. There, she closed the door and pressed her back against it. And sobbed.

21

A quiet rapping sounded at Hannah's door. She'd cried until she was empty, and now she didn't want to speak to anyone. Ignoring the noise, she rolled onto her side and pulled her blanket over her. *They'll go away.* The knocking came again. Hannah tried to ignore it, but when she heard it again, she decided that whoever it was wouldn't leave without speaking to her.

"All right, then," she said, sitting up and dropping her feet to the floor. She stood, glanced in the bureau mirror, tidied her hair, and wiped away remnants of tears. She smoothed her dress as she walked to the door.

Opening it, she was surprised to see Mrs. Atherton. She managed a smile. "I'm sorry it took so long."

"Quite all right, dear. I was concerned about you. Are you ill?"

Hannah did her best to look cheery. "I'm quite all right now. I apologize for leaving church so abruptly. I didn't mean to cause you concern." Hannah knew she ought to invite Mrs. Atherton in, but she didn't have the energy to play hostess or to cope with questions.

"That's all I really needed to know. I was just worried about you." Mrs. Atherton lingered.

Not wanting to appear rude, especially toward her mistress, Hannah asked, "Would you like to come in for tea? There's some left from this morning. It's been on the stove so it may still be hot."

"That would be lovely. Thank you."

Hannah stood aside and opened the door. Mrs. Atherton stepped in. Appearing a bit hesitant, she stood for a moment just inside, then moved to the small table in the kitchen and sat.

Hannah retrieved two cups and saucers and filled the cups with tea. "You do take sugar, don't you?"

"Yes. A small piece." Mrs. Atherton picked up a book lying on the table. "You've been doing some reading?"

Hannah glanced at the book. "Just poetry. It's a collection by Katharine Philips."

"I quite like her." Mrs. Atherton turned the book over in her hands. "Her writing is lovely—refined and straightforward."

"I enjoy poetry. I hope you don't mind; I got it from your library. Elvine said it would be all right."

"Oh yes. You may borrow any books you like."

Hannah set the cup and saucer on the table in front of Mrs. Atherton. "Thank you. I shall."

Setting down the book, Mrs. Atherton picked up her cup. She sipped the warm beverage. "John was quite worried about you today. He said you were rather in a state."

"He was overly concerned. I'm quite all right. Really."

Mrs. Atherton settled a gentle look on Hannah. "When our burdens are heavy, it often helps to share them with someone. I can assure you there isn't much I haven't heard. Since I came to live in this part of the world I've listened to many tragic stories, especially from the women in the prisons."

Hannah longed to release some of her burden, but she feared Mrs. Atherton would be scandalized and reject her. She might even send her back to the factory. She said nothing for a long moment. Dare she speak the truth? "My heart is wicked, mum."

"I don't believe that. You're a dear." She smiled gently. "Perhaps your misfortune isn't so terrible as you imagine."

"I'm not who you think I am. I've done unspeakable evil."

Mrs. Atherton waited patiently, quietly.

"Lydia doesn't even know the entire truth." Hannah's tears were very near the surface. She couldn't speak as she fought to manage her emotions. She gazed at her tea. It was the color of amber. Looking up, she met Mrs. Atherton's eyes and said softly, "I can't speak of it."

"Of course. I'd never presume that you must. But I can assure you I'll not say a word to anyone."

"Certainly, but I'm afraid you'll loathe me when you know the truth."

"I won't. I couldn't." Mrs. Atherton offered a look of reassurance. "I care for you too much."

Hannah wet her lips. "Perhaps confession will help purge my sin." She set her cup of tea on its saucer, then ran her fingertip around the edge of the cup.

"When I lived in London, before my mum died, I had a lovely life. We lived in a small cottage. Mum had her own business. We didn't have much in the way of possessions, but we were happy." Hannah smiled as she remembered those days. "Mum was a superb seamstress. She fit and dressed the best women in London."

She let out a long sigh. "Then one day she got sick, and a few weeks later she died . . . of the sweating sickness." The bereavement she'd felt at the time of her mother's death returned as powerfully as if Hannah had just lost her.

She lifted the cross she wore around her neck. "This was hers. It's all I have left." Tears blurred her vision.

Mrs. Atherton leaned closer to Hannah so she could see the necklace more clearly. "How lovely and delicate it is."

Hannah let go of the cross, then patted it gently and let her hand rest on it a moment longer. "After Mum died, I kept working in the dress shop, but the cultured ladies wanted my mother and not me. They took their business elsewhere. I didn't have enough money to pay the rent and was evicted. I went to work for a judge, Mr. Charlton Walker. He and his wife have six children."

The scene the night Mr. Walker assaulted her roared through her mind. She'd not spoken of it since telling Lydia. She clasped her hands together to keep them from quaking.

"One night . . ." She let out a breath. "One night he came to my room. And . . ." She couldn't get the words out.

"Oh, luv." Mrs. Atherton reached across the table and covered Hannah's hands with her own. "You don't have to say it. I know." She gently squeezed. "I'm certain it wasn't your doing."

"I've thought and thought about it, and I can't remember doing or saying anything that would entice him or make him think that I would want . . . that."

"You must put it out of your mind. Give Mr. Walker up to the Lord. He'll deal with the man. That way you can be free of it."

"There's more." Hannah stood and walked to the small window at the front of the cottage. She stared out at the green lawns and towering trees. The wind had picked up and heavy evergreen boughs swayed. "Mr. Walker was the judge who sentenced me to transportation."

"The blackguard!"

Hannah turned to look at Mrs. Atherton. "He didn't know I was pregnant. I didn't then either, not until later when I was on the ship. Babies were born in that dreadful place, but most of them died. I knew I couldn't have a child, not while I was a convict. What kind of life would that be for a little one?"

Hannah knew she was stalling, hoping to shed some of her guilt by making up reasons for her appeal to God. She swallowed and continued. "I asked God to get rid of it. He did. It was born when I was only four months gone and it was too small to live." Tears spilled onto her cheeks. "I'm despicable. I wanted my child to die." She turned her gaze out the window. "I'll pack my belongings if you like."

"For heaven's sake! Absolutely not!"

"The proper thing to do would be to send me back to the factory. I don't deserve to work for such a fine lady as you."

Mrs. Atherton pushed out of her chair and moved to Hannah. "I'd never send you back there." She pulled Hannah into an embrace and smoothed her hair. "You're not wicked. You were just a child who didn't know what to do. Caring for a baby on a convict ship is the worst sort of situation. You were desperate. I know about that. I've been desperate too."

"You don't hate me?"

"Of course I don't hate you. I've seen the children who live in prison. It's a wretched existence. I'm only angry with a government that sends innocents to prison. It's contemptible."

Hannah felt some relief and thought she could continue. "Lottie and I were already friends. She'd lost her mother and we needed each other. Lottie's a lovely child. Mine could have been too. She could have had a fine life here. I just didn't know." Hannah pushed her hair back from her face. "I hate myself."

Mrs. Atherton held Hannah away from her. "Hannah, I believe you've given yourself too much credit. God makes the decisions about life and death. He and only he is the one who gives life and who takes it away. If it was God's will for your child to live, it would have. You did not kill it."

"I suppose that may be true, but I wanted it dead. I'm certain God finds me despicable."

"Of course he doesn't. He loves all of his children no matter what we do. And he's always ready to forgive a repentant heart."

"I want to believe you, but I'm certain God is angry with me. So many terrible things have happened. The night Mr. Walker attacked me, everything changed. I've felt God's absence. He's stepped away from me. I must have provoked Mr. Walker in some way." Hannah wiped at her tears. "I'm sure God couldn't love someone like me."

"That's not so." Mrs. Atherton held Hannah close. "God's love is bigger than all of our sins. When Christ died, he died for your sins. He took every one of them and laid them upon himself so you wouldn't have to carry them." She tipped Hannah's face up and smiled at her. "God sees you as pure, without blemish."

"If only I could believe you."

"You don't need to believe me. Believe God. His Holy Word states it plainly. He says that while we were yet sinners Christ died for us. And that his Son's sacrifice made us holy and blameless."

So many times Hannah's mother had spoken of God's love and forgiveness. *Why can't I accept it for myself?*

"You've been carrying such a heavy burden. I knew there was something. I could see it in your eyes. The Lord wants you to be free of it."

245

"You truly believe he's not angry with me?"

"Yes. Oh, he may be unhappy about your not trusting him and not trusting the good people around you." She smiled and hugged Hannah again.

Hannah held on to her, feeling as if Mrs. Atherton were her salvation. Her thoughts turned to John. He'd not understand.

"There's something else." Mrs. Atherton gently set Hannah away from her. "What is it?"

"As you know, John followed me home today. He told me that he loves me and wants to marry me."

Mrs. Atherton smiled. "He's a fine man. He'll make a splendid husband. You're to be congratulated."

"I told him no." Hannah hugged herself, rubbing her arms to warm the chill she felt. "I can't marry him. I'd have to tell him the truth. He'll be disgusted by me."

"You know that with certainty, do you?"

"Not everyone is as kind as you. And a man sees with different eyes. He can't accept a defiled woman as a wife."

"How can you know what he'll do if you don't tell him? I find him an exceptional man who would do anything for the woman he loves."

"I pray you're right."

"I only wish you could see yourself from my eyes, or better yet through God's eyes. Let the Lord heal your heart, dear. He's quite good at it."

<hr>

After Mrs. Atherton had gone, Hannah sat at the table and closed her eyes. She tried to pray. She needed to feel God's presence. If only she could believe Mrs. Atherton. Her mother had told her the very things her mistress had. Hannah contemplated on many of the Scriptures her mum had read of God's love and forgiveness. *She and Mrs. Atherton are both faithful believers. They must know the truth*, Hannah thought, and yet she couldn't believe it for herself.

"Lord, I pray you can hear me. I'm a terrible sinner and ashamed to speak to you about my sin. But if your Word is true, even you spent time with the lowest sorts. Will you spend time with me?" She pressed her hands together in sincerity. "I'll do everything I can to please you. I'll not spend idle time in gossip or on thoughtless imaginings. I'll not miss a Sunday service or let my mind wander when the reverend is speaking. I'll do charitable acts. If only you will wipe away my offense." Even as she made the request, she knew that if God forgave, she could never forget or feel absolved. Her iniquity would forever plague her.

When she'd finished praying, she remained at the table. Picking up the book of poetry, she thumbed through the pages, reading passage after passage to find solace for her aching heart. She took the book to her bed and only managed to read a few more entries before falling asleep.

Whistling from outside woke her. Sleepily, she climbed out of bed and went to the window. It was John. He walked up the pathway. After all that had happened and all that had been said, Hannah was reluctant to face him.

Smoothing her hair and her crumpled gown, she moved to the door and opened it, doing her best to appear calm and cheerful. Stepping onto the porch, she said as gaily as she could, "Afternoon, John."

"Good day. You look better." He stopped and planted his hands on his hips. "I thought we might take a walk?"

"It's rather late." Hannah looked at the sky. The sun was low.

"We don't have to go far."

Hannah knew it was unwise to be with him, but she wanted to go. "All right, then. Let me get my wrap."

Pulling her shawl around her shoulders, she asked, "I've not seen Lydia since this morning. Do you know where she is?"

"She and Perry went on a picnic. They haven't come back yet?"

"No." Hannah moved down the walkway. "I must say I'm surprised. I shouldn't think of them as a couple."

"They're not. Perry wouldn't take no for an answer. He can be assertive."

"That's true. And I doubt that will create fondness in Lydia. It's a shame. He's a nice fellow."

For several minutes, they walked without speaking. Finally John broke the silence. "I like it here in Parramatta. I used to travel some, but never did make it to New South Wales. When I lived in London, I dreamed of adventure." He chuckled. "I got it. After being arrested, I decided I'd prefer a more sedentary life. But now it's different. I'm glad to be here."

His jaw hardened slightly. "I would have preferred a different means of arrival, however. I doubt I'll ever see the man who stole my savings and my wife."

"Your wife? You never mentioned that you were married." Although she'd decided to never marry, the idea of John being unavailable stabbed at her heart. "How could you have asked me—"

"No, no. Margaret's dead. I received word just after my arrest that she'd died—an ailment of some sort."

"I'm sorry."

John nodded. "The bloke who stole her from me is very

much alive, at least the last I knew. I hope for an opportunity to see him again. Just once will do."

"You sound bitter."

"That I am. And rightly so. He's my cousin. I took him into the business as a favor. Thought I might be of help to him. His recompense was to destroy the business my father built and then leave me in prison without a farthing." John shook his head. "He should pay for his sins."

"You're right, but it's God who should see to it that he is punished. Bitterness will only destroy you. You must let it go."

As she spoke, Hannah's words penetrated her own heart. She had no right to speak about forgiveness. She couldn't even forgive herself.

"I'll not let him off that easily. I can't." John's eyes settled on Hannah. "What is it? Have I said something to upset you?"

"No. It's nothing. I'm fine. Really."

John stopped beneath an acacia. Its broad limbs reached out toward nearby trees. He leaned against the trunk. "I'm sorry for earlier today. I was too outspoken and too assertive. I shouldn't have pressured you when you were already under duress. But I'd kept my feelings inside for so long they came tumbling out before I could stop them."

He took a deep breath. "I do wish you'd consider my offer. Even if you don't love me, perhaps you could learn to, given time." He studied her. "I was almost certain you had feelings for me."

Hannah couldn't look at him. She did love him. When she glanced at John, the affection in his eyes compelled her to speak. "I do have feelings for you, John. But . . . I can't marry you."

"You love me! I knew it!" He reached for her. "Then marry me. Please marry me."

Hannah longed to be loved, to be held and protected from the world. She gazed up into his hazel eyes so full of devotion. Why would it be wrong to love him? "I do love you, John."

Before she could say more, he kissed her. Months of deprivation, a yearning for affection, and her need for forgiveness drove Hannah. She couldn't resist her passion and returned his kiss, pressing close to him.

When the kiss ended, John continued to hold her. "I've prayed for this moment." He gently lifted her face and searched her eyes. "I love you, more than I can express. I'll make you a fine husband. We'll have a grand life here in New South Wales. One day we'll have a place of our own and children. There will be lots of children."

Hannah sucked in a breath and stepped back.

"What? What is it? Hannah?"

"I can't marry you. I'm so sorry." She backed away. "I'm sorry." She turned and fled.

"Hannah?" he called. "Hannah."

She lifted her skirts and ran. What had she been thinking? How could she have allowed this?

When the forest closed around her, Hannah slowed. She sat at the base of a tree, remembering the feel of his lips on hers. *Oh John, I do love you.*

"Lord, please take this love from me. I can't bear it."

22

John hefted a crate of tools to be delivered to a timber site into the back of the wagon. Watching Hannah, he took a handkerchief from a back pocket and mopped his damp face. Even while hanging laundry, she looked beautiful. Yet the sight of her made his heart heavy. Since the evening he'd kissed her, John had no opportunity to speak with Hannah. She had kept her distance.

He'd replayed their conversation in his mind many times. She'd said she loved him, even allowed the kiss, and then abruptly ran away. What had he done or said that had upset her so? He'd believed she was his, finally. And now, without knowing why, he'd lost her.

Resting an arm on the bed of the wagon, he gazed at Hannah. Perhaps she would look his way. Her dark hair had come free of its pins and softly curled around her face. The effect was charming. John remembered the passion he'd seen in her eyes. *Why won't you allow yourself to love me? What can I do to bring you back to me?*

Mrs. Atherton stepped out of the house and crossed the lawn. "Hannah, I have a number of errands I need you to do for me." She handed Hannah a sheet of paper.

John returned to his work. Best not be caught eavesdropping.

"John and Patrick, one of the roustabouts, are traveling into Port Jackson this morning. I thought you could ride along. There are several items I need."

Hannah stared at the paper and finally said, "Most days I'd be happy to take care of these. But today is washing day. Gwen will need me. There's too much for her to do alone."

"Not to worry. Lydia said she'd help."

"Oh." Hannah fingered her mother's cross. "Well then, of course I'll go."

"Credit the items to our account. William will look after the bill the next time he's in Port Jackson." She started back to the house and then stopped. "Oh, you best take an overnight bag. You'll most certainly need to spend the night."

"Yes, of course," Hannah said. Her voice sounded tight.

John couldn't keep from smiling. Two full days with Hannah. It was more than he could have hoped for. He whistled while hitching up the horses.

Carrying a small bag, Hannah approached the wagon. "Good day, John," she said, using a formal tone. She nodded at Patrick whom she barely knew.

"Good day." John glanced at Hannah's bag. "So, you'll be accompanying me?"

"Yes. It seems Mrs. Atherton needs me to do some errands for her. I hope I'm no bother."

John glanced at Patrick. "He's a good bloke, but you'll add some gentility to the trip."

"I'll be glad for yer company," Patrick said with a grin. "Two blokes together can get tiresome." He climbed into the back of the wagon. "Figure it's a fine day for a nap," he said, leaning against the side and folding his arms over his chest.

John gazed at Hannah warmly. "Your company's always welcome."

"This is business, not pleasure," Hannah said, keeping her tone reserved, but looking disconcerted.

Feeling only slightly deflated, John took her bag and set it in the back of the wagon and then moved around to the front and offered her a hand up.

Hannah settled on the wooden seat, keeping her back rigid and her eyes straight ahead. Her jaw was set.

Perhaps she'll be less standoffish as we go along, John hoped. *If not, I don't know how I'll manage a genuine conversation with someone who'll barely look at me.* Discouraged and trying to come up with a way to thaw her mood, he climbed onto the seat beside her. He lifted the traces. "We're off, then." He flicked the reins lightly, the horses plodded forward. "Warm for August, don't you think?"

"I suppose."

"I heard that August is generally one of our cooler months."

Hannah looked at John with a puzzled expression. "You said *our* cooler months. Do you see this place as home?"

"I hadn't thought on it, but yes. I do." He looked at the patch-work of forest and fields. "I quite like it here. I'm not inclined to return to England."

"But I thought you said you wanted to go back, that is, if you are given a pardon."

"Don't expect I'll have to give that much thought. A life sentence means life." John was unable to keep the dejection out of his voice.

"What about Henry Hodgsson? You spoke of finding him one day."

John found the discussion unsettling, but any conversation was better than none. He glanced back at Patrick. His eyes were closed and he seemed to already be asleep. "If I were pardoned and had the opportunity to find him, I don't think he's worth the journey."

"I'm glad you've given up your vendetta."

"I didn't say that. If I ever have a chance, I'll take my revenge."

Just the thought of Henry and what he'd done made John angry. He hated his cousin. Although aware it did little good to harbor resentments, nurturing the rage felt gratifying. John didn't want to let it go.

An uncomfortable silence fell over the two travelers. Finally, John asked, "Have you plans when you've served your time?"

Hannah tightened the sash on her bonnet. "I haven't decided. It's a long while until then. I only left London nineteen months ago. I've another twelve and a half years to serve." She was quiet a moment, then continued, "When my sentence is fulfilled, I'll no longer be young."

A bird squawked loudly from within the woods. Hannah threw a glance toward the sound. "I've no one left in London. My mum is dead and the friends I had may well be dead by then as well." She sighed heavily. "I suppose I'll live out my years here. If the Athertons will allow me to stay in their employ, I'll remain in Parramatta. It wouldn't be a hardship. They've been very kind."

"They're fine people. Have to admire those who set out on a venture like they did. There was very little here when they arrived. Heard stories of starvation and Aborigine attacks."

John clicked his tongue and slapped the reins, urging on lagging horses.

Once more, John and Hannah turned to their thoughts. The only sound was that of the groaning wagon, the heavy footfalls of the horses, and an occasional squawking of birds. Patrick seemed to be in a deep sleep, undisturbed by the lurching of the wagon.

John couldn't think of anything to say. His mind was stuck on his facing a life sentence. Even if Hannah consented to marry him, he'd remain a prisoner his entire life. What could he offer her, except a cottage on someone else's farm?

Unable to endure his thoughts or the silence any longer, he said, "This road is appalling. Next time we should consider going by river." The words were barely out of his mouth when one of the back wheels thumped into a deep hole. The wagon dropped with a jolt.

"Aye, what's happened?" Patrick asked, sitting up.

"Hit a hole is all," John said. The horses tried to move forward but the wheel was fixed. "Get on with you," John called, flicking the reins. The animals strained in their harnesses, but the wheel remained wedged.

"I'll have to help them." John handed Hannah the reins. "Hold them steady."

Hannah looked at the traces in her hands. "I've not driven a team before."

"Keep the lines taut. If the horses decide to move ahead more than a foot or two, hold them firm."

"I'll do my best," Hannah said with uncertainty.

John jumped down and made his way around to the back wheel. Patrick joined him. Together, the two men gripped the wheel. "When I say go, slap the reins over the horses' rumps," John said.

"All right. Now," he said, and he and Patrick pushed against the wheel.

Hannah shouted for the horses to move and slapped the reins. The men pushed. The wheel nearly came free and then fell back.

"Try again." Once more John and Patrick strained against the wheel, and with a sudden jarring, it broke free. The horses rapidly moved forward and didn't stop.

"Pull back on the reins," John called, running to catch up. With the wagon still moving, he clambered onto the seat and took the traces from Hannah. "You did well," he said with a laugh.

Hannah looked flushed, but pleased. "It was quite exhilarating. I'd like to do it again one day."

"Well, here you are." John handed back the reins.

"Oh no. Not now. I . . ." Hannah shut her mouth and gripped the reins. "All right, then. Will you show me?"

Patrick climbed into the back and stood behind the front seat. "Ye sure she's up to it?" He grinned and nudged his hat back off his forehead.

"She's up to it," John said, then patiently demonstrated how best to manage the team and instructed Hannah in the skills of driving, taking the reins only when the roadway became too challenging.

The rest of the trip passed rapidly and pleasantly. Patrick returned to snoozing while John and Hannah settled into casual conversation, chatting about home, music, horses, their daily lives, and even some of their dreams.

When they arrived at Port Jackson, John wished they had farther to go. He stopped the wagon in front of an inn. "You can get settled while Patrick and I see to the team. I've business to take care of. Do you need assistance?"

"No. The millinery shop is just down the street and the mercantile is nearby. I'll make my purchases and ask the proprietor to have them ready to be picked up tomorrow morning."

"Very well. I'll see you then in time for dinner, eh?"

"That will be fine."

John watched as Hannah stepped into the inn. He wished for more days like today. *If only she'd allow my devotion.* He turned the horses toward the stables. *No use thinking on it.*

John left Patrick to care for the team, and he walked down the street toward a company Mr. Atherton had recently started doing business with. He'd explained to John that the proprietor had offered the best prices to distribute tools and lumber and was also willing to export raw logs.

Like much of Port Jackson, the building was new and unpretentious. John opened the door and stepped into an office. The room was small and a bit shoddy, but that was of no consequence. Businesses here had little use for pretense. A man worked at a desk in the back.

"I'll be right with you," he said without looking up.

John tensed. The voice sounded familiar. He knew the set of the man's shoulders and the way he bent over his work.

The proprietor looked up. "Sorry 'bout that, I . . ." The color drained from his face and his jaw went slack.

Rage thundered through John.

Henry Hodgsson straightened and then stood.

John wanted to lunge at him; put his head through a wall. Somehow he managed to maintain a composed exterior. He needed to think rationally. How could he best make use of this encounter?

"Henry." He pushed his hands into his pockets and loosened the set of his shoulders. *Stay calm*, he told himself. "What an unlikely place to find you."

"Yes, indeed." Sweat beaded up on Henry's upper lip. "Glad to see you looking so fit. Didn't know what had become of you."

"Is that right?" John's tone was caustic.

"After that night, I waited for you."

"You did, eh?" John clenched his teeth. "Didn't strike you as odd that I just disappeared? You saw no need to inquire as to my whereabouts?"

"Of course. I was gravely concerned. I searched for you. Later I found that you'd been transported so I liquidated the business."

"You liquidated before I was transported, long before."

"I'm sure that's not correct."

"It is." John barely managed to keep his fury reined in.

"I can't imagine how that could have happened." Henry grabbed hold of the edge of the desk.

"You managed to get your hands on the funds before my trial." John seethed inside. "My attorney tried to access them and discovered that the accounts had been emptied."

Henry fidgeted and looked toward the door as if contemplating escape. "That's not how it was. Your attorney must have made an error, or the people at the bank." He took a step toward the front of the room. "It was a long time ago. I don't remember how it all happened." Folding his arms over his chest, he asked, "So, how is it that you came to be free?"

"I'm not. I'm under bond to Mr. Atherton. He sent me here

on business." John mulled over the idea of giving Henry a thrashing, but common sense won out. Prisoners who caused trouble were severely punished. He didn't want to hang for someone like Henry Hodgsson. Still, the idea of smashing his fists into the man's face was tempting.

Henry's look changed from fear to superiority. "A convict, eh? Quite a change of status for you."

"That it is." John took a step closer to Henry. "I suppose my money paid for this venture?"

"It was our money, John. And with you in prison, what was I to do?"

"Perhaps my wife would have wanted a bit of it."

"Yes. But poor Margaret succumbed to fever."

"I got word of that while I was in the gaol in London." John stared at the little man. He loathed him. But now was not the time to take revenge. He'd find a way that would punish Henry without jeopardizing himself.

"What can I do for Mr. Atherton?" Henry asked.

"He said he'd corresponded with you about a shipment of logs, as well as the distribution of milled lumber and tools."

"Right. I recall receiving an inquiry from him." He moved to a file cabinet. Opening a drawer, he thumbed through several files. "Here it is." He scanned the letter. "I can have his supplies shipped in good time and at a fair price." He handed John several documents. "Have him look these over, and if he's so inclined, he can sign them. Get them back to me. I'll make sure his wares are well taken care of."

John took the papers and quickly looked them over. The prices were good. Perhaps too good. He studied Henry. Could he be trusted? "I'll see to it that he gets them," he said, then turned and walked out.

John strode up the street, barely able to contain his anger. *That loathsome beggar deserves to die. I have a right to retribution. There must be a way to give him what he deserves. Lord, I must have my revenge.*

That night over dinner, John still hadn't completely reined in his anger. It consumed his thoughts. He'd looked forward to time alone with Hannah and had even managed to sidetrack Patrick. Now all he could think of was Henry. He sat glumly across the table from Hannah.

She set down her fork and knife and looked at him. "What is it? You've barely said two words since we got here and you look quite distressed."

"I saw him today."

"You saw who?"

"Henry Hodgsson."

"Your cousin?"

"Yeah." John picked up his knife and stuck it into the wooden table. "Never a word from him. He's been traveling about, spending my money." He clenched his teeth. "And it seems he's prospering."

"Dear heavens. What is he doing in Port Jackson?"

"He's transporting goods, and Mr. Atherton is doing business with him." John stared at the knife. Calmly and deliberately he said, "I want him dead."

"He may deserve it, but you'll hang if you touch him. Leave it be, please." Hannah lifted her napkin off her lap, folded it, and set it on the table. "Perhaps Mr. Atherton can have someone else deal with these business matters."

"No. It'll be me. And I want it to be me. I don't trust Henry. I'll see to it that he doesn't cheat Mr. Atherton. And if I get my chance . . ."

"Give your bitterness to God, John. He'll deal with Mr. Hodgsson. Revenge brings nothing but trouble. You'll be much better off if you can forgive the wrong done to you. Forgiveness is good for a person's soul. The Scriptures state clearly that vengeance belongs to the Lord."

John was in no mood to hear sermonizing from Hannah. He stared at her across the table. "You speak of forgiveness, but you've demons of your own. I've seen your anguish." Gripping the handle of the knife, he looked at her. "Who is it you can't forgive, Hannah?"

"Whatever do you mean?" Hannah picked up her napkin and refolded it. "I bear no grudge against any man."

"Something plagues you. You can't hide it. I see it lurking inside."

Hannah looked at him, but didn't hold his gaze and turned her eyes back to her napkin folding. She compressed her lips. "I dare say, we all have shadows from our past—things best left alone."

John immediately felt badly at confronting Hannah. It was clear that whatever beset her was too painful for her to speak of. He gently grasped her hand. "My apologies for prying. I didn't mean to upset you."

"You haven't. Not at all," she said, but her dark eyes said otherwise.

23

It had been weeks since John had last seen Henry, but he was even more certain that he was corrupt. Hands clenched, he stepped out of Henry Hodgsson's office. *He's depraved. He can't be trusted.*

In spite of his anger, John felt triumphant. He'd managed to convince Henry that he'd forgiven him and that their bad history had been set aside. He smiled. *A day will come when he receives what he deserves. All I need do is wait and watch. He'll reveal his treacherous heart.*

John headed up the street toward the stables. He hoped to be home before dark. Perhaps he could convince Hannah to take a stroll with him. Since their trip into Port Jackson, the rapport between them had improved. They'd spent many hours together. He smiled, remembering her competitiveness and her laughter as she'd learned the games of chess and cribbage.

She turned out to be an adept pupil at cribbage, but chess was another matter. She'd furrow her brows and study the board, making cautious moves and building strategies, but she'd yet to best him. *Perhaps she'll join me for a game of chess tonight.*

I could lose on purpose, he thought and then decided against it. She'd know.

Thinking about spending time with Hannah, he pushed away thoughts of Henry. *We're closer*, he thought. *I know I'm not imagining it.* He considered their recent exchanges and was convinced that she loved him. She'd said as much that one evening. What held her back now he could only guess. Something or someone had hurt her. He could see it in her eyes. *I must convince her I can make her happy and will never cause her harm.*

John planned to ask for her hand again. He'd been waiting for an opportune moment.

So occupied with thoughts of Hannah, John nearly walked into Gavin Brice, a local businessman.

"Good day, John." Gavin grasped him by the shoulders. He grinned. "Your mind elsewhere?"

"I guess so." John focused on the big man. "Shall we begin again?" He reached for Gavin's hand. "Good day to you."

"I've missed seeing you 'bout the work site."

"Mr. Atherton has me busy with business. I planned on stopping by your place next week. I've nearly finished the tools you ordered."

"Good." Gavin lifted his hat, swiped his hair back, and then settled the hat on his head. Glancing at a hazy blue sky, he said, "It's a hot one."

"Bit unusual for September, I'm told."

"We're only two days from October. Heat usually starts settling in 'bout now." He rested a hand against the side of a building and leaned. "Heard William's business is thriving. From what I've seen at the docks he's shipping out a good deal of lumber."

"Right. We're doing well. There's a great need for raw timber as well. I'm managing some of the shipments. In fact, that's why I'm here. Had paperwork to sign for Mr. Hodgsson on a shipment of logs."

"So William is also selling logs? Thought he dealt mainly with sawn lumber."

"He did, but diversification's a good idea."

"Right smart of him." Gavin folded his arms over his chest. "And you're working with Hodgsson, eh?"

"We are."

"He handled a couple of transactions for me. I've yet to receive payment. In fact, as far as I know the shipment hasn't yet made it to Newcastle."

"Didn't make it?" John's curiosity piqued.

"Hodgsson told me there was a delay getting the goods out. He assures me everything's in order."

John couldn't quiet his suspicions. "What kind of delay?"

"He didn't say exactly. But it shouldn't take more than a week or two."

"How long's it been?"

"A good three weeks."

"Did you contact the buyers?"

Gavin nudged his hat up. "You know how it is in Newcastle. It's still a fledgling settlement, nearly all prison trade. That's the trouble, can't connect with anyone up there."

"You hear of anybody else having difficulties with Hodgsson?" John asked.

Gavin scrubbed at a day-old beard. "Blanchett had some trouble. Maybe another fellow too."

John's suspicions grew. Most likely Henry was up to no good. "You might want to do some more checking on that

shipment. I don't completely trust Mr. Hodgsson. He's a du-
bious past."

"How so?" Gavin narrowed his eyes.

John let out a loud breath. "Hate to admit it, but he's my
cousin. We were partners in a machining business back in
London. After I was arrested, he liquidated the company and
disappeared with the assets. Never saw him again until he
showed up here. I'd hoped he'd changed."

"Why didn't you say something?" Gavin's tone demanded
an answer.

"Wanted to be fair-minded. It's possible he's legitimate." The
more John thought about the circumstances, the more alarmed
and the angrier he became. "But I'm going to have a talk with
him now. Right now."

"I'll go with you."

The two marched back to Hodgsson's office. Hands clenched,
John stopped at the office door. "Best to be subtle," John warned
Gavin, who had a reputation for a hot temper, but the warning
was as much for himself as well.

Gavin nodded.

John opened the door and stepped in with Gavin right behind him.

Henry slid a file drawer closed. "John, did you forget something?"

"No. Just have a few questions."

"So do I," Gavin said. He moved closer to Henry. "I got tired
of waiting for payment on those goods you shipped so I tried
to contact the company. Couldn't find them."

Henry smiled easily. If he'd been up to no good, it didn't show.
"No worries. All that happened was the ship that your goods
were scheduled to go on was overloaded. Had to wait for the

next one to go out." He rubbed his chin. "There's a lot going on up that way. There's still work being done on the prison, plus they're trying to get some housing up for the administration. It's not easy communicating with those blokes." He rested a hand on Gavin's shoulder. "It all takes time." He turned back to the file cabinet and opened a drawer.

"Let's see here." He pulled out a shipping order. "Yes. Here it is. That shipped on the first of September. Not so long ago. As I said, deliveries have been held up. And the weather's given us a little trouble—heavy seas. Your shipment will get there. Be patient."

"It's nearly October. Those crates didn't ship out of the country; they were hauled up the coast."

"If it will make you feel better, I'll look into it," Henry assured him. He focused on John. "Now, what can I do for you?"

"I want you to hold off on the shipment for Mr. Atherton."

"It's too late for that. They're loaded and scheduled for departure tomorrow. I'm not about to unload all that timber. Unless, of course, Mr. Atherton doesn't mind paying the cost of labor and storage."

John wasn't sure what to do. He needed to speak with Mr. Atherton. If he was wrong about Hodgsson, it could cost his employer a huge sum. "I'll be back tomorrow. The ship better not sail until I speak to you."

"It'll go with the tide. I've no control over that." Henry's eyes were hard.

"I'll be back," John said and strode toward the door, certain Henry was running some kind of swindle.

"I expect payment," Gavin demanded. "If I don't have it in a week, consider our contract invalid." He followed John out.

The men headed down the street. "You think he's taken those

supplies for himself?" Gavin asked. "And he's selling them and keeping the money?"

"Could be. We have to see if your goods were sent out, and if they were, when and where." He walked faster. "I've got to speak to Mr. Atherton." He stopped in front of the mercantile. "I'll see you here in the morning. With a bit of luck we'll get some answers. See what you can find out about your shipment and if anyone else has been having trouble with deliveries or payments."

Late in the day, John rode into the Athertons' yard. He hoped it wasn't too late to save his employer's goods.

After explaining what he knew, he and Mr. Atherton headed back to Port Jackson. John felt responsible. He should have voiced his suspicions sooner.

Contemplating the consequences Henry faced if he were caught in a swindle, John smiled. He'd pay dearly, and the thought of that gave John satisfaction. Retribution would be sweet.

The sky turned pink and when the last of the sunlight faded, John and Mr. Atherton were forced to stop for the night. They tied their horses, lay out their saddle blankets, and settled down. The air was warm so there was no need for a fire.

The night was filled with sounds of the bush—cicadas thrummed, frogs chirped from the nearby river, and a dingo yipped in the distance. John rested against his saddle and chewed on a piece of dried meat. Staring up at the night sky, apprehension stirred in him. He'd acted hastily. What if he were wrong and had dragged Mr. Atherton all the way to Port Jackson without cause? He'd be a laughingstock and maybe worse. One word from his employer and he could end up back in prison. And Henry would be free to continue spending his money.

"I thought his prices were a bit too reasonable," Mr. Atherton said. "I'm usually more cautious in my business dealings." He let out a breath. "I'm grateful you were keeping an eye out."

"I should have said something about his past. And I would have, except I wasn't sure if he'd changed. I didn't know with certainty that he couldn't be trusted. We're still not sure."

"You're right there. I hope this is all a misunderstanding. If not, there are a lot of fine gents who've been dealing with him and who have a lot to lose."

"I hope I'm wrong," John said, but he didn't mean it. He wanted his revenge. This was the perfect opportunity. He'd hoped to catch Henry in wrongdoing, and now it seemed his need was about to be satisfied. His actions hadn't been unselfish.

<hr/>

The morning air was cool and damp. While John and William Atherton downed a dry biscuit and water, chattering birds serenaded them.

They saddled their horses and headed toward Port Jackson.

"I've a bad feeling." Mr. Atherton rested a hand on his saddle horn. "Hope we get there before that ship sails. I'm not about to let that timber go until I know it's heading to the right people for the right price."

As they approached the colony, John tightened his hold on the reins. *God, let the ship still be in the harbor.* The two men crested a hill overlooking Port Jackson and the bay.

"There it is," Mr. Atherton said.

John blew out a relieved breath. Even if he was right about Henry, at least the timber was safe.

They tied their horses and walked to Henry's office. Something felt wrong. The building looked dark and the door was ajar.

They stepped inside. The room was in disarray. Cabinet drawers stood open, papers littered the floor. Henry was nowhere to be seen.

"Seems you were right," Mr. Atherton said. "He's run. And it's a good assumption he's gone off with whatever funds he had, including my money."

"You still have your timber."

"I do at that. And I'd best see it remains here." He headed for the door.

"I'll find Henry. The money's sure to be with him." John faced Mr. Atherton. "Sorry, sir. This is my fault."

"No use blaming yourself. You didn't know he'd do something like this."

"I suspected."

Atherton stared at John, but there was no anger in his eyes. "Go on, now. See if you can get someone to help you hunt him down."

John went straight to the stables.

"He left at first light," the stable hand said. "Headed north on horseback. Told him he was a fool to try. It's rough going, no roads." The man shook his head. "He'll end up a pile of bones."

"You think I'd have any luck following him?" asked John.

"Doubt it. The brush is thick that way and there are canyons and the like." He shrugged. "He might leave a trail to follow."

The man scratched stubble on his chin. "Ye could try a black tracker. They know their way, and if Henry stays with his horse, a tracker can find him."

"Right then. Thank you." John went in search of Gavin.

⬥

Gavin had no difficulty finding a tracker who was willing to trade his skills for a modest amount of tobacco. By late morning, he, John, and another man named Jack had set out after Henry. Jack's boss had been having trouble with Hodgsson, so when he found out a swindle was in progress, he insisted one of his men go.

In spite of the tracker, John felt ill at ease riding into the bush. He had no weapon and there were stories about those who'd tried to find their way through. The word was that none had made it.

He eyed the Aborigine tracker. He was small of stature, but he moved fast and seemed to have no difficulty following Henry's trail. Obviously he was skilled; John just hoped he could be trusted.

By late afternoon, the sun blazed hot and merciless. The brush seemed to close in around them. And while they fought for every foot the tracker seemed tireless. The horses blew air from their nostrils, tossed their heads, and shied from stickery plants and scuttling lizards. Their coats glistened with sweat.

"We're gonna have to lead the horses," Gavin said, pulling to a stop and dismounting. John and Jack did the same. The tracker kept moving. There was no rest.

They pushed their way through heavy underbrush. Stubby branches with barbed leaves caught at their skin and clothes.

As they moved along a narrow ridge with a deep crevasse falling away below them, Jack said, "Keep an eye out for snakes. They'll get ye before ye know what happened."

John eyed the ravine and thought snakes were the least of his worries. He wondered how Henry had made it this far. The man had no stamina or courage.

The three men stopped. John drank from his canteen and then asked Gavin, "Is the tracker sure Henry came this way? I can't see him getting this far, not in this kind of terrain."

"He's a fine reputation," Gavin said, watching the black man move ahead easily. "We can't afford to lose him."

Gavin moved on, rocks and dirt skittering down the cliff side.

"I'm not so sure this was a good idea," Jack said. "Maybe we ought t' go back." He wiped sweat from his face. "Henry's gonna die out 'ere anyway."

John knew Jack spoke the truth. It made sense to stop and let Henry simply destroy himself. But he wanted to face him, accuse him, and then turn him over to the authorities. "He couldn't have gone much farther," he said. "He's never been a good rider, and this kind of country will do him in. He can't be moving very fast. We're probably close."

Silently, the men followed the tracker inland and away from the ravine. Abruptly the Aborigine stopped. He squatted and motioned for the men to remain out of sight.

"He's found something," Gavin whispered, peering ahead.

John couldn't see anything. He glanced at the setting sun and hoped they'd found his cousin. They couldn't go much farther before the night turned black.

The Aborigine motioned them to move forward. The three joined him and peered around a eucalypt. There, sitting in the dusk, was Henry. He'd found a small clearing and had started a fire. Resting his back against a log, he picked sticks and leaves from his clothing and then used a knife to dig slivers out of his hands. A pistol rested on his lap.

"We found him," John whispered, feeling exhilaration. He nodded his thanks at the tracker. The black man moved back and rested against the bare trunk of a grass tree.

"What should we do now?" Jack asked quietly.

"We ought to go in there and arrest him." Gavin brandished his musket.

Jack's eyes widened. "What about the pistol? He might shoot us."

Gavin scowled at Jack. "He's one man. We're three."

"Let's wait until dark," John suggested. "That way he won't see us until we want him to."

The three hunkered down and waited for the last of the light to withdraw. John kept an eye on the tracker, wondering if he might go off into the night and leave them. He leaned close to Gavin and whispered, "Can we trust the black to stay with us?"

"Like I said, he's a good man. I've known him awhile. No worries there." Gavin walked back to his horse and lifted a length of rope from around the saddle horn. Holding it up, he said, "We'll likely need this."

"I could use a pistol," John said.

Gavin gaped at him. "Right. I forgot you're a prisoner." He grabbed a pistol out of his holster. "I'll say nothing 'bout this."

As it got darker, they watched Henry nervously eye the brush around him and continue to add wood to the fire. He took something out of his saddlebag and sat back to eat it.

"He'll manage to set the whole place ablaze if he's not careful," Jack whispered.

Remaining out of sight, John stood and stretched his legs. "How's he look to you?"

"Tired," Gavin said with a smile.

"Ought to be easy," Jack said.

"I'd say it's time to surprise him then, eh? What do you say?" John savored the idea of the confrontation. He'd dreamed of it. His hand on the pistol, he approached. Jack and Gavin followed, muskets ready.

As they moved closer, Henry heard them. He picked up his pistol. "Who is it? I'll shoot!" He stood and waved the gun about.

"Not a bright idea," John said, stepping out of the shadows. "There are three of us and only one of you." He smiled.

Pointing his pistol at John, then Gavin and then Jack, Henry's hand shook. "What are you doing here?"

"We come to talk to ye," Jack said, his voice hard.

John smiled. "You got yourself caught this time, Henry."

"Caught? What do you mean? I'm just on my way north. Nothing wrong with that."

"What fool would try making the trip overland? There's ships that can take you. Unless you were in a hurry." Gavin grinned.

John stepped closer. "We went by your office. Looks like you left in a rush."

Henry didn't respond.

"You on your way out of town with someone else's money perchance? Figuring on setting up another swindle farther north?"

"I've business in Newcastle."

"That would explain the condition of your office?"

"My office? I don't know anything about that."

John fingered the pistol. "Perhaps you ought to head back to Port Jackson, then, so you can see the damage done by the hoodlums who must have broke in. You'll need to tend to it."

"I'll see to it when I've completed my business."

"You've business to attend to in Port Jackson." John stepped closer to Henry. "You can die here or you can come with us."

"I'm going nowhere with you." He brandished his firearm.

His pistol trained on Henry, Jack edged around behind him. "Don't figure ye want a brawl, now do ye?"

Henry's eyes narrowed as he looked from one man to the other, then he settled on John. "You're the cause of this."

"No. I'd say you're the culprit." He glanced at the men with him. "Now, would you like to argue or will you let us truss you up nicely?"

Gavin pulled himself up to his full height and grasped the rope he had draped over his shoulder. "I can assure you that you don't want to fight us."

Henry looked about like a cornered animal. He took a step toward the bush, then seemingly realizing the futility of any escape plan, he dropped his arms and his gun and held out his hands. "This isn't the end of it."

"That's right, it's not." Gavin tied his hands, pulling it tight with a jerk and then knotting it. Henry winced. "You'll be paying me every farthing you owe."

"I don't owe you a copper." Sweat on Henry's face glistened in the firelight. "Take up your complaint with the blokes who got your shipment."

"And who might they be?"

Henry hesitated and then said, "I don't keep all that in my head. I'd have to look at the records." Sweat trailed into his eyes. He looked from one man to the other and finally settled his gaze on Gavin. "Your goods are safe. And so is your money."

"Fine then," Gavin said. "Good thing we came along to see you back to Port Jackson safely." He smirked.

A broken man, Henry Hodgsson stood before the magistrate. John tried to relax the muscles in his shoulders. This was the moment he'd been waiting for. He'd dreamed of the day Henry paid for his crimes. He deserved a harsh sentence. Not only had he destroyed John's life, but he'd deceived and stolen from several New South Wales businessmen, freeing them of a goodly sum. Gavin had retrieved most of his funds, but the shipment was never returned.

The judge glared at Henry. John had always thought his cousin to be of small stature, and now with his shoulders hunched forward and his body trembling, he seemed shriveled and was clearly no longer a menace.

"Henry Hodgsson, for your crimes you shall spend fourteen years hard labor in Newcastle Prison."

Henry sniveled. "Please. Have mercy on me."

"You've shown no mercy and none will be given," the judge said with finality.

Cheers broke out from several who'd been cheated and had shown up to witness Henry's hearing.

Henry was dragged from the courtroom.

John stood in place for a long while. Rather than feeling satisfaction, he was aware only of the bleakness of a life lost. Finally, he walked out. It was time to go home.

While John traveled back to the Atherton farm, his mind pondered something Hannah had once said. She'd quoted Scripture from the book of Romans. *"Beloved, avenge not yourselves, but rather give place to wrath; for it is written, Vengeance is mine, I will repay, says the Lord. Therefore if your enemy hungers, feed him; If he thirsts, give him a drink; for in so doing you will heap coals of fire on his head. Do not be overcome by evil, but overcome evil with good."*

He knew the verses, but they'd never meant much to him before. Now in light of what had happened, he realized vengeance provided no peace. What he'd wanted and waited for so long offered only emptiness.

Forgiveness is good for the soul, Hannah had told him.

But how do I forgive a man who has stolen my life? Regretfully John knew he'd attained nothing by Henry's punishment. He still couldn't forgive him for what he'd done. *There's nothing more I can do,* John decided. *I give it to you, Lord.*

John left it at that. Thinking on it would do little good. Besides, he was weary—more so than he could remember. All he wanted now was sleep.

When he rode into the yard, Mr. Atherton stepped out of the house to greet him. *Perhaps to send me back to prison,* he thought. *Deservedly so. I let him and everyone else down.* When word got out that John and Henry were related, a handful of businessmen who'd lost money and goods had wanted him returned to Port Jackson. However, they had no say. It was up to Mr. Atherton.

"Evening, John," Mr. Atherton said, walking up to him.

276

"Good evening." John slid off his horse.

"What was the outcome of the trial?"

"Henry's going to prison." John's hands were sweating. He moved the reins to one hand and wiped the palm of the other on his breeches. "Only a small portion of the moneys were recovered. Most the men who did business with him were not compensated."

Mr. Atherton nodded. "Too bad. But I'm glad Hodgsson will pay for his crimes." He clapped John on the back. "I owe you a debt of gratitude. If not for you, my timber and my money would have been lost."

"If I'd told you straightaway, you would have stopped doing business with Henry as soon as I knew who the proprietor was. And I wanted to catch him. I needed revenge."

"In similar circumstances I might have done the same."

"No. You wouldn't. You're an honorable man."

"And so are you." Mr. Atherton patted John's horse. "Henry took a lot from you."

"Right you are there." John loosened his hold on the reins. "I ought to put the horse away."

"Before you go, I have something for you." Mr. Atherton reached into his coat pocket and retrieved a document. Handing it to John, he said, "Your papers. You're a free man."

John stared at the document in Mr. Atherton's hand. "You're freeing me?" John knew he didn't deserve to be rewarded. It had been his need for revenge that had brought trouble on Mr. Atherton. "But I've a life sentence."

"Not anymore. You've been pardoned." He smiled. "You're a fine man, John, and don't deserve to be imprisoned. The King's orders were unjust." He grasped John's shoulder. "You've earned your freedom."

John couldn't believe what he was hearing. "Thank you," he stammered. "I don't know what else to say."

Mr. Atherton smiled. "Just the look on your face says it all."

"What do I do now?"

"To begin with, you might want to talk to Hannah." He tipped his hat and walked toward the main house.

24

John finished his first cup of coffee and refilled the tin. It was early and the rest of the men in the barracks were still sleeping. After cooling down the horse and putting it away the previous evening, it had been too late to speak to Hannah. Even Perry had gone to bed. He'd told no one about his new freedom.

Wishing there were someone he could share his good news with, John had gone to bed thinking about all it would mean to him. He didn't sleep; instead, his mind wound and rewound Mr. Atherton's words. Hands clasped behind his head, he'd stared at the bunk above his and considered what to do. He was free to make his own choices. After months of captivity and believing freedom would never be his, the reality was almost too much to grasp.

Sipping the coffee, he stepped onto the front porch and quietly closed the door behind him. Heated morning air rose like a mist in the dim light. A hush lay over the earth; even the cicadas were quiet. He ambled down the steps and sat on the bottom one.

A loud squawk emanated from the forest and then others

joined in. A cow needing to be milked mooed her distress. Patrick moved toward the barn. He nodded at John as he passed.

Lifting a hand in greeting, John wanted to shout, "I'm free!" Instead, he silently watched the man disappear inside the barn. *Perry and Hannah ought to be the first to know.*

The door creaked open and Perry stepped onto the porch. He scrubbed his face with one hand and squinted at the light beyond the trees. "Coffee smells good," he said, hitching up his pants.

"Tastes a bit rough, but it'll wake you up." John nodded toward the inside of the barracks. "There's some cooked." He smiled.

"What ye grinning 'bout so early?" Perry asked as he moved off the porch and stepped around to the side of the shack to relieve himself.

"There's a dunny not ten paces from where you're standing," John said.

"This is easier and smells better." Perry chuckled and walked back to the porch. Leaning against the railing, he asked, "Why ye up so bloomin' early? Ye came in late."

"Just after dark." John rested his forearms on his thighs and thought about how best to share his news. Should he just blurt it out or work up to it?

"So, how'd the trial go? Did Henry get what he deserved?"

"Fourteen years at Newcastle."

"Well then, that ought to set him back a bit." Perry grinned.

John took another sip from his coffee. "Mr. Atherton said he's grateful for my part in Henry's arrest and for keeping his goods and money intact."

"Ye did a fine thing. Especially goin' off in the bush after him the way ye did."

"Figure I'll wait until there's a road before I venture up that way again," John said with a chuckle. He studied the brown liquid in his cup and then looked up at Perry. "Mr. Atherton gave me my freedom."

"He what?"

"He applied to the Governor, and I've been pardoned. I'm free."

Slack-jawed, Perry stared at John. "Free? Yer free?"

John nodded.

With a whoop, Perry leaped toward John. Ignoring his friend's coffee, he dragged him off the step, hugged him, and then danced him around the yard.

John laughed and held his cup away from him. "All right. Enough. Enough. You've spilled my coffee."

Perry slung an arm over John's shoulders. "Blessed Mary and Joseph! Who cares 'bout yer coffee?" Grinning, he shook his head. "Ye deserve it. Ye never belonged in a gaol." He squeezed John's shoulders. "What will ye do now, eh?"

"Don't know for certain. I can do most anything, I guess." He looked at Hannah's cottage. "First thing, I'm asking Hannah to marry me . . . again."

"Fine idea." Perry ran a hand through his hair, leaving some of it standing on end. He shook his head back and forth. "Free. Can't believe it." His voice had taken on a hint of longing.

John felt a flush of guilt. It didn't seem right that someone like Perry was still a convict and he was free. "It won't be long for you. You've only a few years left."

"That's right. And I work for one of the finest men in New South Wales. Not sure I'd want to leave even if I could." He tipped his mouth sideways and raised his eyebrows. "But it would be grand to have a choice."

John looked at Hannah's cottage. "I think I'll speak to Hannah. What do you think she'll say?"

"She'd be a fool to turn ye down, that's what *I* say."

"She's already done so." John set his nearly empty coffee cup on the railing. "I've no reason to wait longer." He glanced down at his coffee-stained shirt. "Better change first."

✦

John stood in front of Hannah's door staring at it. He'd thought all night about what he ought to say. But he still wasn't certain. How should he ask for her hand? What could he say different from what he'd already said? Somehow he must convince her that marrying him was the right thing to do. He knew she loved him.

Well, you'll get nowhere standing here. He smoothed back his hair and knocked.

The door opened and Lydia smiled out at him. White powder dusted her apron, and she looked like she'd put her mahogany-colored hair up in a hurry. "Good day, John. Yer up early."

"The sun's up. Figure I ought to be as well."

Lydia looked out. "It's barely light. Wouldn't exactly say the sun's up, it's more like it's just waking up."

"I was hoping to speak with Hannah. Is she in?"

"That she is." Lydia eyed him. "What's on yer mind? There's a glint in yer eyes." She folded her arms over her chest.

John smiled. "Nothing. Just need to talk with her." He looked past Lydia. "You said she's here."

"She's dressing." Lydia opened the door wider. "But ye can come in."

282

John stepped inside. He stood in the center of the main room, feeling awkward and still trying to work out in his mind just what to say.

"I'll tell her yer here." Lydia disappeared into the bedroom.

John moved to the window and gazed out. His heart hammered wildly. Dare he hope? He tried to concentrate on the distant fields. Already the summer heat had sucked most of the green from them. Golden grasslands shimmered beneath the first touch of morning sunlight.

He glanced at the bedroom door. *What will I tell her of my plans? I don't even know what they are.*

The door opened. "John?" Hannah stepped out. "It's a bit early to be calling. Is something wrong?"

"No. Nothing's wrong. And sorry. I didn't mean any inconvenience. I've been awake awhile and it didn't feel early to me." His thoughts were in a tangle. "Would you take a walk with me before the day heats up?"

"I'd like to but Mrs. Atherton's expecting me."

"We won't go far."

Hannah didn't answer right away. "All right, then." She turned to Lydia. "If I haven't returned when you go to the house, please tell Mrs. Atherton I shan't be long."

John opened the door and stood aside while Hannah walked out. The sweet smell of lavender followed her. "I thought perhaps we could walk along the river. It's a bit low this time of year, but it's still agreeable and calming."

"It is lovely there." Hannah considered him thoughtfully. "Are you in need of calming?"

"No. Not at all." John sucked in a breath, hoping she couldn't see his nervousness.

He walked beside Hannah, fighting off the desire to take

283

her arm. Although it would be proper, he feared she would see it otherwise.

They strolled along the river, talking about crops, the weather, and an upcoming social gathering the Athertons were hosting. The trees and plants hugging the riverbank were still lush and green.

"How lovely it is here." Hannah looked up into the canopy of trees. She breathed deeply, her eyes closed. "Mmm. I love the smell here. There are so many different kinds of flowers." Wearing a whimsical expression, she said, "One day I shall plant flowers about my home. That way when I'm sitting on my veranda I can enjoy their fragrance."

"I rather like that idea."

Hannah plucked a yellow blossom. She held it to her nose and then brushed the petals against her chin. Moving toward the river, she said, "It's nice here—cooler."

Birdsong interspersed with the squawks of magpies and cockatoos resonated all around them.

"I thought you'd still be in Port Jackson."

"I rode back after the hearing. Henry was sentenced to fourteen years at Newcastle."

"Newcastle? Isn't it the most dreadful prison in New South Wales?"

"That's what I hear." John picked up a pebble and tossed it into the slow-moving river. "He tried to make it there on his own, now he's getting a little help."

"How do you feel about all that's happened especially now that Henry's received justice?"

"I don't feel anything, really. The whole thing is rather depressing." John tossed another pebble. It plunked into the water and ripples washed into widening circles. "I expected to feel pleased or relieved. But I keep seeing him, dismal and sickly. What a waste it all is—his life and mine."

"Your life is not a waste. Not at all."

"You're right. It's hard to change my thinking after so many months of believing I'd lost everything—all my father worked for, my life in London."

"You have a life here now. And your father would be proud of you."

"I believe he would be, yes. But I still feel badly about his life's work being ruined."

"It seems to me the work he cared about most is you. You are his life's work."

"Quite right." John smiled. "When I was arrested and convicted, I lost hope in ever having anything good again. And now to my amazement things have turned out rather grand."

Hannah leaned against a tree. "I understand. There've been incidents that have made me feel all was lost. But I've found peace here." She grabbed hold of a low-hanging branch. "There are things I'd change of course if I could, but in truth I've received better than I deserve."

The wounded look John had seen many times before touched Hannah's eyes. It cut to his heart. If only he could lift away her sorrow. Bracing a hand against the tree trunk, John moved closer to Hannah and gazed into her dark eyes. Remembering the kiss they'd shared, he longed to take her into his arms again. Instead, he stepped back. "I've some news."

"Something more than Henry's sentencing? Pray tell, what is it?"

Tension building inside, John gazed at Hannah. "Mr. Atherton set me free."

"What?"

285

"He's set me free. I'm no longer a prisoner."

Light in her eyes, Hannah gazed at him for a moment. "You're truly free?"

John nodded and smiled. "I am."

"How grand!" Throwing her arms about John, Hannah hugged him. "I'm so happy for you!"

He pulled Hannah closer. She pressed in against him, then her body went rigid and she stepped away.

Tugging at a dress cuff, she kept her eyes down. "I'm sorry. That was quite forward of me." Looking at him, she added, "I was carried away with joy." She smiled. "I'm so pleased for you. Have you made plans?"

"No. Not yet."

Uncertainty touched Hannah's brown eyes. "Now that you can, will you return to England?"

"No. As I said, there's nothing for me there." He glanced around. "And I rather like it here."

She visibly relaxed. "I'm glad. I value your friendship. It would be dreadful to have to say good-bye to you."

John nodded. He needed to ask her. He moved closer and took Hannah's hands in his. "Now that I'm free I can work anywhere. I can own a home, have a family. . . ." Hannah's creamy skin, her dark brown eyes, and the lips that liked to smile made him yearn for her. "I want you to share my life. Will you marry me?"

Hannah searched his face. Her eyes brimmed with tears. "I wish I could say yes. But I can't. Especially not now. You're free. I'm not. And I won't hold you back. I couldn't do that."

She looked at their intertwined hands and disengaged hers. "There are things you don't know about me, John. And I'm certain that if you did, you'd not want me for a wife."

"Tell me what it is." He cupped her face in his hands. "You've not given me a chance."

Hannah pulled away and moved toward the riverbank. She gazed at the meandering water. It seemed so peaceful and quiet. She wanted to feel like that. Without looking up, she said, "I can't tell you." She turned and studied him. "I want you to know that I wish I could say yes. You'd make a fine husband."

Frustration spread through John. What good was freedom if he couldn't have what he wanted most? "I'll stay here and work for Mr. Atherton, then. I'll remain a prisoner until you're free. I'm content with that, if only you'll marry me. Freedom doesn't matter if it means living without you."

"I don't want you to do that. Not for me."

"I will do it. Right now." John turned and walked toward the house, his steps determined.

Hannah watched him go. As he moved away, she caught a glimmer of the depth of his love. How could he give up so much for her? A Scripture her mother had read many times came flooding back. *This is my commandment, that you love one another as I have loved you. Greater love has no one than this, than to lay down one's life for his friends.*

"There is no greater love than this," she whispered. *Oh, John, I'm not worthy of such love.*

She sat on the bank and watched the river as it flowed by, washing toward Sydney Cove and the ocean beyond. She remembered the days in the cottage with her mum. So often she'd talked of God's love. She'd explained that he'd given all there was to give without asking for anything in return other than to accept his gift of love—his Son.

Truth seeped into Hannah's spirit. There was nothing she could do to earn God's love. Did that also mean there was nothing she could do to repulse his love? Even as ugly as she was, did God still love her? Were there no conditions except that one accept the Savior's gift?

If receiving was all she need do, then she'd done that long ago. Like a sunburst, understanding and joy spread through her. God had never left her. His love had remained steadfast. It was she who had rejected him. The gift had always been hers.

Hannah's eyes brimmed with tears. *No matter how soiled I am, I'm still yours. How could I have been so blind?*

John had been set free and was now willing to relinquish that freedom out of love. "If he's willing to give up so much for me, I must give him my heart. I love him." Hannah pushed up off the ground and hurried toward the house. She needed to tell him.

Hannah found John in the shop. Quietly closing the door, she stepped into the room. "John?"

He looked up from a tool he'd been sanding.

She moved toward him. *What shall I say? Lord, give me the words.* When she was only a step away she gazed up at him, delighting in the devotion she saw in his eyes.

"No one has loved me so deeply, except my parents." She smiled. "And my heavenly Father.

"I don't deserve your love, but I'm grateful for it. And I accept it." She stepped closer. "I will be honored to become Mrs. John Bradshaw." She rested her hands on his arms. "My heart breaks to think that you'd give up your freedom for me, but I'm swept away by your sacrifice."

He enfolded her in his arms.

Hannah couldn't hold him tightly enough. "I love you. Thank you for loving me."

25

Anticipation and fear coursed through Hannah. Tomorrow she would become Mrs. John Bradshaw. She stared at her reflection in the mirror. She looked different. Her skin and eyes seemed more vibrant than usual.

Closing her eyes, she tried to imagine how it would be. To be sure, John would be well-dressed and handsome. He'd stand in front of the church, tall and broad-shouldered, and his eyes would follow her as she stepped into the church. She'd be wearing her lovely new gown and be quaking inside. While gazing at each other with adoring eyes, they'd exchange vows and then be declared husband and wife. Hannah smiled softly at the thought.

A celebration would follow with delectable foods, drink, and sweet treats. There would be congratulations and kisses and possibly even dancing. And then they would begin their new life together.

Apprehension swept away Hannah's imaginings. She'd not told John about her past. *If he knew, would he still want to marry me?* she asked for the thousandth time. Just the thought of telling him made her stomach churn. She tidied her hair and her hands trembled.

Her eyes went to the wedding gown hanging in the corner of the room. It was exquisite blue silk with a brocade center front panel. Mrs. Atherton had provided the fabric. *I still cannot believe how the Lord has blessed me. In spite of my little faith and my protesting, he's given so much.*

Lydia stepped into the room. "Ye'll make a beautiful bride." She crossed to the gown and lifted it off the rack. Draping the dress over one arm, she moved to Hannah and held it up to her. "The color is perfect."

"Do you think John will like it?"

"I doubt he'll be able to keep his eyes off ye." Lydia returned the gown to its stand. "Ye nervous?"

Hannah nodded. "I don't know what kind of wife I'll be. What if I'm terrible at it?"

"Of course ye won't be. Ye can cook and clean and ye love him, right?"

"I do."

"Then ye've nothing to worry 'bout."

"I can't wait to be his wife and at the same time I'm frightened."

Lydia grinned. "Then I'd say yer like most brides."

Hannah touched her mother's necklace. She'd worn it every day since her death. *I wish she were here.* An ache swelled at the base of her throat. "I miss my mum. She should be here."

Lydia put an arm over Hannah's shoulders and squeezed gently. "She's here in yer heart. From what ye've told me ye have fine memories."

"I do. But it's not the same."

"Course not." Lydia hugged her. "Nothing will be the same now. Not even for me. This little place will feel big without ye sharing it with me. I'll miss ye."

Hannah had to smile. "We'll see each other nearly every day. I'm still working here."

Lydia's eyes shimmered. "Right. I'm being silly." She blinked away tears. "I'm happy for ye." Her expression turned tender. "It's just that we've shared so much, the two of us."

"That we have."

Lydia glanced out the window. "I suppose I ought to go. Perry's waiting for me." She let out a sigh. "I don't know that I ought to see him anymore. I like him well enough, but not the way he wants me to."

"He loves you."

"I know. But I don't love him, anyway not the way he needs me to. He's a fine man, but . . . I want to feel about someone the way ye do 'bout John."

"You'll find the right man some day." Hannah hugged Lydia. "But you should be honest with Perry. Let him know how you truly feel."

A knock sounded at the front of the cottage.

"Now who might that be?" Lydia moved to the door and opened it to Mrs. Atherton. "Good day, mum."

She greeted Lydia and then her eyes settled on Hannah. "I was hoping to have a word with you, dear."

"Certainly. Please come in."

"I'm looking forward to seeing you in your gown tomorrow. I'm sure you'll be absolutely stunning."

"Only because of your generosity. I never dreamed of wearing something so elegant on my wedding day. Again, thank you."

"You're quite welcome. I'd say you've a right to it. Especially after all the dresses you've made for others." She glanced at Lydia and then back at Hannah. "Would it be possible for us to speak privately?"

291

Lydia moved to the door. "I'll be on me way. I'm supposed to meet Perry." She stepped outside.

Mrs. Atherton moved to the tiny table in the kitchen and sat down. She clasped her hands in front of her. "Please do sit, dear."

Hannah couldn't imagine what her mistress wanted to speak with her about, unless she felt a responsibility to offer advice to a young bride. She sat across from her. "If you're here to tell me about the ways of husbands and wives, I already know *too* much about that."

"I do have something to say about it." She smiled. "But I doubt you know much in regards to it at all. The intimate bond between a man and woman is not what you've experienced. When two people love each other the way you and John do, the union is much more than physical. Although that part of it is a blessing and it can sometimes be bliss. It's not at all ugly. And it's my prayer that what's been perpetrated against you will not spoil what ought to exist between you and your husband."

"I pray not. I must admit to being afraid. But not about what you might think." Hannah clasped and unclasped her hands. "What if John should realize . . . that I've been defiled? What shall I do?"

"You've not told him, then?"

"No."

"It would be best if you did. There should be nothing hidden to cast darkness upon your marriage."

"I couldn't bring myself to tell him. I'm afraid."

Mrs. Atherton reached across the table and grasped Hannah's hands. "I'm certain you've no need to fear. John is a fine man. And he loves you deeply. Go to him. Tell him."

The thought of it made Hannah's stomach do flips. "You're certain he'll understand?"

"I am."

Hannah didn't want to think about it. She'd made up her mind not to tell him. He'd never have to know. God loved her no matter what had happened. He'd forgiven her. Isn't that all that mattered?

"Not telling him would be deception."

"Why must I? I've told no one but you."

"You've said nothing to anyone else?"

"Lydia knows about Judge Walker and she helped bring the child into the world. But I didn't tell her that I asked God to take the baby from me."

Sadness and concern touched Mrs. Atherton's eyes.

"God has forgiven me," Hannah said. "It was a horrible sin, but I understand now that I've been rescued from my offenses by my Lord." She looked straight at her mistress. "I don't want anyone else to know. They may not be as forgiving as you or my heavenly Father."

"It's your decision, of course. Either way, I'm sure you and John will find happiness. And there will be more children."

Mrs. Atherton reached into her reticule. "There is another reason I've come." She withdrew a document and extended it to Hannah. "This is yours."

Hannah stared at the paper. "What is it?"

"Read it." Mrs. Atherton smiled slightly as if holding on to a pleasant secret.

Hannah unfolded the official-looking paper. She scanned it and then sucked in a breath. She looked up at Mrs. Atherton. "My freedom? You and Mr. Atherton have given me my freedom?"

"Yes, we have. We want you and John to begin life together without encumbrances."

Hannah read the document again. "How shall I ever repay you?"

"You're dear to me, Hannah. Just remain as good-hearted as you are."

Remembering what Mrs. Atherton had said about the women in the prisons being like daughters to her, Hannah thought she understood why she had done this kindness. Her heart swelled with gratitude and devotion. She stood and reached across to Mrs. Atherton, hugging her. "I shall be forever grateful."

Smiling kindly, Mrs. Atherton gently pressed her hands against Hannah's cheeks and kissed her forehead. "I'll pray for you." She moved to the door. "If you need me, I'll be up quite late."

With her document of freedom pressed against her chest, Hannah closed her eyes and focused on slowing her breathing. Her stomach churned. Her emotions were a jumble. She was ecstatic about being free and at the same time terrified, because she knew she must tell John about her past.

———

He'll understand. He loves me, Hannah told herself as she walked toward John's cottage.

She approached the front door. Tomorrow this would be her home too. She liked the cottage. It was small, but she was used to that. She'd already planned on some of the flowers she would plant in the front and had looked at drapery material at the mercantile. She'd start with the front windows first.

At the foot of the porch, Hannah stopped. What if John

rejected her? Her plans and her heart would be shattered. She didn't know if she could bear to lose all that she'd hoped and prayed for. For so long she'd given up on ever having a husband or a family. To lose the dream now would be a profound and unbearable sorrow. At the thought, a spasm of pain burrowed into her chest. She felt the sting of unshed tears.

Taking a deep breath, she thought, *You must compose yourself. Trust the Lord. He is with you.*

With trepidation, she made her way up the steps. So beset by thoughts of what she must do, Hannah had forgotten the document in her hand. She stared at the door. Tomorrow was supposed to be a glorious day. Was she about to ruin it? Ruin everything?

Perhaps I should wait. God sees me as pure, so what does it matter? She lifted her hand and knocked.

A moment later, John opened the door. "Hannah. This is a pleasant surprise." He stood in the doorway. "What is it? Something's wrong."

"No. Nothing's wrong." She searched for the right words to say, but all she could think of was that when he knew he'd see her as contemptible. "Everything is right," she finally said, holding out the document proclaiming her freedom. "I'm free—no longer a prisoner. It's incredible! Utterly unbelievable! We're both free!"

John looked at the paper. "This is astonishing." He smiled broadly and pulled Hannah into a jubilant embrace. "My life is full to overflowing."

"Yes. It's wonderful good news."

A shadow touched John's eyes. "I asked Mr. Atherton to rescind my pardon."

"No."

"Don't worry yourself. He refused. He and Mrs. Atherton want us to begin our lives anew without burdens." Hannah smiled up at him. "God has blessed us." She withdrew a step and wet her lips. She needed to tell him. No need to put it off longer.

"There's something else I wanted to speak with you about." She moved down the steps. "Perhaps we can walk. I don't think it appropriate for me to go inside with you."

"Of course." John closed the door and joined Hannah. He took her hand and the two strolled toward the river.

"There's something about me that you need to know," Hannah said softly.

"I know all I need to," John said, pulling her into his arms and smiling down at her. "You're everything I've ever wanted."

Hannah took a deep breath. "I love you, John, but there is something more . . . I'm not the person you think I am. And when I'm finished, you may change your mind about marrying me."

"It's not possible."

Hannah couldn't keep from trembling. She gazed into John's trusting eyes. She imagined the hurt and disgust she would see in them when he learned the truth. "There are things that have happened to me—ugly things . . . " Hannah felt dizzy and nearly fell. She grasped his arm.

"Hannah, are you all right?"

She tried to clear her thoughts.

"Luv, if what you have to say is so distressing to you, please don't say it. Nothing you can tell me will change how I feel about you."

Hannah pressed her hands against his chest. "But I must tell you."

"What I know is that I love you and that you love me. Have your feelings changed?"

"No. I do love you. I always will."

John's hazel eyes searched Hannah's. "That's all that matters to me. We're free to do with our lives whatever we wish. We can begin again, together. It will be splendid, just the two of us." He smiled down at Hannah and enveloped her in his arms.

Resting her cheek against his chest, she could feel the thump of his heart. Not so long ago her life had been in ruins. Now it was complete. There was no need to tell him about her past. He'd said it didn't matter. What good could come of telling him now?

She looked up at him. "I can scarcely wait for our wedding."

John kissed the top of her head and then gently pressed his lips to hers. "Tomorrow my life will truly begin."

Hannah remained in his arms.

"We can do anything we want," John said. He looked out across an open field. "We might even have our own farm. We could grow wheat . . . or we might even raise sheep." He smiled. "How would you like that?"

"It would be splendid."

He stepped away from Hannah but kept hold of her hands. "Shall we discuss our life together, then?"

"By all means."

Bonnie Leon dabbled in writing for many years but never set it in a place of priority until an accident in 1991 left her unable to work. She is now the author of several historical fiction series, including the Queensland Chronicles, the Matanuska series, the Sowers Trilogy, and the Northern Lights series. She also stays busy teaching women's Bible studies, speaking, and teaching at writing seminars and conventions. Bonnie and her husband, Greg, live in Glide, Oregon. They have three grown children and four grandchildren. Visit Bonnie's website at www .bonnieleon.com.

Continue the adventure ...

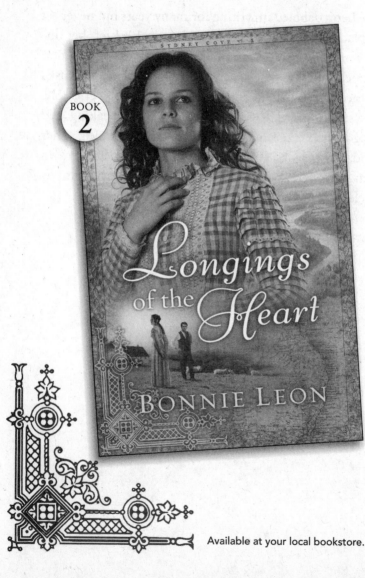

BOOK
2

Longings
of the *Heart*

BONNIE LEON

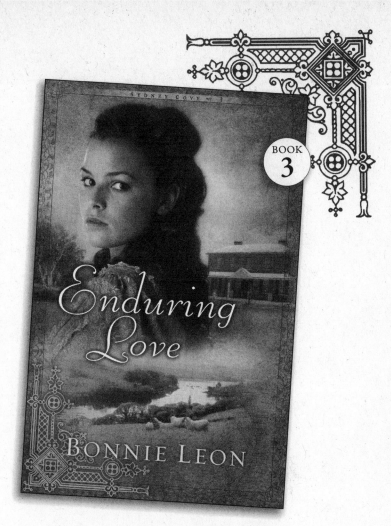

SYDNEY COVE 3

BOOK
3

Enduring
Love

BONNIE LEON

with the
Sydney Cove series.

Get lost in these heart-gripping stories of
two people journeying toward forgiveness and love.

Revell
a division of Baker Publishing Group
www.RevellBooks.com